Also by Rachel Callaghan

Under Water
Devils Knob

GRAB THE GROOM

Rachel Callaghan

First published in the United States in 2024 by Angry Alfie Press

EPUB 979-8-9909865-1-0
Paperback 979-8-9909865-0-3

Angry Alfie Press

Contents

CHAPTER ONE

Movements traceable by the ghostly glow of her cigarette, Mabel DeVine hovered in the chill air. "A 'reality' show? Coming here?" She paused for a long, deep drag and ruefully shook her translucent white-blonde head. "*Déclassé* hogwash brought by magic into the dismal dwellings of morons, now to be staged in my house?" Twin streams of smoke gusted from her nostrils. "Dead or not, I can't let that happen!"

Once upon a time, she'd been The Divine DeVine, siren of the silver screen, toast of Hollywood, her signature ciggie holder always on her left middle finger. Now, as she floated above the manor house, perched high on the cliffs of Normandy, her thin-penciled brows spiced with bitterness, she was a spectral figure, gossamer in the moonlight.

Waves crashed against rocks below, heralding a storm blowing down from the North Sea. Tossing the loose end of a trailing scarf over her shoulder, Mabel wailed a haunting crescendo, "Ohhhhhhhh, ohhhhhh," movie-ghost noises designed to drive the living mad with fear. The cry was interrupted by a rumbling smoker's cough. "Ohhhhh...kah, kahhh, kah...ohhhh!"

She disappeared into the tumble-down turret of the ancient convent at the far end of the manor. The only sounds then were the surf, the wind, and a distant, but distinctly undainty loogie being expelled behind stone walls.

Her image blurred, the molecules of incandescent ectoplasm scattering like a pyrotechnic display, then reassembling into a flapper, complete with glittering headband across her platinum blonde hair. "In my day, the audience dressed up in their Sunday best, just to see me on the screen. No words needed—my face expressed the emotions. Thank goodness there was no television then, no people lounging in undergarments, their couches covered in stale taco chips and nacho cheese. And to watch what? Stars of the silver screen? No, just ordinary hoity-toity skanks..." She shrugged. "...maybe pretty enough, but it's all baloney. No story, no actors. And certainly, no reality!"

She sighed, wishing the dead nuns would exorcise the intruders, but all they did was mumble prayers, day in and day out. Not a damn thing else. Hell, they ignored her completely, as if *she* were an interloper!

Twisting herself into a screw of smoke, Mabel spiraled down to the manor house, boring through the wall. Once inside, she resumed her ghostly form, drifting past the maids, their swollen feet up, lounging when they should have been cleaning. Watching Grab the Groom dubbed in French—the very show coming to Mabel's home.

She floated up the stairs to the only occupied bed chamber, where a young woman was unpacking a suitcase. Mabel lingered, just a puff of dust against the pale gray wall, before passing through the woman's body.

The young woman shivered. "Friggin' drafty old dump!" she said to herself. "For fuck's sake, Diana, what *have* you gotten yourself into?" She resumed sorting through clothes, unaware she was no longer alone.

Selecting a dress, she turned to the mirror, admiring her image.

Mabel, however, was not impressed. “Look at her, all big tits and hips like a broodmare. Can’t hold a candle to my body. I was elegant. Sleek as a greyhound. In my day, the men fought over me!” Pouring herself through the air, she waved her hand extravagantly, dropping sparks on the floor to die like fireflies. “Forget it, toots! No one will ever be the star I was!”

* * *

Far away across the sea, five-year-old Hortensia’s tall, beautiful mommy slammed a pair of fuzzy sleepers into a half-packed suitcase. “I’m warning you—give me even an ounce of grief, and you’ll be sorry. Go get dressed right now.”

Hortensia groveled on the rug, begging, “Please, please, puh-leeze, don’t make me wear those pink shorts… Summer’s over! School’s already started!”

Mommy shot her an angry look. “What is wrong with those absolutely adorable shorts? Anyway, it’s not jeans weather yet—didn’t you say it’s so hot the sun burns your head and that’s why you stay inside for recess?”

Hort could tell what Mommy was thinking, because she’d said it often enough: *Recess on the very fancy playground of your very expensive school.*

Hort would have loved to be with the others, out on the jungle gym or flying high on the swings. In all the time she spent wearing the teacher down with pleading, she had never told the real reason she drew alone in the art room—what the other kids called her: mostly the names of large, clumsy animals.

Shorts made things worse when it came to

teasing. “But they’re so tight,” she whimpered.

Mommy shook her head and held up the horrid pink-flowered outfit. “It’s all that greasy stuff my mother makes you. If you get fatter...” Mommy sighed deep, like her heart was breaking, all because of Hortensia. And then some muttered Spanish words Hort didn’t understand. Without seeing her grandparents, her Spanish was getting spotty, but Hort knew that *Abuela* loved her so much she couldn’t stop cooking her favorites. Everything she made tasted so good! Hort could have as much as she wanted. which was why she wasn’t allowed to visit her grandparent’s almond farm anymore.

Mommy couldn’t understand what it was like to love food so much. She only ate things that were good for you. Worst was the kale smoothie that looked just like the algae growing in the fish tank, the one the housekeeper refused to clean. The pet fish were dead, anyway, drifting upside down.

Mommy took lots of good care of herself, always buying new dresses and getting her hair done. As Hortensia’s used-to-be best friend Alicia said, “Your mommy looks like Barbie.”

After she tossed Hort’s clothes in the suitcase, Mommy packed her own outfits for a trip on her new boyfriend’s boat. He didn’t want Hort to go with them. She’d begged and begged to be sent to her grandparents, but Mommy said, “It’s time that son-of-a-bitch father of yours did his share.“

“But I don’t know him.” She tried to keep from whining.

“You’re going.” And that was that.

When Hort realized there was no use protesting, she squeezed herself into the shorts and the matching top that rode up over her belly. And then she scraped a bunch of the algae from the fish tank and put it in the blender when Cook made Mommy’s breakfast. One of Hort’s

True Beliefs was that getting even was only fair.

The next thing she knew, she was in the back of a limo, her thighs oozing out from her shorts like the lard her *abuela* squished into masa.

Though the limo was air conditioned, her bare skin stuck to the leather seat. When she lifted a knee the sound of her sweaty skin pulling away from the leather was like ripping open the Velcro on her sandals. The *fff-thip-thip-thip-thip* was interesting, diverting her from worrying. It hurt a bit, but still she lifted one leg then the other, over and over. *Fff-thip-thip-thip-thip!*

After about twenty *fff-thips*, the driver's eyes in the rear view shot to her. She locked on his gaze, inserted one finger as deeply as possible into her left nostril, and dug vigorously. His eyes returned to the road.

Hortensia looked out the side window, just in case her father appeared. She'd seen only one photo of him, the only one that hadn't been ripped to shreds. He was almost as pretty as Mommy.

How could he be Hortensia's daddy? *Someone* had to have brought the ugly in.

* * *

Brad Hudson stood at the window of his office, hands in the pockets of his jeans. The sidewalks below his L.A. office were emptier than usual. There wasn't even a derelict pushing a stolen Von's shopping cart with the trash bag-shrouded detritus of a wasted life. In the record heatwave, the only things moving were cars driving by on Sunset Boulevard, the sunlight glittering on their metal shells, like the carapaces of very expensive beetles.

He squinted, tilting his head. The new angle distorted the traffic's faint reflection, simulating the opening of *Bosch*. Only the wailing horns were missing. How much had the creative geniuses behind that sequence cost? "You know, Irwin," Brad said to his partner, "*Bosch*, now that's class."

"Ah, yes," Irwin also longed to put out that kind of intellectual shit, but, what with the writing and giving actors time to learn lines, it would cost more than they could manage. As producer, Brad had to keep firm control over expenses and delays, or the new streaming network wouldn't work with them again. Their sweet contract would be void. *Grab the Groom* might then be dead in the water.

"Classy." Irwin didn't give up dreams easily.

"We can't afford to give a crap about class, not yet. Maybe what we do is trashy, but it's what the public wants."

Unlikely as it seemed, one day American tastes could become more BBC-ish, but until then, *Grab the Groom* could go on year after year, bringing in a steady income. Best of all, the contestants worked for free, hoping to win a man and a quarter-million-dollar prize—a mere pittance compared to paying actors each time they appeared, plus residuals forever. Actors were trained extortionists. Give them a career-making role and they'd thank you by jacking up their demands.

And then, Brad's reward: the girls out in the hall, flashing ballooning breasts and long bare legs that went from the hem of their tiny skirts to the inevitable platform stilettos. Stretching and yawning with nervous energy during the competition, revealing teeth whitened until they let light through, they fluttered, birds worrying they'd be ordered to fly away.

Keeping them waiting would jump-start their rivalry, and rivalry, especially petty backstabbing, was reality TV's bread and butter. Tomorrow, once the last selections took place, the girls would be en route to their new location: Normandy. The show's crew would help them settle in. The Groom would remain tantalizingly hidden away, that very fact, the mystery of him, stirring the pot.

Brad and Irwin, the director, accompanying the most important investors, would arrive later by private jet.

Down on the street, a limo slowed. At the sight, Brad jerked forward, banging his nose on the glass. His head bounced back. "Ow!"

The car sped up, turning at the intersection.

"Your kid here?" Irwin had been fretting that her arrival would disrupt their schedule.

"Not yet." Brad's voice broke as if he had reached adolescence.

Irwin sighed. "Come on, little boy, buck the fuck up. You've got to act glad to see her. You know, acting like a dad."

Bosch still keening in Brad's head, the L.A. traffic still flowing by, disordering his thoughts. He'd never wanted to be a daddy, not if "daddy" meant being saddled with the care of an actual child. The money for those damned expensive schools—and to keep his exes quiet—was painful enough.

Without knocking, Brad's uber-competent assistant Suzanne entered. Her flat-footed walk, flat-chested body, and forlorn demeanor made Brad wince, and she knew it. She didn't waste time flirting.

"The last one's waiting." She shifted her iPad from hand to hand. "She's pissed all the others have been vetted."

"Thanks. Be a minute." Brad turned back to the window.

"This final girl's B-level, more the 'entertain the investors' type than camera-ready," Suzanne said.

Brad sighed. "We'll let her know. Find out how much entertaining she's willing to do."

Suzanne cleared her throat, but neither man asked what was on her mind. "I'll tell her to keep waiting." But she didn't leave the room.

* * *

Meanwhile, back at the manor...

CONTESTANT #1—DIANA

Diana hadn't waited for the other contestants to travel from L.A. She'd gotten on a plane to France as soon as she'd gotten the email, complete with electronic contract saying she'd made the cut. Hot-footing it to the show's location on her homeliest cousin's mileage—Zelda wasn't going anywhere fun, anyway—her goal was first pick of accommodation before the other girls arrived. They all thought they would win the show, and any little advantage, like better sleep in an out-of-the-way room, could tip the scales in her favor.

But really, nobody had a chance against her. No, sir, Diana wasn't there to be Miss Congeniality. She planned to fight for the win, tooth and nail. She had pride in being a lone wolf.

Maybe really a lone fox. Sure, all the potential contestants she'd met at the auditions were good-looking, but only one was truly sexy—a tall brunette named Isabella. Not that the 'ho had been friendly or introduced herself. Snooty bitch.

From the first try-outs, the cutesy, high-pitched voices—as well as the undercurrent of bitchiness—drove her crazy. Well, maybe not the bitchiness, but the squealing put her in a bad mood that only meaningless sex could relieve. She sighed, missing the Golden State's opportunities. A heroic teacher of underprivileged barrio youth—that's how blonde all-American Diana sold herself to that gay director. It would play well on TV when she was intro'd and again, once she won.

If the show's executives thought Diana would wait to get laid until The Groom was in play, they were sadly mistaken—a girl had her needs.

She was a dedicated teacher, just unable to resist the best L.A. had to offer. L.A., where a romp with a group of high school cholos, fortunately not "too young for their teacher to seduce," attracted no condemnation. Just the proud appreciation of the boys' fathers. And it wasn't like the kids complained. Those boys, with their dreamy, long-lashed dark eyes, full of disinterest in English composition. "Hell, all they want is for us to write how crappy our 'hood is! That shit get old!"

The best, the creamiest one of all was in her two-p.m. composition class. His lack of interest in creative writing was balanced out by a lot of interest in creative fucking, access to mighty good Molly, and a papa proud he was gaining useful experience with a teacher, an older, golden-haired gringa!

She'd driven him in her BMW convertible to Griffith Park, hiked to the HOLLYWOOD sign, and spread the blanket on the ground. Afterward, she'd dropped that sticky blanket at the drycleaners.

Diana had only arrived at the manor yesterday but, sad to say, already found this French manor's maintenance staff even less motivated than her students. She'd called for extra towels and a carafe of plain hot water—to brew her hibiscus facial—and they hadn't been seen again. Perhaps her room was *too* out of the way.

The staff members were not only incompetent, they were unappealing. The damp climate and depressed economy had left the young men wan and unhealthy, with pallid, acned cheeks.

The effect of her last sexual gymnastics had worn

off. The producer and his weird little partner were arriving any day now. There was no time to wait if she wanted a final, secret romp.

Wandering about, Diana happened upon two youths moving dividing panels. If they'd been around before, she would have noticed. Her attention made them glance about with nervous energy, speaking some sort of native patois—the local equivalent of the street Spanish in L.A. Who cared? Like she was going to *chat* with them!

They were stalwart and handsome, with velvet skin uncrinkled by age, smoothly covering muscles that writhed like snakes with the effort of lifting.

"Bonjour, jolie demoiselle!" one said.

"Anglais! All the time in Anglais! How else will we learn?" the other said, elbowing his friend in the side. He turned to her with a charming smile. "Please, very pretty lady, help us to practice the English. We are not very *acomplis*."

Fortunately, she was able to communicate enough to convince them to sneak up to her room, located at the far end of the third floor, for private lessons. She slipped away, back to her quarters to wait, like a spider in her web.

But spider or not, the web needed to be alluring, and this place was a real pain in her ass. She was barely visible in the round mirror above the dressing table. The bulbs in the ceiling's petite chandelier were probably 40 watts at most.

Something irresistibly drew her to the wall's elaborate sconces. The sconces didn't seem to have bulbs in them, so they must be some fancy French technology gussied to fit the "ancient"—and musty—décor of the place. Mildewed wasn't conducive to romance. Lacking Glade plug-ins, she doused two of her silk thongs with perfume to drape over the sconces—the heat would fill the room with scent intense enough to drive any male wild with desire. Then she turned the little tab on the fixture. There was a small hiss in response.

Five minutes later, it was almost time to let in her guests. But at the onset of a severe headache, she decided to get rid of the migraine by taking one—just one—tab of the Ecstasy she'd hidden in her birth control pack. Well, not so much "get rid of the headache" as remove herself from caring about it.

The perfume smell was a bit much, even without heat. She never could stand smells with a migraine. She grabbed the thongs as quickly as she could, stuffing them in a Ziploc.

Sleepiness pulled at her, especially her eyes, which longed to close. She'd lie down for a just a minute, waiting for her two eager swains to knock. By then the E would kick in and she'd be ready to go. She'd never had a bad reaction to the stuff.

Her head was so muggy, she couldn't think straight. Sure was warm in the room. Hot, not warm. Hotter than hell. Hotter than L.A.'s hills in the summer sun. She longed for a cigarette, but the odor might turn them off. Who knew if a beautiful woman should smell like an ashtray, even in France?

Just a short nap to recover, to let sleep cool her down. Her last pre-show bang should go out in a flame of desire. Maybe she'd have that cigarette; a girl's got to please herself first. But where was her lighter? She scrounged in her purse. Her head was heavy as a stone.

* * *

The two workers knocked on the pretty American lady's door. Discreetly, as the management restricted them to the building's first floor. Discreetly, as ghosts were said to roam the ancient convent. The tales of lonely nuns longing for satisfaction of their thwarted desires had been part of their upbringing, the local version of Grimmer Than Grimm's fairytales. No one had ever seen a specter, but you couldn't be too careful.

It was chilly near the door. Clammy, if they were being particular. Almost made them want to turn back. Almost. But the building was old and drafty.

There was no answer to the knock. "Lucien, you moron," one boy said, cuffing his companion on the head. "For this we risk the only work we have?"

"But such a woman, with those big American breasts, up so high!" the one named Lucien exclaimed. "And I can smell through the door—like the boudoir of a high-class *courtesan*!"

"As if a sophisticated lady would be interested in an ignorant, callow youth like you!" the first said.

"And you?"

"*Shut up!*" was the answer. He sniffed the air. "*Mon Dieu*! That is not just perfume—that is the gas!"

Lucien shoved his shoulder against the door, but it didn't give. The other lad grabbed the knob and turned. The door opened. Coughing, they rushed in and shut off the valves on the ancient fixtures.

Shaking, they inched toward the bed, where Diana lay face up, her eyes wide with mascara…and wide open. She was very still. Glancing at each other, they raised their left eyebrows and cried out, "*Merde*! She is dead!" and rushed from the room.

Halfway down the servants' stairs, they remembered their positions as new hires at *Couvent de la Mer*. Not to mention the crappy local economy. "We must return," Lucien whispered. He pulled a handkerchief, lovingly ironed by *cher maman* in celebration of him landing a position at last, used it to wipe the knob and, inside the room, the fixtures of all prints. "See, unlike you, I watch le CSI!"

* * *

Mabel DeVine levitated out of the way, letting the two young men pass. After the Great War, there'd been so many like them, dark and muscular, with a burning gaze. But she'd only had eyes for Maxim, her beloved husband. Max had made her Countess de Summer. She'd finally had a real "de." Not bad for a girl from Bedrock, Arkansas.

She sighed. "Maxim, my darling..." Another sigh nearly dislodged the binding on her breasts—threatening her sporty physique. "Where are you, Max? Are you in Heaven or in Hell? Whatever, our property's got to be protected."

The youths turned back toward the room's door. One wiped the doorknob with a handkerchief. Mable passed between them, trailing the smoke of *Gauloises* and the scent of her signature perfume, narcissus and orange blossom. That odor replaced the lingering smell of coal gas.

"*Sacre bleu*!" The young men shivered and stopped, turning their bodies back-to-back, like swordsmen defending from an unseen enemy. "What can that be?"

"Max, my darling, look at these weaklings, neither one half the man you were." Mabel circled the workers.

"You see anything?" the one named Lucien asked. The other shook his head.

Mabel floated above them, against the ceiling of the hall, until bumping into a light fixture, knocking her tiara askew. She settled onto a chair to ensure the safety of her coiffure. "Oh, Maxim, remember our safari, back in '34? Even when a rhino charged, you stood your ground." She'd only had eyes for him, as he played for her at their campsite, diamonds flashing on his snowy cuffs above the piano keys. How romantic he was, insisting they bring the instrument! "I Only Have Eyes for You," the last song he sang to her.

The next day that damned rhino gored him. "Brave, you were, Max, but a crap shot." She shook her head. "I would have drilled that beast."

But that song! Swoon! She continued to swirl about and, though the two workers saw nothing but the faintest haze, they froze in place, their backs still against each other. Mabel concentrated her insubstantial being into her eyes, until that was all there was of her. The young men reached back to grab each other's hands, squeezing assurance into their bodies.

"Lucien, I feel like something is watching us."

Lucien shivered. "I feel it too. There, in the corner, near the ceiling, a shadow!"

"*Le fantôme*!" They broke apart and raced toward the stairs. As they ran, the taller one squealed. "We never come to this corridor again!"

"Fuck!" Mabel grumbled. After eighty years of effort, all she could evoke was foggy grayness, cold spots, and subliminal fear. To be seen, a star needed to shine brightly!

In a swirling mist, Mabel streaked down the hallway after them, screeching to a halt when she saw herself in a mirror. A white-blond, marcelled curl had escaped from under her headband. She tidied her hairdo and lit another ciggie.

Ah, perfection again! No sense having regrets, not while there was work to be done, more competition to dispose of with what little encouragement she could make.

One down, twenty or so more to go.

CHAPTER TWO

In the office on Sunset, Suzanne shifted from foot to foot, all too obviously waiting for some further recognition from Brad. Irwin felt a twinge of sadness in his chest. He remembered all too well what it was like to long for someone out of his league. He wanted to intervene, to say something, but that would be self-defeating. She was the best hire they'd ever made, hopelessly loyal to Brad and hence to the show. And Irwin didn't have to worry about his partner's chronic womanizing when it came to her.

Irwin stood on tiptoe, looking over Brad's shoulder. "At the risk of being repetitious, the 'no touch' rules apply to all the girls." The curb was still unoccupied.

"I heard you. No *Me Too* scandals," Brad chanted in falsetto. "No new child support."

Their show's schtick was finding love, not getting laid, though that was usually the only thing that happened. Onscreen drama, rivalry between the girls, carefully released, was internet gold, but avoiding dissension, and drama *offscreen*, were the only ways to protect from delays, from the ravages of underfunding. From the need to keep the new streaming network, IntertainMint, and the investors on the hook, promising nothing more than stock options. "Easy for you but not for me." Brad said, without turning his head, his eyes still fixed on the street.

"I may be gay but I'm not dead. Some of the crew's pretty hot," Irwin said.

"Ehh." Brad looked over his shoulder with a soft chuckle. "Fernand's not coming, you know."

Season after season, Irwin had eyed the handsome gaffer, who was so skilled with lighting that a contestant could stay up all night hurling from drink and sex yet appear the next day fresh and desirable if you stayed up wind. He wanted to say, "You know I'd never cheat on Guglielmo," which was the truth, but instead found his mouth hanging open. Like a fish longing for its fatal hook. "Why, for God's sake?" he blurted out.

"A French great-aunt of his lived near the location. She claims everyone knows the place is haunted. Made it impossible for us to get a full local crew."

"It was easier to find locals in the islands."

"Yeah, but Normandy's cheaper, especially off-season. The place is isolated. There won't be tourists interrupting or paparazzi peeping through the bushes. Not to mention that finding love is too easy in paradise. This place is more realistic. Lousy weather will help them concentrate on the show." Brad's phone *blonged.* He pulled it from his pocket and looked at the text.

The blood drained from his fresh-shaven cheeks. "She's almost here."

* * *

Brad elevatored down to the sidewalk. He held a brand-new Barbie, one he'd bought after his assistant purchased a *thing* that could only loosely be described as a doll—ungainly, misshapen, with a squashed oval head atop a tiny body and gangly outsized limbs. A train wreck, a victim of toy-body dysmorphia, though Suzanne said it was the latest, all over the kidfluencers' sites. Suzanne had horrible taste.

He rubbed Barbie's body with his thumb, absentmindedly sliding up over teeny-weeny, pointy breasts and back down the slick flat belly. Though only plastic beneath his fingers, it was familiar as his ex's in its lack of yielding. Sex with her was like copulating with a knothole in a one-by-twelve.

Why hadn't Ana Maria had a simple, easy to understand boy? Female children were mysterious, junior versions of their mothers, taking to any new fad, no matter how hideous, as long as it was with his money.

Hopefully, little Hortensia would view these gifts as a positive introduction to the stranger called "Daddy."

The thought that her mind had already been poisoned by her mother cricked the back of his neck. Damn his exes! Why did they hate him so? Why make his children despise him? He was a bigshot, a successful producer, he sent money, lots of money. Even Brad Jr., now a sullen and pimply adolescent, acted as if he were irrelevant. And if his youngest, Hortensia, arriving by limousine any minute now, was anything like her mother, she was sure to loathe him. He felt the rising steam of resentment competing with his fear.

Indignation was his strongest paternal feeling.

He'd met Hortensia's mother, Ana Maria, at Lake Oroville, up above Sacramento. Dripping after a swim on the fiercely hot day, she lay on the North Forebay—which he afterwards thought of as "North Foreplay"—beach. Her shirt's thin cloth, bright orange and yellow, was nearly transparent on her damp tan skin. She'd done that magical woman-thing, removing her bikini top from beneath her shirt, rummaging around to get the cups down. Freed, her breasts had bounced like eager little bunnies longing for a bite of carrot.

She lived with her parents on an almond farm. "They are very strict, Mami and Papi," she said, her slight Spanish accent charming, her eyes dark and seductive. "Today I told them I am with our priest. It may not be possible for me to see you again."

This was his only chance with her, a diem to carpe!

"There's a quiet spot," she continued. "An almond grove in full bloom—falling petals white and clean as snow. No one about, just trees and flowers and *buzz-buzz* of the bees." She stretched her arms to the sky, that magical shirt riding up over a taut rib cage. "Take me in that pretty, pretty car." She pointed to his parked Lamborghini.

And so they'd set off, her hair fluttering in the breeze, the sparkling sun shining down. Pushing a hundred at times, the Lambo made the 2-hour drive in an hour fifteen.

The grove was fragrant, the hum of dancing pollinators adding to the intoxication of her skin's sweetness. Sweet and yet with the faintest of feral undercurrent, tangy and wild.

What a day that was! What were the odds of her getting knocked up the first and only time they'd do it?

Apparently, pretty high. Now she needed to unload the kid, whom Brad hadn't seen for…he wasn't sure--oh, yes, not since Hortensia was about three months old.

Ana Maria's neglect of maternal duties really made Brad sick. He shelved the erotic memories to relish years in the future, in the long cold winter of his Viagra age.

A text from Irwin: WHEN U COME BACK IN?

Brad tucked the toys in his armpit and texted back: KID ARRIVING.

A sleek black sedan pulled up to the curb. Brad rocked on his heels with anxiety. He had no idea what to expect of a five-year-old girl or what she'd look like.

Maybe he should have opened the emails from Ana Maria—one might have included a photo. Last time he'd seen the kid she'd been a baby and babies all look the same. But he'd never been able to correspond civilly with his exes, so the rule was: forward everything to the lawyer without opening—damn the expense. It was cheaper in the long run than getting into a fight.

The driver took out two pink suitcases from the trunk, deposited them on the pavement, and opened the passenger door. A short figure slid from the seat and into the sunlight. Standing before him, glowering from beneath lowered brows and an unfortunate mid-forehead fringe of deep-black hair, was a tiny version of the fat girl from the Oblongs cartoon. Decades ago, he'd watched the Oblongs while giggling, stoned and slightly drunk with his—as the family maid complained—delinquent teen friends. The ones who brought the beer.

What was the name used on the Oblong show for the blighted cartoon child he and his friends had mocked? It took a moment and then it came to him: Helga Phugly.

A voice, paradoxically both high-pitched and gravelly, interrupted his reverie with, "Are you my daddy?"

That's when it hit him. This little toad-like Helga clone was the offspring of his loins, the product of his genes. DNA analysis had proven her to be his. Against all logic, his and the gloriously sublime Ana Maria.

Ana Maria had won a good chunk of Brad's income for the next eighteen years, more if the kid went to college. He needed to get a little of his own back, as unappealing as that now seemed. He needed to win. Win her over, that was.

He held out the doll he'd bought. "I picked this one out myself," he said, thrusting the Barbie at her, and letting the other doll dangle.

Looking up into his face, Hortensia hesitated a moment and then grabbed both dolls, clutching them to her rotund torso. She headed toward the doors of the office building.

"Well, thank you, Daddy," Brad muttered under his breath, and then called aloud, "Just a minute!"

When the child turned, he snapped a photo with his phone. "I want to remember this moment," he said to Hortensia. When she looked confused, he plastered a smile on his face, and, without looking down, texted the picture to Irwin—otherwise, the surprise that was little Hortensia might be too great. Then his long legs took him ahead of her to open the heavy brass and plate-glass door.

* * *

As Hortensia crossed the threshold behind her father, she let the Barbie slip from under her arm without a backward glance. The door closed with a dull whoosh, beheading the tiny plastic beauty. Her dad was busy yelling to someone called "mailroom boy" about the luggage. He didn't stop to pick up the Barbie.

The elevator whisked them to the fifth floor, where a man, much smaller than her daddy, was waiting in the hall. Hortensia pointed toward him. "Who's he?" she grumbled.

The man crouched down to her level—not that far for him—and said, "I'm Irwin, your daddy's partner."

Hortensia swung the remaining doll at his face. The man fell on his ass, feet up off the ground. She almost gave herself away by laughing.

* * *

Brad's mouth dropped open as Irwin hit the floor. "What the...!" He looked down and saw one of Hortensia's pudgy little hands was empty. "And you dropped your Barbie! I'll go back and look for her."

"'s okay," she said, hugging the remaining toy. Whoever had bought that doll *understood.*

The mailroom boy came from the service lift, wheeling Hortensia's two suitcases. "Mr. Hudson, want the luggage in your office?"

Brad nodded, noticing the Barbie strapped atop one case. "Wait a sec," he said, grabbing the doll. The torso was now a disc that flopped over at the waist and the pointy little breasts were flattened under the torn pink prom dress. Worst of all, the head was missing.

Hortensia shrugged and gave a look that seemed designed to be reassuring. "Barbie's no good now. She's broken." She smoothed the cloth doll's head. "Kimmie threw her away. Kimmie don't like Barbie."

"Who the hell's Kimmie?" Irwin asked.

Hortensia held up the weird doll Suzanne had bought. It was grinning as if demented, its pastel limbs flopping in the air. "This is Kimmie. I loooove Kimmie."

They continued past the row of offices. Hortensia fell silent, eyes scanning the photos of previous years' winners. She only acknowledged one person: after looking Suzanne up and down, she cracked her first smile, a huge one. "You got me Kimmie, didn't you?"

The path to ridding himself of responsibility for watching the kid was suddenly clear. Brad gave Hortensia a shove—just a little in—toward his assistant.

Hortensia planted her feet in the deep carpet and stood her ground, turning to her father. "Really," the rough-edged, squeaky voice said, "Kimmie and me both hate Barbie. And maybe you!" She glared at him and reached out for Suzanne's hand.

Flustered, Brad ducked into his office. Then he snapped his fingers and waved to Suzanne. "Seems the little darling has taken to you. Keep her entertained. Irwin and I've got a ton of work."

* * *

An hour later, Irwin and Brad were having a finance meeting when Suzanne returned.

"Arrangements set? You get Fernand to change his mind?" Irwin knew it would be hard to find someone as talented as Fernand. Especially one who looked like a young Sidney Poitier, his boyhood celebrity crush. While other kids adored the cast of *Friends,* Irwin had spent family dinners holed up in his aunt's bedroom, watching her ancient DVD of "To Sir with Love." While the family gobbled brisket in the kitchen, he imagined himself alone in a classroom, getting help from a man he called "Sir." Thank God his aunt had a chenille bedspread. A lot of body fluids could be hidden in the grooves of good chenille.

"Nope," Suzanne said. "Ferd's dead set on leaving."

Pain sharp as an arrow shot through Irwin's right eye. Losing Fernand as eye-candy? A cluster headache! He clapped a hand over the side of his face.

Brad poured them each three fingers of scotch. He asked Irwin, "Offer him an extra ten percent?"

Irwin whispered, "Maybe make it fifteen? We're due to leave in two days. Hard to replace anyone at this late date!" The throbbing in his head increased and his eye watered. Fernand, his *Sir*, was drifting away, the possibilities unexplored.

Dammit! How many times had he approached

Fernand only to stumble at the last moment, too shy, asking a stupid question as an excuse for talking to him? How many times had Irwin let his always-busy husband's offer of an open marriage slide by?

"Need a pill?" Suzanne asked, concern making her face even plainer. When Irwin gingerly shook his head, she went on. "I found a substitute gaffer."

Irwin's heart sank.

"Not Fernand, but almost as good." She began to check things off on her iPad. "Everything else is moving along—several of our guys are already in place (*check*), hiring locals to arrange the partition walls and make sure the electricity works (*check*)... The full crew arrives later today (*check*), they'll start setting up (*check*). The contestants come tomorrow on Virgin Atlantic (*check*). We booked the whole plane so no paparazzi…"

"What about our flight?" Brad asked.

"Tomorrow, around the same time as the Virgin flight, private jet for you guys and the biggest investors." She glanced at the iPad. "And a few girls to keep them happy."

Irwin said, "Good. I wanted to make sure everything was top-notch." He waved his hand toward the door, to indicate that Suzanne was dismissed. Instead of leaving she remained, looking worried.

"Something else?" Irwin's eye was running now.

"Some of the crew are threatening to follow Fernand's lead. They aren't going. They hate the new location. Want to go back to the Caribbean. I had to explain about the interfering tourists and last year's bootlegging of our content. But they claim they're afraid of ghosts."

Brad slammed down his Glenmorangie. "That bullshit again?"

Despite the pain movement caused, his brain sloshing from one side of his skull to the other, Irwin reached out blindly for the tissues.

Suzanne grabbed the box and handed them to him. “Bullshit, maybe, but they say those who don’t see the ghost can smell a scent in the air…”

“That air, of course, is always extra chilly?” Irwin, longing to lie in a dark room, couldn’t keep the irritation from his voice.

“…a complex fragrance of narcissus…”

“Huh?”

“Daffodils, Brad,” Irwin snapped.

“…and orange blossom…”

“Ick.” Brad furrowed his brow.

“Not really,” Irwin gasped. “A classic from the ‘20s.” At the moment, imagining that odor gagged him. “Changed my mind, Suzanne. Get me narcotics.”

Suzanne hesitated a moment. “If you’re wondering where Hortensia is, the little darling was so wiped out, she fell asleep on the couch in my office. If you want, we could go see her together.”

Brad shook his head. “Got too much to do. You’ll need to hire a nanny while I’m away in France. Can’t leave her by herself, I guess.”

Suzanne’s mouth pursed and her scanty bosom rose in a sigh. “I’ll work on it. When will she be going home?”

“Her mother’s going to be in Bora-Bora for three months.”

“And didn’t take her along?”

Brad shook his head. “I’m as shocked as you are.”

Suzanne half-raised her hand as if asking why, but instead said, “I almost forgot, Brad, your attorney called. I’ll get him on the phone now, if you’re ready.”

“Legal? Franchise? Employee relations?”

Suzanne shook her head. Brad’s face sagged. “Personal?”

When she nodded, he shrugged. “May as well.”

“Thank God you’ve been a good boy, Brad, so I

don't have to worry," Irwin snarled. "Though that's more due to those condoms from Pleasure Treasure. Without them another child-support settlement would be a twinkle in its mother's eye."

* * *

Hortensia swiped her hand across the back of her mouth to remove the sticky drool. Kimmie was still tucked in the crook of her elbow, the imprint of the doll's head pressed into the pudge of her upper arm. She blinked in the sunlight shining through the large windows and yawned. Her mouth was dry and her tummy, as usual, hungry.

Suzanne's room in the office building was nice, a pretty yellow color. The couch was squooshy and had big pillows. The window's light was soft through shades. A bookcase held as many kitty statues as books. The room had a kind feel, like "it's okay to be a kid in here," that the rest of the place—and most of her mommy's house—didn't have.

Getting even hungrier, Hort went to the desk and opened the drawers. The third one down on the right, the deep one, had a pile of granola bars. Probably healthy but not as much as her mommy's food. Mommy said granola bars were just expensive candy.

Real candy, like Sour Patch Kids, were a lot tastier, but granola bars would have to do. She took one and used the butter-knife-looking thingie to tear the plastic. Dropping the wrapper on the floor, she crammed as much as would fit into her mouth and looked around the room.

The desktop held a big computer monitor. When she touched a key, it sprang to life, asking for a password. At home, her iPad used HORT. She tried but it didn't work. That had been silly. Suzanne didn't know Hort, though the doll had been just right for her. Why would her name be a password here?

When she was getting Hort ready to go, Mommy should have let her take the iPad so there was something fun to do. But instead, she'd snatched it away, saying, "That lazy sack of shit. You take electronics, he'll let you play on them the whole time. Your father has no conscience."

Hort didn't know what 'a conscience' was, but it sounded bad when Mommy said that, like not having a leg or something. She really, really wanted her daddy to get one. Especially if it meant he'd love her enough to get a new iPad. Maybe she'd save her allowance and buy a conscience for him. Had to be less money than something electronic.

Mommy was busy throwing clothes into Hort's suitcases. "That worm's not getting out of one minute of daddy duty!"

Hort would be with her daddy for weeks! Weeks without Candy Crush? It would be awful. "Puh-leeze!, " she begged, "Promise to just do educational!" but that hadn't worked.

She did manage to smuggle a few books into the bottom of her case, including her favorite. *Charlotte's Web*. The one with Wilbur, the pig, and the spider who shows the world how special he is. She read it herself a lot when nobody was looking. She didn't want Mommy to know she could get through it by herself.

After packing the book she'd gone to her mommy's room and opened the little bag holding the pills meant "to keep Mommy from having another little burden," which Hort knew meant another kid like her. One pack almost finished, two brand-new. She'd left the open pack alone and carefully opened the new ones. Popping out the pills from their covering had been fun, like bubble wrap. They flushed down easy, and the covering had smoothed down pretty well. Good luck getting more in the middle of the ocean!

Out in the hall outside Suzanne's room, photos of beautiful ladies hung on the walls, one after another, some prettier even than her mommy. They made her feel more worried about time with her daddy. Looking too long at them made her eyes feel tight and scratchy. She went back into Suzanne's office, picked up the granola wrapper and put it in the trash can.

Thirsty, Hortensia stumbled out along the hall's deep carpet, looking for a water fountain.

* * *

"You're being sued for more child support. Not just by one of your kids' mothers. By both." His lawyer couldn't keep the amused tone from his voice.

"Brad Junior's mom, too? Coraline?" Coraline had married a billionaire! Apparently, money didn't have the charm to soothe the silicone-enhanced breast of that savage beast.

And Ana Maria—she of the mouth-watering, cajeta-colored titties—was joining Coraline in holding him up for an increase? He knew what kind of bitch Coraline was but had thought better of Hortensia's mother.

He could ill-afford to give more money to Ana Maria and Coraline. And what if others were conspiring, waiting in the wings? A film of sweat erupted on his brow. There seemed to be an open pit at his feet, leading to a hell suspiciously resembling San Bernardino.

"An additional contingency to little Hortensia's visit..." The attorney cleared his throat, and then went silent. Another trick to squeezing more time out of the call: never finish a thought.

Ding! Brad had no choice but to play along. "What now?"

"You've got to care for the kid yourself. No leaving her in Los Angeles while you go away. Take her with you. It'll be cheaper in the long run."

"What the hell? Can she do that? Extort me?" Brad sighed. "Never mind. I get it—I'm screwed."

A chuckle, hastily disguised as a cough, echoed in his ear. The attorney's voice softened. "You really ought to keep it in your pants, Brad. Not that I don't appreciate repeat business."

Pity from a lawyer was always bad. Brad's eyes rolled up toward the ceiling, only to drift downward, as if of their own accord, to rest on the empty picture frame he kept on his desk.

What the hell was he going to do, trailing a five-year-old kid around with him? He'd look like a schmuck. No matter, he was stuck unless he handed over everything he owned. "Send my assistant the details."

A six-minute call. At six hundred dollars, the most expensive screw job Brad had ever experienced. And his lawyer hadn't even undressed.

CHAPTER THREE

Deep in the bowels of the jet, inside the false bottom of a black leather case, perforated to allow airflow, Cleopatra lay, sated by her last meal. Her metabolism slowed as low as it could go, lethargic in the chill dark.

The thrumming of the plane's engines would have upset her if she'd been warmer. Unlike the repeated movements of her human, these vibrations were anxiety producing, similar to those of a big cat's rhythmic chuffing when prey is trapped. And, in jaguar country, Cleopatra would be a tasty, if dangerous, meal. Ancient memories activated easily in the deepest, most primitive parts of her brain.

She had no thoughts of where she had been or where she was going, concentrating instead on the digestion of rat pelt and succulent flesh, down to the bones. In the cold, her gut moved as sluggishly as her mind, compacting the indigestible into a pellet she'd vomit up later.

* * *

Irwin was trying his best to relax as they headed to the airport. He and Brad had four eager investors and an equal number of girls in tow. Not to mention Suzanne and Brad's kid—the lawyer had made sure of that. Their private jet was waiting.

The production staff and crew were already on location in France, getting things set up with the help of the local hires they'd been able to snag. The contestants were traveling across the ocean via commercial jet. The Groom, the principal player, their prized leading man was hidden in a locked suite, awaiting the Big Reveal. That way, neither the paparazzi nor the contestants could get a sneak peek to post on every trash celebrity site.

The main investor, the moneyman, the Sausage King, wasn't fat, as Irwin had pictured a sausage king would be, not even as chubby as Irwin's departed father, whose hairless limbs had been like an overfed baby's. The Sausage King was tall and saturnine, towering over Irwin's five-foot, seven-inch frame, and thin in a peculiarly boneless way, making him sway like kelp when he moved. His face was long and oddly shaped, almost crocodilian. But he had billions and an unquenchable desire to associate with the glamorous world of celebrity, so he had become one of the new network's biggest sources of ready cash.

The King continued, "My wife finds your partner devastatingly handsome—sees his picture on all those celebrity sites and on TV discussion shows. But I guess putting up with her hopeless crush is easier than having your girls trying to bed him."

"Ain't it the truth?" Irwin answered, flicking his pen between his fingers. Something had to be the truth, but he didn't want the investors figuring out how scarce that something was. They were all from places like Omaha, where they shipped the steaks sold online. They'd learned the Beverly Hills lifestyle from the *Actual Housewives* series and loved the lowbrow glam of *Grab the Groom*, which they watched with their chronically dissatisfied wives. Most of all, they loved the girls who were so… How should he put it? So unchallenging, so retro, so Miss America. So overly-lipsticked and nail-polished and decked-out—in a way that hinted of a desperate desire to please men. Or please desperate men willing to put dollars where they wished their dicks could go.

The agreement *Grab the Groom* had with the contestants was: anything a girl made by entertaining them was hers to keep—but only after the Groom eliminated her. It was all laid out in the contracts.

Irwin sighed and ran his fingers through his thinning hair. The extra effort he'd gone to for this trip, locking down their privacy, would be casting pearls before swine. But they still had to provide the expected luxury and glam: Kobe beef, Fourchu lobster (butter-poached), and coddled baby vegetables, tender and precious. The plane's seats were upholstered in supple unborn lambskin, the cabin crew a visual delight in striking black and white designer outfits.

But the Sausage King... He always stirred memories of Irwin's chronically disapproving father, making him a tough sell. Where was Brad, who usually did the charm, the bon-vivanting? Irwin was assigned the scheming and Hebraic penny-counting. Both playing to expected stereotype. Neither set of tasks difficult as the Grab the Groom franchise was wildly successful.

The investors had yet to lose money and Irwin was determined that they never would. No Ponzi scheme shit for them. No prison. Glamour enough to go around—the funds skimmed off the top weren't at the expense of the backers' profits.

And as for the inconvenient kid Ana Maria was foisting on them? Irwin would just tell everyone Brad refused to be parted from her, turning a misdeed into a mitzvah, a blessing. People who didn't know him might believe it.

In the spirit of friendliness, he turned back to the Sausage King. "Have you ever considered investing in a real artistic production?"

* * *

Crossing from the deluxe airport lounge to their private plane, Brad was followed closely by Suzanne with Hortensia. They'd almost reached the jet's stairs when the little girl halted, leaned back on her heels, and screamed, "Kimmie!"

Brad wheeled around. The loathsome doll was lying fifty feet back on the tarmac, face down with arms and legs splayed out as if flattened by a heavy weight. Depressed by the sight of the ugly thing, he froze as Hortensia pulled away to get the doll.

Suzanne ran after Hortensia and hoisted the kid to her chest, staggering under the weight. As they moved closer to Brad, Hortensia, holding Kimmie, sagged in Suzanne's arms, dropping lower and lower, weird LED-lighted sneakers twinkling on and off, pink, baby blue, and yellow. The stockholders looked on, aghast.

"Brad," Irwin hissed, "get down there and help, for crissakes!"

That broke the spell. Brad darted down the steps. He grabbed Hortensia's middle and tugged. But his kid refused to let go of Suzanne, and the three of them did a clumsy waltz before awkwardly stumbling as one. Finally, they made it into the plane. The entire time, Brad played to his audience, plastering a smile on his face, despite breathing harder than he had in months.

He collapsed into one of the seats, wondering how he could lift weights five times a week with a personal trainer and still be exhausted after carrying a five-year-old.

“Kids,” the Sausage King, said with his weird reptilian smile. “Dead weights. Millstones around your neck. Always in the way. Got three myself, all boys, home with the old ball and chain. Should’ve left yours home.”

Why did Brad have the overwhelming urge to tell this guy to shut his pie hole? Irwin’s hand crept over his back and patted his shoulder. That calmed him enough to handle the situation.

His daughter was in Suzanne’s lap, arms wrapped around her neck like a baby orangutan around its mother, and his assistant was smiling beatifically down at her. He felt a sudden longing to be next to them. Should he move to the long couch and ask them to join him? He shook his head to clear those thoughts away. Business first. Schmoozing. Irwin had done his part; time for Brad to do his. So instead of moving, he locked his seatbelt and settled in for the flight.

When the door closed and the plane taxied down the runway to a smooth lift-off and an even smoother cruising altitude, Brad turned his attention to the investors. He walked back and slid into the seat next to The King. “So, sausage, eh?” Brad said. “Interesting. Tough to slide the casing on, I imagine. Two- hand job.”

“Got automation now, but yeah, tough to do right. Fortunately for me, we have good workers. Let’s me move on to creative work.” He sucked on his teeth while Brad kept his eyes from rolling. “My granddad’s whole family made sausages. He built a factory in Omaha and we continue his traditional flavorings. Particularly delicious blood sausage! White sausage, too!”

A sudden thud. The Sausage King’s body snapped forward and bounced back. They’d been told to anticipate turbulence but no one else seemed disturbed.

“You okay?” Brad asked.

“Yeah. Must have been a bump but felt like

someone kicked my seat." The Sausage King turned to look behind him. The nearest seats were too far away for anyone's leg to have reached him.

Snapping his fingers for the air hostess to bring more drinks, Brad was mystified, too.

He moved across the aisle and motioned, oh so discreetly, for a girl to sit next to the King.

* * *

Mabel DeVine wandered the manor house, sucking down one cigarette after another. The local staff had tarted up the place to welcome the show, replacing the high-deco style on which her darling Maxim had spent so lavishly. No one had discovered the dead girl, whose corpse should be scaring off the living, so the infestation of human reality vermin was still on its way.

The manor had been merely a stage for her in the old days. Countess Mabel de Summer, the Toast of Gay Paree, the Queen of Hollywood, hostess extraordinaire for endless hot summer weekends, when louche champagne drunks motored up in limousines to cavort in the surf. Meanwhile Mabel stood smoking cliff-top, a slender vamp, glittering diamonds adorning her turban, looking down on her guests, the star of her own show.

That was then, this was now, when the guest rooms had all been split in two so the contestants would have private rooms with en suite bathrooms replacing the old chamber pots. The beds sported tacky brocade counterpanes to keep away the night air—perhaps the chill Mabel could generate would counter that coziness and spark fear at staying the night.

One of the public areas, a massive room in which Mabel had once held balls for royalty, was set up as the main filming area, sectioned with movable walls faux painted to appear old. There were towering fake flower arrangements and potted plants that brought color and life to the beige walls. They also created "private" nooks for assignations. Interesting. Plenty of places to find the enemy alone and waiting to have the pants scared off them.

* * *

From the middle of the plane's cabin, Irwin saw little Hortensia dart behind the Sausage King, lift one leg —with astonishing grace for someone her height and heft —and kick the rear of his seat. She twirled about as she landed and, as she passed on the way back to Suzanne, stared at Irwin with a peculiar steady gaze from beneath lowered brows. Sweat broke out on his brow. It was obvious she dared him to call her out. "No fuckin' way," he muttered under his breath, forcing his eyes away.

Mid-Atlantic, they hit the predicted turbulence, more dramatic than anticipated. Bumps caused steaks, champagne and lobster to bounce about the cabin and spilled expensive booze onto expensive suits. One of the contestants seized the opportunity to throw her arms around the neck of the closest investor, who clutched her in return, a bit lower than the neck.

Everyone was queasy or outright vomiting. Everyone but Hortensia. She raced, shrieking with delight up and down the aisles. Her low center of gravity protected from falls as the plane bounced its way through the clouds. Heavy weather obscured the tumultuous sea far below. The pilot took the plane higher, above the storm until the descent, where they encountered even more disturbance.

* * *

Their trip wasn't to go as planned—another huge storm was brewing in the North Sea, extending to the English Channel, making landing at Le Havre's airport perilous. They diverted to Paris, with transportation arranged to Normandy, though there was still no guarantee they'd reach their destination.

Brad wiped the sick sweat from his forehead. Someone tugged his sleeve and waved something in his face. It was Hortensia with a drawing of two large figures, monsters from the look of them, one small but even more monstrous figure between them. "Mommy, Daddy, and Hort," she crowed.

A fresh bump. His mouth filled with bile and he pushed her away, only to be startled when she returned to snuggle next to him. She looked up into his eyes and fluttered her eyelashes in what seemed a mockery of adoration.

Returning to his chat with the Sausage King was impossible. His daughter was humming, the sound almost mechanical like the grinding of small stones underfoot. It made his thoughts swirl.

In one of the two seats across the aisle, practically drooling over the girl next to him, the King really did look menacing, a dragon in disguise. He raised one eyebrow and sent Brad a half-concealed smirk.

To Brad, it was like a huge and precariously hung sword above him. He cut his glance to the contestant, a bit of redheaded pulchritude at least two degrees too slutty for the show. She got the hint, purred up against the King like an adolescent cat in her first heat. Brad smiled with gratitude, trying his best to telepathically convey the images of a Mercedes convertible and condo in Vegas, the King bringing sausage to her on gambling trips.

Her eyes wide and fixed, Hortensia also appeared to study the King and the girl. After what seemed an eternity, she held up her doll, pointed at the redhead and exclaimed, "Look Kimmie, that lady is just like Barbie!"

In response, the contestant practically twinkled. She cooed, "Aren't you the cleverest little thing! So, so sweet!" The Sausage King put his arm around her shoulders. "Did you hear that? She thinks I look like Barbie!"

For the first time in Brad's life, a beautiful, all-too-available girl repulsed him. And yet he couldn't pull his eyes away from the russet tangle about her face. He pictured the King huge as Godzilla, ripping off her head and crushing her torso into a pancake.

Hortensia's humming grew ever more dissonant. She smiled into her father's face, then left his row to curl up against Suzanne. Looking for a moment like an innocent child, she yawned and fell asleep. And, for a moment, Suzanne looked like the mother he'd like to have for his kids.

* * *

The old convent's nuns were right where Mabel had left them. Under the protection of the cloister's roof, they faced each other in two lines, hands folded, drab black hoods covering all but their moving lips.

"Come on, ladies!" Mabel said. "Can the chanting. There's work to be done. A lot of cardinal sins will be played out here. You could save quite a few souls."

The susurration continued without any sign they heard. Praying was all they could do, stuck in the same place for almost four hundred and fifty years. If all their praying hadn't set them free, didn't let them contact the living, what chance did a libertine like Mabel DeVine have?

Depressing, but there was no one else to talk to and that had nearly driven her cuckoo. A star needed an audience, so she'd talk to them until someone else arrived. Someone who could see and hear her.

That day might never come. Mabel lit another cigarette and thoughtfully blew smoke under the veils. No reaction. She headed up the crumbling bell turret, to ring the ghostly bell, the original having been melted down to make cannon balls. The sound was low and mournful, like the distant rumble of a coming storm. Maybe that would sow a soupcon of fear in the approaching horde.

* * *

There wasn't room in the limo for everyone. Irwin begged and pleaded with the rental agency but was told that, due to the storm, there were no other cars to be hired. Nothing to be done but send some of their group on the chartered bus with the contestants.

He gritted his teeth at the wasted expense of the private jet. He and Brad conferred, selected the two less attractive girls of the four they'd brought and sent them, with Suzanne and Hortensia, on the bus. Then they climbed into the limo with the rest of their party and opened a bottle of champagne.

CHAPTER FOUR

The plane ride was fun. Hortensia had felt fine the entire time, even laughing when the others were bent over, faces in throw-up bags. But the bus was different. Right after she scarfed down several 3 Musketeers, Hortensia's tummy began to bubble and squeak. She'd smuggled the candy from her grandparents' place in her little wholesome snack bag. Her *abuelo* knew they were her favorite, knew how she loved peeling the slippery, silvery wrapping from the chocolate coating, holding the bars in her hands until they were soft and bendy but not yet melted. He always had a small stash waiting for her visits. Not even her *abuela* was in on the secret. She was too afraid of Ana Maria, her *hija elegante.*

Suzanne grumbled that the bus booked for the contestants had been streamlined and well-appointed, and now the French were taking advantage of the storm's demands on transportation to supply something far different. Without a discount. "They're giving us foreigners their worst, a smoke-belching thirty-year-old piece of crap!" Then she smiled down at Hortensia and squeezed her hand reassuringly.

As they boarded, a contestant elbowed Suzanne out of the way and Hortensia was knocked onto her knees on the muddy ground. The guilty woman was the tallest, with a teeny middle and long legs like Barbie's, and hair even blacker than Ana Maria's. She was really, truly the most beautiful lady Hortensia had ever seen. She was also probably the meanest—she didn't even say, "Sorry!" for bumping into them. Instead, she turned to the lady next to her and said, "Homely kids just make me sad."

Hortensia would have kicked her, just like the man in the plane, but a scrape on her right leg was throbbing. She pressed her hand against it. It was sticky with blood. She must have hit a stone.

After Hortensia and Suzanne took the seat in the very back, the mean lady tossed her small bag next to them. The sparkly strap hit Suzanne's shoulder. "That kid's mom is just crew, pretty useless. Only good as a luggage rack."

Suzanne didn't say the thing about being Hortensia's mom was wrong, and, at that, Hort's heart soared and her resolve strengthened. She wriggled even closer to her.

The other ladies followed, putting their carry-ons where the mean lady had, until Suzanne and Hortensia were squished together, surrounded by a mound of perfume-y bags. As if the exhaust seeping into the bus wasn't bad enough.

Hortensia watched the black-haired lady like her abuela's chihuahua watched a squirrel, with sharp eyes and murder in her heart. But how could she get even? She couldn't think straight with her belly aching so. "Who's that lady?" she asked, pointing.

"Oh," replied Suzanne with a big sigh, "that's Isabella."

"She's awful."

"Yes, honey. Yes, she is." Suzanne looked how Hortensia felt in the schoolyard, when the other kids were playing, and she was alone.

Hort's heart burned with the desire for vengeance. She slouched, pushing the travel bags to the side. The bus swerved around curves through countryside with high trees that looked fake as giant green Q-tips. The road went up hills and down into valleys. The black smoke from the tailpipe worsened mile after mile, looking the way the stinkiest farts she could imagine would look.

At one sharp curve, the melted 3 Musketeers, sickly sweet, squooshed up from her stomach into her mouth. She was going to be sick, couldn't keep it in. Desperate, she scrabbled through the little bags until she found the one with the sparkly strap—Isabella's. A short while later she was asleep, leaning against Suzanne's arm, feeling so much better.

She awoke. Snuggling warm and deep into her *abuela's* soft belly, the happy chihuahuas dancing around, had been a dream. The belly beneath her was only a little round one. Suzanne's. They were still far from home, and she was still stuck with her daddy.

Suzanne slid away from her seat next to Hort, who stretched and yawned. There was now lots of room on the seat since the satchels around her had been taken by the pretty ladies. Suzanne waited for her toward the front of the bus.

"Yucky trip," Hortensia said, rubbing her eyes.

"Yup." Suzanne nodded. She smiled. "But you throwing up into someone's overnight case was the highlight of the day. Do you know whose bag it was?"

Hortensia felt a giggle rising through the sick feeling. "That mean lady's."

Suzanne patted Hort's hand. "Don't you worry a bit. I zipped it back up. She won't notice until tonight."

Hortensia smiled her first Continental smile.

* * *

The redhead was doing her best to amuse The Sausage King, but his attention was fading. Irwin, on the limo seat facing them, was glum. Even if it was to *Grab the Groom's* advantage, it was depressing that women sold themselves so cheaply. Why didn't they go to college and become nice teachers or accountants? Maybe even doctors or lawyers, though Irwin doubted this lot was smart enough. Or to be honest, pretty enough to find a sugar-daddy.

Oh, well, they were doing the job of making things go smoothly. He and Brad had sat these girls at the office conference table, photos of the other contestants laid out. Those headshots made it obvious there was no way they could compete to win The Groom. They had a choice: drop out or come along as assistants to entertain the investors—no strings attached, chat and flirt only. If they struck a deal of some sort on their own, the show's executive staff would never, ever invade their privacy.

And so, the now ex-contestants had sized up the situation and agreed to ride with the Meat Packers, as he and Brad called the moneymen.

Looks, he mused. They mattered much more than ever these days for women. Much more than talent did, especially in L.A. The gay scene there was the same. He remembered his young self, vowing to make a difference in the world. Create art, not schlock, where actions and deeds counted. He longed to write and direct a major art-film, his reinterpretation of a classic.

What if his husband—who really had become a doctor, who really did something for the world—noticed his insignificance? Looked elsewhere for love? There were lots of young male nurses these days, traipsing softly in and out of the operating suite in their little rubber clogs and easily removable scrubs.

They'd been married ten years and Guglielmo spent evenings on the internet watching medical symposia with sound-canceling earphones. Blocking out the "Tones and I" Irwin played while dance-monkeying around the living room. That would once have been regarded as come-hither cute.

Sometimes Irwin felt he faded into their $250 a roll wallpaper. Nagging self-doubt squirmed through his chest like a worm in an overripe peach, growing longer and longer until it strangled the pit of his heart. His husband deserved better than the man Irwin was. He deserved a famous intellectual, a renowned maker of timeless classics, not a crap reality TV schlock-meister.

To finance an art film, *Grab the Groom* needed to continue as a cash cow. Or at least a cash calf as it had been for the past six seasons

Lost in thought, wishing his husband had come with him to France, he paid little attention to the downpour and howling wind outside his window. Then, with breathtaking speed, the car lurched suddenly, flinging him from one side of the hip-bruising seatbelt to the other. He clung to the seatback in front, stiff with fear.

The car skidded and fishtailed. The world whirled about as the limo hydroplaned across the road on a small lake of rainwater. Irwin's head cracked against his window. The girls screamed and clutched the Meat Packers. Irwin screamed along with them.

The driver desperately turned the wheel. The vehicle didn't respond. His loud cursing rang out, "*Fils de pute*! *Merde*! *Encule toi Salaud*!" In another half-second he switched to English with, "Fuckshit! Fuckshit! Fuckshit!"

The limo ricocheted side to side, tilted to the right, almost flipped, then stabilized and shuddered to a halt. The whirring of wheels sounded, but without movement. Everyone's eyes were wide, their anxious breath fogging the windows. No one said a thing. The driver hopped out, walked around the car, and finally kicked its side. Hair streaming water, he returned to lean in the open driver's door. "For what did you *connards* make me leave Paris? To come to fucking Normandy in such a storm?"

Then the driver shook like a damp poodle, climbed in and said, "Get out. Out! And push. We are stuck in the mud!"

"Can't we wait for a tow truck?" Irwin asked.

Maniacal laughter answered him. "*Zut alors*! Look at the weather! A tow truck? In a monster storm? There will be no tow truck! Push or die!"

Brad was pretending to be deaf, so, regretting his white buck Salvatore Ferragamo loafers, Irwin got out and surveyed the situation. The right rear wheel was mired. When he crouched to look closer, the driver gunned the motor. *SPLAT, SPLAT, SPLAT*! Irwin was covered in mud from the chest down. But the limo hadn't budged.

No other vehicle was in sight. There were no locals around. Drenched, he opened the passenger door and said with a smile, his tone hard and bright and no-nonsense as a shiny franc, "Not to worry, ladies! Your manly escorts and I will push us out!"

CHAPTER FIVE

Hortensia hopped out of the bus. Outside was colder than she'd ever felt in California, rain mixed with white flakes like the showers of almond petals in spring, but icy. So this was snow. But not picture book snow, ready for good moms and daddies to make angels with their kids. Instead of covering the ground with white, this was melting as soon as it landed on the gray stones.

The ladies were waiting for the driver to unload the big suitcases. Isabella was in front, complaining loudly. "Where's a porter? We can't go up to there without one and we can't leave our luggage. If we don't fucking watch, that fucking driver might steal our stuff."

Hortensia's *abuela* would smack her for that language. That made it extra nice to see the shiny strap on Isabella's shoulder and think about her opening the bag later.

The driver didn't seem to care about what she said. Humming happily, he was standing at the stone wall, his back turned toward his passengers. "I don't believe this," one of the contestants said, her face red with anger and slick with sleet. "We're freezing! What the hell is he doing?"

Hortensia liked the way his baggy jeans sagged

beneath his tiny butt and liked his humming. Nice to see someone happy who didn't care what other people thought. "Looking away from ugly things," she said.

Suzanne's face reddened. She put her finger over her lips. "Shhhh. Don't be rude."

Hortensia shrugged and hummed along, her voice as bad as the driver's, loud and enjoyably out-of-tune.

Up the drive was an old building, pinkish like raw pork, peek-a-booing through the blowing mist. The wind was whistling in her ears and, with the sound of crashing waves, made Hortensia shiver.

The driver was waggling his hips back and forth in time to the tune. The shivering and complaining of the passengers, as well as the steady rain, seemed to be of no interest to him.

The bus was still running, pumping black smoke out its rear. The white mists from around the manor mixed with and swirled the blackness into ominous shapes. A few low, bent-over trees creaked and thrashed, threatening to pull out of the ground and walk toward Hortensia. She put her arms around Suzanne's leg, twisting her fingers in the hem of the skirt. Suzanne was kind of weak and small to hold off what was surrounding them, if there were bad things like monsters.

Her daddy was big. She wished he would come.

"Hurry up," the nearest contestant called. "We're freezing."

"Oh, that French guy's just a bum!" another woman said.

The driver's clothes were kind of old and wrinkly, but he didn't look like a poor bum to Hortensia. Just happy.

Ignoring Suzanne, Isabella turned to the other girls. "Surprised a French guy actually works a job." She walked toward the driver, waving a pack of cigarettes.

Like magic, he turned and moved back to the bus.

"Why the hell didn't you drive up to the door?" she asked.

"Why the hell you didn't offer tobacco sooner?" He pointed up at the mansion. "The drive, it is too small for the bus to go." He pulled two cigarettes from the pack, put both in his mouth, hunching over enough to get them lit in the wind. He held out one to Isabella, but she made an *ewww* face. The driver shrugged, pinched the end, tucked it in his shirt.

After a puff of the other, he lifted one eyebrow and took out a giant ring full of keys. He sorted through the keys, murmuring "*non*" over and over. At a final "*oui*," he unlocked the cargo hold.

Two men came down the drive with a rattling wooden cart. They put the bags and equipment on it.

It was hard to walk. The drive was made of big stones—slippery in the freezing rain—and it was colder, the chilly wind stronger. Hortensia's hair was dripping rain down her back as she trudged along with her hand in Suzanne's.

She looked up. Behind the pink building was a tower with a top like jagged teeth. Between two of those teeth, stood a woman, all gray like a dirty cloud. Hortensia pointed and cried, "Look up there! A lady!"

Suzanne and the cart stopped. "Nobody's there, Hort."

Hortensia hated when people didn't believe her. She pushed her lower lip out. "But she is. I see her."

The men pulling the cart looked at each other in a funny way, shivering. "*Non*, little girl. There cannot be no one up there. The stairs, they broke two hundred years now." They jabbered away in French, pulling a bit faster. Hortensia didn't understand a word, but they were leaving her and Suzanne behind.

She waved at the lady on the tower, who jumped back as if surprised. The figure lifted a hand but quickly disappeared behind one of the stony teeth.

* * *

The little girl had seen her. Mabel was sure of it. She swirled rapidly down the tower, bouncing from one wall to another, to discuss it with the nuns.

She snapped her fingers under a veil. “Someone saw me, girls! What do you think of that? Just a little ankle-biter, but still someone.”

Their chanting grew louder, more understandable now, the *Adoro te Devote*, but they didn’t otherwise respond. They seemed to entirely lack curiosity. Perhaps it was simply the way they were, their essential nun-ness.

Or perhaps it was the way they’d died. Some of the veils were empty, the heads inside missing. Lord knew that wasn’t simply death itself. Mabel always wanted to know what was what, but those nuns never told her anything. She snorted.

Who needed them if someone could see her? That someone might prove useful. Depending.

* * *

The jostling was very unsettling, coming out of the chill dark of the jet and into the foul air and rough bumps on the road. And then, once removed from the cargo hold of the bus, the fierce wind and frightful cold made Cleopatra coil her body protectively over her head. Her case bounced on the cart and then up the stairs until it came to rest on the floor in a dark place. Flicking her tongue, she detected a faint but fresh trace of her owner and was momentarily reassured.

* * *

Safe from the storm, Brad had settled in at Couvent de la Mer. The location was atmospheric, the executive suite spacious with a view of the churning, crashing surf below. Brad had almost forgotten the horror of the trip, the fear and dread in Irwin's eyes every time the little guy looked at Hortensia. He shook his head. No matter that his child was a girl, no matter that she was scary, he had to hand it to her. The kid had balls.

In anticipation of the cast's arrival, the production staff had spent their time wisely. The grand ballroom, with its patterned marble floor and Louis Quatorze gold window trim, was divided by moveable panels. The library's gargoyle-encrusted fireplace held a roaring fire, welcoming and dignified, a new concept for the show. A hot tub, yes, but no poolside tiki bar like the island seasons. Dignified.

Irwin was such a serious little dude, longing to produce art. Perhaps, with this set design, they could win Outstanding Production Design for a Reality-Competition Show on the next Webbys. As the Webbys were the pinnacle of internet reality show art, that might make him happy.

Suzanne came in, her damp shoes *squinch, squinch, squinching* on the carpet. "I haven't even had time to unpack. The contestants are in an uproar, upset hair and makeup weren't immediately available. Don't know what they're whining about," she said, turning to go. "The Groom is hidden away in his suite and won't be out until tonight."

"Do you think I should soothe their feathers?" He meant to sound boss-like but fumbled, feeling a tinge of guilt. He'd arrived in luxury and, while she took care of his five-year-old child and arrangements for the show, he'd lounged in a dry robe, warmed for him by the manor's staff.

Her response was a look with a clear message: there were lots of things he should do. Possibly some involving the kid. He ignored her, making his voice extra-chirpy. "I promise to be on time for tonight's Reveal of The Groom. Without any reminders."

She stopped at the room's threshold. "When will you read to Hortensia?" Shit, he'd been right. "She wants milk and cookies. With you."

Shit once more! Milk and cookies with a five-year-old? Or scotch and soda with the gorgeous contestants? The second sounded better, much better. Yawning, he dodged that bullet with praise. "I fell asleep. Jet lag, I guess. I knew I could count on you. Efficient as always!"

She gave him that look again.

"Little kids love adult dress up, right?" he asked. "Bring her to the reception."

"Not sure your daughter's the dress-up type." She turned to go, her stiff back accusation enough. "But be sure and spend some of the time with us."

Confused thoughts swirling in his head, he lost all longing for a snack. A wash of melancholy swept across him. But why? Things were going fine, weren't they? And waiting for his appearance were wine, cheese, Irwin, and all those women.

His mental discomfort must be due to the gloomy weather. He freshened up hastily and went down the stairs.

* * *

The reception was a kaleidoscopic swirl of satin polyester and décolletage beneath gold-leafed ceiling medallions of fat cherubs, disporting with naked nymphs.

Regency France. Even Hollywood was no longer that tasteless.

"Baguette slice with brie?" A waiter asked.

Irwin shook his head. He surveyed the room where other waiters circulated with mini pastries, little marzipan apples filled with Calvados, and marrons glaces, which the contestants avoided. A sticky candied chestnut down the cleavage was only good if someone rich were there to lick it away.

The Meat Packers tried to mingle, hoisting their champagne flutes at passing females. For the most part, they were ignored, except by the girls who'd traveled with them. Still, good thing they'd lost interest in discussing business, giving Brad and Irwin a breather to relax and oversee the build-up to the Reveal of The Groom.

Irwin walked up to a cameraman and nudged him. "Focus on Mr. Hudson as he makes his way through the crowd!" But the camera's angle was on the blonde opposite Brad, the one engaging his rapt attention. The woman seemed to have forgotten to tape down one edge of her cleavage, failing to keep her right breast under control. The nipple was winking in and out of sight like a shy kitten. Its peekaboo appearance would need to be blurred but odds the uncensored shots would be bootlegged. Oh, well, they wouldn't go to waste. Any publicity was good publicity.

Irwin worked his way across the room, bent on weaning Brad off the teat.

* * *

After introducing The Groom as an entrepreneur in Silicon Valley, Brad stepped aside. The Groom took the microphone and, in a voice smooth and seductive, said, "Hello, ladies! I look forward to getting to know each and every one of you." A pointed hesitation and then, "Intimately." He gave a charming laugh and stepped aside.

Brad returned to center stage to introduce the contestants. The first one was Isabella, tall, inky hair swept up, imperious, and almost unreal in a shimmering, low-back, skin-tight fuchsia gown.

The second was petite Jocelyn. Almost a mini-Isabella. Then came a blonde Southern giggler.

One by one the girls stepped up and received a chaste kiss on the cheek from The Groom.

CHAPTER SIX

CONTESTANT #2—HAILEY

Hailey wasn't as stupid as Irwin thought. She'd carefully fastened her plunging décolletage, making sure only one side played it close to the chest. The other fluttered loose with each breath she took—her thirty-thousand Instagram followers would appreciate that. And she was just getting started.

As Brad Hudson headed to the stage, she let her hand linger on his arm until he moved out of reach. Nothing stirred a man's heart like competition, so she made certain The Groom was looking.

"Whatever you're thinking, you can forget it," a hissing voice said in her ear. That black-haired bitch, Isabella.

"Bet you want to jump on that gorgeous specimen. Drag him off to your web." Hailey nodded toward the stage.

"If you mean The Groom, uh-uh, not him."

"You're not here for The Groom?" Hailey replied. When they'd gone to costuming, Isabella had pissed Hailey off. One good thing about this show, compared to the others, was that outfits were supplied for the contestants. Isabella grabbed the dress Hailey'd picked out and insisted she'd seen it first. Hailey gave it up. But when the second gown fit Hailey's hips like a latex surgical glove, Isabella tried to rip it off her. That's when they became mortal enemies.

"He's not my type. Too pretty-boy. I like a bit of maturity."

"Ah, come on. Poo-pooing The Groom? The lady—using the term loosely—doth protest too much."

"Fuck off."

Hailey snorted. The bitch was trying to convince her The Groom wasn't worth it, as gorgeous as he was. A snort wasn't feminine, but no one was close by—even that boring twerp Irwin had moved off. He thought he was invisible, but he'd triggered her gaydar. Obviously, the little guy was queer as a two-dollar bill, as her family always said. Probably had the hots for his partner.

Isabella wasn't done goading. She hooked one long talon on the cloth of Hailey's dress. "Having a wardrobe malfunction?"

Hailey ignored that jibe. "Hear you're going by 'Isabella Imbriglio' now. Isn't that a bit Faux-talian, Ms. Britney Woodcock? As if dyeing your hair dead-Mafia black was convincing."

Hailey was counting on rage being the result. Instead, Isabella broke out in peals of laughter. "Speaking of 'faux,' we can chat more about this later. In fact, I think we will."

The other girls shushed them. The Groom was about to speak and, even more important, he would show the gifts to be given each evening to the date of his choice.

"Thank you, thank you," The Groom said to Brad, who was still clapping. On the folding table next to him was a shiny leather box. It held everything from the first night's braided gold hoop earrings to the two-carat diamond ring for the contestant chosen as The Fiancée.

Hailey had the inside track on the diamond. Her bestie at the Rodeo Drive jewelry store, where Grab the Groom previously sourced the prizes, said this year's ring was purchased on overstock.com. Still, that final reward, even if cheapened, made total winnings worth three-hundred thousand. Nothing to sneeze at for a few months in a drafty old hotel, eating French food.

Funny, she had the impression that the Isabella creature, the serpent in the garden, the worm in the apple, thought the producer, Brad Hudson, was the prize—Isabella sashayed by him, working her hips, a dozen times or more. Hailey prided herself on never missing a trick, and she'd turned enough of them.

The Groom was still going on about his search for love. It was all Hailey could do to keep from laughing. As if someone who looked like him had trouble in that department.

Hailey smiled at him, ducking her head coyly, but not before catching a glittering response in his eyes. That's enough for tonight, she thought. She pushed her way out of the crowd.

In the corridor, she again bumped into Isabella, who promptly moved from the wall she was leaning against to block Hailey's progress. Isabella' grabbed either side of Hailey's plunging neckline with firm roughness. One side stayed in place, pulling on the skin. The other came up easily, with no sign it had ever been taped down.

"Nice tits, right?" Hailey asked with an innocent smile.

"Natural-looking," Isabella said with one eyebrow raised. "Nipple's still a bit small."

Hailey pulled the fabric from her grasp. "You'll stretch it out, just like the ass of that rag you're wearing." She started back to her room but was called up short by

Isabella saying, "No matter how hard you try, how much makeup you slather on, you're gonna blow it. I'll see to that."

"Oh, I'm gonna blow it all right." She winked, pursing her lips to pop a little kiss at her rival, and headed to the stairs.

In her bedroom, Hailey shucked the dress, exclaiming a loud "Ouch!" as she removed the taped side. In an outrageously expensive lace bra and satin thong panties, topped with a sheer silk robe, she paced the floor. Could that Isabella whore take her down? What did she know and how?

The game was on—other contestants were no match for them—and the game was no holds barred.

So, she, Hailey, didn't follow the rules. She could satisfy The Groom—or any man. She could. At least long enough to make off with the prize money!

But how she regretted leaving the glorious, well-hung Hans and aptly named Peter, silver-tongued and gold-fingered! What turn-ons!

With sudden fierceness, her skin flushed and sweat poured from her, darkly spotting the pale mauve of her lingerie. Her room was overheated now, when it had been cold and drafty before. Why?

A hot flash! Worse than any sadomasochist scenario imaginable. Her breath came tight. She'd forgotten her estrogen shot! No wonder she was dripping. Her damn doctor had gotten the flu just before she boarded the plane. She'd missed getting her prescription. Hell, France was awash in estrogen and she'd thought a dose would be easy to come by. But not in this deserted pile of rubble, not in a godforsaken hurricane! What cowards, to close the whole area down. No wonder they'd lost…some war or other…

Air, air! Go out on the balcony! The pressure built in her head.

Perspiring like mad, she flung open the doors that led to her balcony, stepped out into the maelstrom of Arctic winds, finding instant relief. Far below, the North Sea waves crashed against the cliff. She stepped farther out, spreading her silk-encased arms, like a Valkyrie in the Gotterdammerung. It was hard not to break into Brunhilde's aria.

What stopped her was how fiercely her balls itched. Sweat always did that to them.

As she adjusted her panties, a sudden powerful gust blew shut the doors with a clap as loud as thunder. A fierce cloud swirled around her. Hailey, startled, fell back, her arms reaching out for the railing. She lost her balance, failed to gain a hold. Another gust and she tumbled over the edge.

* * *

Mabel perched on the ornate metal railing, musing how times had changed. Back in her time, when "anything goes" was the motto, lots of men dressed as women. Why, there was even that famous madame over in Oxnard, where *The Sheik* was filmed. Rumor had it that madam and her girls serviced Valentino in every way possible. And the drag balls, what fun they'd been! It took skill to create the illusion. it was a grand performance, but with enough work, often quite successful.

These days, everything was simple. People changed sex like they once changed costumes. But what irked her the most was how easily they gained fame. No hard work, no lines to learn, just show up and be your irritating, declasse self, mugging in front of a laptop's camera. Bingo, you're a celebrity!

On the other hand, that dive had been spectacular.

For a brief moment, gusting on the wind, Hailey's robe swirling upward like wings—she'd appeared a creature from ancient myths. And then the storm tore off that beautifully styled, real human-hair wig as she spun downward to the bare and jagged rocks below.

Mabel stood and clapped her hands, crying, "Bravo! Bravo!"

CHAPTER SEVEN

The misty lady floated in through the closed window, just as Hortensia got to the drawing of all the people admiring Wilbur, who stood under Charlotte's web with the words "SOME PIG."

"You can really see me?" the lady asked.

"If seeing all the way through you means I can see you, yeah,'" Hortensia said. "Why?"

"Because I'm a ghost. *Booo*!" The lady's "*boo*" sounded more "I don't care" than scary. She fiddled with the cigarette in the holder on her finger and took a big puff.

"That's funny!" Nice to have a visitor since Suzanne was busy. "People sure smoke a lot in France. Smoking's bad for you."

The lady laughed. "'I'm a ghost' means I'm dead. So smoking can't hurt me."

Hortensia closed her book. Adults thought kids were stupid. The lady was rude, too, coming into Hort's room—didn't she know what "private" meant? But Hort was curious enough to keep the conversation going. "My name's Hortensia. What's yours?"

"Mabel DeVine." The ghost lady tilted her head.

"You know, you'd remind me of me, if I hadn't always been a beauty."

"That's mean." Adults also thought you wouldn't get what they really meant. Hortensia opened the book and put her finger on the first word of the page, to pretend she was reading when she was really spying on Mabel.

The lady moved around the room, going straight through the furniture if it was in her way. That made it hard to concentrate on the letters, which went all squiggly. Hort made sure to keep looking down at the book, anyway, saying "Some pig" very softly to herself.

Mabel DeVine zoomed around the ceiling, then scattered in a sparkly cloud, spreading to every corner of the room. Hort dropped her lower lip and kept turning the pages, determined not to seem impressed.

At last Mabel pulled herself back into the shape of a person. "What are you reading?"

Hort sighed and showed the illustration on the cover.

"Huh, a book about a pig and a spider living in an old barn on a farm. To make it a good book, there's gotta be a glamorous gold digger who saves the day and marries the farmer who's secretly a very rich guy."

Hort rolled her eyes. That sounded like one of her mother's books.

"Would it make a good movie?" Mabel asked.

"Already was a good movie. Long, long time ago. Before I was born. But I still saw it on TV."

"TV." The ghost lady snorted through her nose, letting loose two streams of smoke. She settled on the couch next to Hort. "Why don't you read with a computer thingie? Everyone who comes here seems to have one."

"They don't feel like a real book. They don't smell like real paper."

Mabel's hand reached out toward the book. Her fingertips went straight through the cover. She tried again, sneaking up on the pages like a timid mouse and the same thing happened. She sniffed. "I remember that smell. The nice weight of a book in hand. Fitzgerald, that handsome devil with the loony wife..." She sounded sad and Hort forgave her for being rude. She was meeting a lot of grownups who weren't very grown up.

Mabel licked one finger, which didn't help her turn the page. She frowned. "You'll have to read it to me," she said. "If you know how."

Hortensia considered pretending she couldn't read yet, just like she did with her mommy and the au pair. But maybe a ghost could see inside someone and know when they were lying. "I like to be read to instead."

"Why ever?"

Hortensia looked down. "That's the only way I get to snuggle. The words make them forget to go do other things."

"Well, all you have to do is turn the pages and I'll..." Then Mabel's mouth went all crooked. "No, that's okay. Just looking at the pictures would be ducky." Ghostly tears showed on her cheeks. Maybe they made it hard to read.

"We only have time for a bit. I have to see my daddy." Hortensia opened the book. "And you can call me 'Hort'."

* * *

When Brad reached the landing, Hortensia was waiting for him in footie pajamas. Strangely quiet and demure, she leaned against the handrail, her fleece clad legs dangling on either side of the baluster. When she saw him, she stood and led the way back to the room she shared with Suzanne. The small, resolute figure drooped a bit—was that from being tired or from knowing she was impinging on his time? The after-reception party was in full swing.

In the pastel pink pajamas, she made him think of a shrimp-filled Chinese dumpling. An ambulatory dumpling, trundling along with a determined air, swish, swish with each step. Shrimp pink. But Hortensia was no shrimp, not in size or attitude, so maybe piglet pink.

As soon as they entered the suite, she clambered under her covers, burrowing like a little sow in a mud bath. He shook his head. No, not a little pig—that thought was cruel. He went back to shrimp, as she was so much littler than him. Shrimp pink.

"Where's Suzanne?" she said, looking past him.

Ouch. "She's still taking care of things downstairs." He felt the pang of rejection. Wasn't he good enough? Wasn't her *father* enough? "Let's see what we have here," he said in his best "jolly presenter voice," the one used to intro contestants. That tone always won people over.

He settled next to her—atop the covers with his back propped up against the headboard—and picked up *Charlotte's Web*. Just feeling the slick cover made him proud. He was going to read to his kid, like a TV daddy. His own daddy had never read to him. Nor had his mother. When he was little, nannies read to him at bedtime. Which one was it who read *Charlotte's Web*? He flipped through the book's pages. "This is awful long."

Hortensia snorted and pulled it from his hands. She moved restlessly, her feet, in their footies, crossed and uncrossed, made a rubberized *squeech, squeech, squeech*. Did she want him to leave?

Suzanne came in and, for a moment, he half-hoped his kid would want her to take over. "You still want *me* to read the story?" Brad liked to think of himself as confident, sophisticated, and smarter than most, but now a little kid threw him off his game. Made him feel like a buffoon in a way no grown woman had.

"Yes, she does," Suzanne said, settling on the bed on Hortensia's other side. Above the kid's head, her shoulder met his. Her weight felt just right against him.

On his other side, Hortensia leaned forward to look around him. She said to Suzanne, "If you want him to."

"Not *Charlotte's Web,* maybe this." Suzanne held out a book with a beautiful cover illustration.

"Read dat boog!" Hortensia had put the Kimmie doll over her mouth as if it were speaking in baby talk, her expression daring him to object.

The book was *Beauty and the Beast,* but not the cartoony Disney version. "I bought it for Hortensia when I got the doll," Suzanne said.

The volume was reassuringly slim. He'd read rapidly—but with feeling—planning to tuck her in and be back to work in a jiffy.

"Once there was a wealthy merchant..." The story went quickly at first, starting with Beauty's request for a rose. Little Hortensia sat upright against the headboard but, as he read on, she slipped back down on the pillows. Drawing after drawing, her stubby fingers reached out to touch the images of Beauty and her romance with the Beast.

"The Beast is nice." She had morphed into a harmless, small child, slowly leaning against him, warm and solid, smelling of milk and cookies. Tension leached from his muscles.

At last Beauty returned to find the Beast dying of love, until Beauty's tears dropped onto his face and he transformed into a handsome prince. "They lived happily ever after," Brad announced. He snapped the book shut with a cheery, "OK, then!"

But Hortensia's face was like a mask of horror. "NOOOOO!" she shrieked and shot upward.

"What's the...?" Brad pulled her back toward him, but she struggled away, sobbing as bitterly as an eliminated contestant.

Brad moved toward his daughter. "Aren't you happy the prince was released from his spell and Beauty loves him?"

Instead of agreeing, Hortensia continued to wail, her two little eyes like Craisins in a bowl of oatmeal. Her cries crescendoed, blending into the howling wind outside, as if a ghostly horde surrounding the house had finally gained entrance.

Voice trembling, body trembling, Brad stood, saying, "I better return to the party."

Suzanne gave him a puzzling look. "I'll stay until she falls asleep." She slid close to Hortensia. Close enough to hug his daughter.

Hortensia looked at Suzanne and then him, and back to Suzanne again. Hort pooched out her lower lip, pointed at the door, and said, "No. Go with him."

* * *

After Suzanne and her father left, Hortensia tore the pages of the book one-by-one, tearing them into tiny pieces. She was sobbing and the bits got wet from her damp little hands. The rug was a mess.

Mabel hovered over the little girl's shoulder. "What's up, buttercup? Why the waterworks? What's the deal with your daddy and that bug-eyed Betty?"

Hortensia stopped ripping and glared through her tears. "Her name's Suzanne, and that's not very nice."

She turned her back on Mabel.

Mabel tried to distract her. She blew smoke rings that danced in and out of each other, gradually widening until they dissipated near the ceiling, but got no response from Hortensia. "The truth is often not very nice."

"Beauty loved the Beast. Why did he have to die?" Hortensia covered her eyes with grubby little paws.

Someone needed to teach that kid hygiene. And, anyway, the Beast in the story hadn't really died. Instead, he came back to life, revived by Beauty's tears. Not just back to life, but no longer beastly! "Wasn't it better for Beauty to have a Handsome Prince instead of a hideous monster? You think the Beast would have loved Beauty if she wasn't a beauty?"

At that, Hortensia began to sob more vigorously, her eyes reddening more, her upper lip streaming with snot. Tragically homely. Mabel felt an inkling of something unfamiliar, a funny sensation beneath her sequins. Just a little, as if her heart was an egg tapped gently against the counter, but not quite breaking.

Hortensia dropped her hands and snuffled snot back into her nose. "And when the truth's not nice, you don't gotta say it."

"Sorry." The alien word nearly choked Mabel, and empathy swelled in her heart until, when she looked down, she could almost see it beating. "How about you forgive Aunty Mabel? Okay, ducky?"

Took a moment, but Hortensia nodded. "'K, but promise to be nice to Suzanne. She's my only friend."

Mabel looked away, taking another drag. The empathy turned to ice.

"Besides you."

The chill surrounding Mabel's heart lessened a little. "Sure, kiddo, do my best."

* * *

Later that night, cozy in his bed, Brad pulled out *Charlotte's Web*, the first thing he'd swiped in decades. He sank into the pillow, turning pages. The story made him think of his beloved Nanny Lan in her soft gray uniform, reading while he lay tucked between the starched sheets. Her voice was hard to hear over the happy, drunken noises wafting up from his parents' parties.

Those parties meant she'd rush through a few pages each night before leaving to serve hors d'oeuvres. He'd been on tenterhooks, worried that Wilbur would be made into char sui bao like the wait staff carried on silver trays downstairs. Lan had taken Brad to the dumpling factory, where men with giant cleavers hacked at pig carcasses and dead piggy eyes stared at him, so he worried about the fate of pigs, despite his guilty pleasure in the savory filling.

His mother fired Lan, saying that she'd broken an antique vase. Brad told her he was the real culprit, but his mother stopped meditating to say, "Don't be ridiculous. You were at junior yoga."

The next nanny was Adelita, who continued *Charlotte's Web* when she wasn't serving *tamales de huitlacoche* from her sister's taqueria. But Adelita scorched one of his father's silk shirts.

With Adelita gone, the story was taken up by Mamie, whose brother, Mo'n BBQ Bubba, provided boiled shrimp skewers, clever little spoons of cheesy grits, and miniature fried green tomato sliders. Wilbur's story was read aloud in a soft Southern accent. A giant of a woman, she let him nuzzle in her capacious bosom as the spider wove the web to save the little pig.

Brad loved his nannies, in all their rainbow variety, even if none of them lasted. He could never get enough of their attention.

It took months to get through *Charlotte's Web*. Meanwhile, the animal noises of couples staggering to the house's bedrooms were terrifying. He'd push a chair against his door and sit leaning against it, listening for the latest nanny's footsteps on the wooden back stairs.

Relaxed at last, Brad lay in the dark, dreaming of a giant, benevolent spider watching over him.

* * *

The window shutters banged in the shrieking wind; hail rattled against the windowpanes. Hortensia woke up, alone.

"Jeez Louise!' Mabel came together from different sides of the ceiling: her head from above the window, body from over the door, arms and legs from each corner. "Storm of the century. And I should know—been stuck here a hundred damn years." She shivered.

"Storms scare you?"

Snort! Mabel blew two streams of smoke from her nose and cackled. "The flooding scares me. Nobody can get out—that means I might be stuck with these grifters forever."

"What's a grifter? Am I one?"

"No, honey child, you're the bee's knees."

Bugs were small and she was fat. Hortensia wasn't a bug. She was a girl. But bugs weren't cute, and neither was Hort.

She'd never be as special as Mabel. Mabel was beautiful. Mabel was magic. She flew through the air, came apart into sparkly bits, swirled back together like chocolate and vanilla soft serve. Best of all, she was hidden from everyone else, what Hort always wished for —a friend who was all hers. *A secret nobody believed was real. Just like Kimmie.*

"I'm real but that ugly toy isn't, even if you give it a name."

Hort realized she'd whispered the last bit aloud and now Mabel was mad, but she still blurted out, "Kimmie's not ugly. Not to me."

"Real, indeed!" Mabel leaned against the window frame. She looked like a movie ad. "I'm real. Hell's bells, even the nuns are real, or they were, even if nobody can see them."

"The nuns? What are they?"

"Bunch of dried-up old crones, raisins that used to be grapes."

That was even more confusing.

"You better go have breakfast before that Suzanne person comes looking for you." Mabel fiddled with her cigarette and blew out another puff. Without another word, she walked out through the window glass, slinky as a snake, though the ground was way below. The wind blew dancing dust right through her.

* * *

In a paisley silk robe over boxer briefs, Brad was reading scripts, checking for spontaneity.

The door slammed as Irwin blew into the room. "We got a problem."

Brad retrieved his reading glasses, hastily chucked onto the floor at the sound of someone coming. "Oh? I thought everything went very smoothly last night."

"Just come!" The last was in Irwin's whiney "backseat of the family Lincoln" voice, the one Brad figured he'd used on family trips when he was young. Irwin was perpetually kvetching about those.

First Suzanne and now Irwin treating him like an underling. Brad didn't disguise the testiness from his voice. "Why?"

Irwin's narrow shoulders rolled as if he had the world's stiffest neck. "Because it's important!"

"Not good enough."

Irwin shut his eyes. "Okay. Important because the house staff found a body below the cliff. They risked life and limb climbing down to retrieve it. Good thing they weren't swept away. Gale force winds out there and massive waves."

"What does this body have to do with us?"

"A contestant. The blonde girl with the peek-a-boo tit. The one you were talking to last night."

"She's dead?" Brad pushed himself out of his chair.

"Just fucking get dressed!"

The basement of the manor house held the now-unused Victorian pantry. The concierge stood over the rough-hewn wooden table. "*Monsieurs*, I assure you, nothing like this has ever happened before! My staff, they are not supposed to go down the cliffs. Especially not in the stormy weather. *Dangereuse*!"

"If you please…" Irwin pointed to the lumpy pile of burlap.

The man drew back the covering over the top part of the body, exposing the head.

"Is it her? I'm not sure." Brad's brow furrowed in consternation and he cocked his head side to side for different angles.

With delicate tugs and an even more delicate sigh, Irwin pulled until a torn, lacy bra exposed a pink-nippled breast.

"That's her, all right," Brad said.

Irwin said to the Frenchman, "Call the gendarmes. We'll report this immediately." When the concierge turned to go, he added, "Some blankets to cover her."

As soon as they were alone, Irwin whisked away the remaining burlap. "We have a bigger problem." He pointed to the dainty thong. Beneath was a large bulge. Fluttering out the left side edge was a length of tattered tape, attached was the nether end of a very impressive penis.

"What the fuck!" Brad gasped. "I can't believe…" He hurried to cover the body again as footsteps echoed on the servants' stair.

The concierge returned, panting from unaccustomed exertion. "*Monsieur* Irwin, *Monsieur* Brad, we cannot reach the *Gendarmerie Nationale*! Another storm has come from the west. It is hanging up the one from the north, so we are at the weather's mercy with no end in sight. The town, it is flooded and the roads, too, and the cell towers down from the wind. All telephone in this area is *fini!* We are—how you say it? Cut off! On our own!" He wiped his brow with a handkerchief pulled from his pants pocket. "There is nothing we can do but to stay alive—now I must go! We will keep this body here. It is cool enough." He ran back to the stairway, stopped, and said, "Oh, I have forgot the blanket!" He left them alone.

"A dead contestant!" Brad's usual flattery and platitudes would fall like the dull thuds of farts. "You said I was talking to her last night. That doesn't mean that you think I…?"

"Of course, not. You were tied up at the Reveal. Anyway, you weren't the last person seen with…" Irwin coughed, "...the deceased. I saw her in a heated conversation with another girl. Isabella, I think." He gestured at the corpse's lingerie. "But look at what she's wearing! Maybe entertaining…um, rough trade and things got heated—why else would she be wearing underwear and out on the balcony in this storm?"

Brad risked a more thoughtful peek at the body. *Forensic Files* had taught him a lot about evidence. The body was battered and bruised, consistent with a fall. Or a violent fight. "Not our fault, but maybe it's better the police can't get here right away."

"You think we should keep it quiet? A death could be bad for the brand."

Brad rolled his eyes. "Don't be silly. Accidents happen on sets all the time. A death would up ratings—audiences love death. Just shoot a couple segments of weepy girls bemoaning her loss. 'What a lovely friend she was,' and 'If I couldn't win, she's the one I would have voted for!'" He sighed. "The problem is we don't want the audience thinking that we knowingly offed our first trans contestant rather than picking one of the other girls. ... God, if she'd only told us! We'd have marketed the hell out of it. But how were we to know? She did such a good job…" Brad shrugged and made the Gallic expression he'd practiced, the "*comme çi, comme ça*" face. She acted so stupid, so totally believable as a woman…And anyway, who cares these days?"

"How could we not have known?"

"Well, Irwin, you're supposedly our resident expert on things LGBTetc."

"You mean you're allegedly 'Brad, the Expert on Women'."

"Look on the bright side—flooding means no police investigation to shut us down. We'll wrap up next week before the weather breaks. Save us millions." Brad rubbed his chin, moral qualms fizzling away like bubbles in the Reveal party's champagne, leaving his conscience flat. "With a couple hundred Euros, the concierge would keep things hush-hush."

Irwin dropped his hand, his gesture frantic with disgust. It was the hand that had touched the filthy burlap covering the body.

CHAPTER EIGHT

CONTESTANT #3—TAMARA

Tamara, the contestant from West Virginia, seethed at breakfast, though she kept a tight smile for the cameras. That awful Isabella had draped herself over The Groom, until he was practically wearing the witch like a shroud. It wasn't enough she'd called Tamara low-class trailer-trash right before yesterday's taping, right in front of the other contestants, throwing her off her game.

Isabella must have sensed her looking, as she winked and licked her lips in a suggestive manner, close to The Groom's ear. Had she been with him after The Reveal? He'd been MIA at hot tub time, despite being contractually required to cavort with contestants while "getting to know them." Tamara planned to be the one to remove her top first, so she'd be the stand-out, the daring one whose breasts were blurred on America's TV screens.

She'd waited in the slightly oily pool of disappointed girl stew, fingering the button of her bikini bra while pretending to scratch a mosquito bite. Counting on the others being too dumb to realize what she was up to, she lolled like a croc in the tropic-temperature water, ready to whisk off that scanty bit of cloth. But The Groom was a no-show. When the wind had picked up again, buffeting the Plexiglas paned walls, the women had been evacuated with nothing to do but slink back to their lonely quarters.

The waiter put another basket of croissants on the table.

"What shit!" Tamara said to the table in general. "Everyone makes such a big deal about French food, but it's so fattening. Completely non-Paleo." She grabbed the waiter's arm. "Hey, don't you have any carb-free protein bars?"

The waiter, whose name tag read "Lucien," answered her with "The storm, it has cut off our supply routes, and so the cooks, they must make do with what is on the hand."

Isabella had moved on to the executive table, chatting with the handsome—and rich—producer. And The Groom had moved on to that hoity-toity skank Jocelyn, who was tossing back her hair. The movement focused Tamara's attention—there was something practiced about the gesture. Something familiar, more suggestive than the flurry of hair-flipping all the girls did. A certain sluttiness to its style.

She knew Jocelyn, but from where? Clanging her spoon against the inside of the coffee cup as if she'd added sugar—another dietary no-no—she stirred up her own memory: a dimly-lit club, lines of cocaine, music with a pounding beat, fat blunts in the fat hands of Chinese businessmen, big tips, and another girl in the party. But the girl's name wasn't Jocelyn. It was something trashier, alcohol-y, like Brandy or Chardonnay. Maybe Chablis?

Same shape face, same wide brown eyes and plush-as-velvet lips. Hair different—the girl at the club had streaks of red woven in the fake blond. The rear was familiar, too. That's what made it certain—Tamara never forgot an ass like the one sported by this Jocelyn-Chablis, or whatever her real name was. Juicy. Heart-shaped with a slight, gelatinous wiggle.

Tamara was sure the other "escort" in their party had been Jocelyn. Did Jocelyn recognize her? She'd used her real name that night just like now.

A warm flush of embarrassment rose up her neck at her own stupidity. As if getting a fake I.D. would have been tough. Jeez, she'd had real good driver's licenses at fifteen! Couple different ones in case some bartender caught her out and confiscated one. Fake credit cards, too.

Certain that the real criterion for picking contestants was looks—and so any investigation into their pasts would be cursory—Tamara had declared herself "a bank teller come to Hollywood to act." Thank God she'd been able to get her arrest record expunged.

Who the hell would've thought she'd meet someone she knew here? What were the odds of another phony good girl? Jocelyn must also have revised history to be acceptable. But, judging by the dazed look in The Groom's eyes, she was practiced in the tricks of her trade.

They weren't supposed to have sex with him, just make it seem they were. Tamara had been waiting for her opportunity to break the rule—but obviously, Jocelyn had gotten a leg up on her. As well as on The Groom.

She gritted her teeth against a slice of toasted brioche. There was room for only one "escort" under that flower-bedecked end-of-season trellis. Only one girl to get the two-hundred-fifty-thousand-dollar prize, the jewelry, and the man. The man to whom she'd say, "See ya, sucker!" And that girl had to be Tamara.

Half an hour later, she was upstairs, away from the rest, standing in her bare feet—panting with excitement—behind the door to Jocelyn's boudoir.

The shutters were closed, keeping out the eerie light of the storm's eye. Tamara switched on the bedside lamp and gasped, startled as she saw someone move. But it was only her reflection in the Louie the Fourteenth armoire's mirror. "Christ!" she muttered. "Whoever decorated this dump must have shopped at the French Salvation Army."

The armoire was the size of the shitty little closets in her childhood home. Part of her winnings would go to building a huge walk-in, with a darling settee and a center island on which to lay out jewelry, just like on *The Real Housewives.* She opened the armoire, revealing a big leather valise. She rolled the bag out and rummaged through its contents. Nothing but dresses, bras, panties, cosmetics… No pajamas or nightgowns, which, considering the drafts in this moody wreck, meant Jocelyn believed she'd be sleeping naked, someone keeping her warm. Tamara patted down the lining, but nothing lurked in secret compartments except generic Restoril. Damn! No keeping Jocelyn from the competition by dumping several into the carafe on her night table. The stuff would just settle to the bottom, chalky and easy to spit out.

She slid the bag back inside and shut the door with a loud creak. The mirror reflected the room, which was neat. Too neat. To Tamara, such tidiness meant an attempt to hide the truth. Growing up, before her parents' divorce and her mother's descent into straight-up alky, their house had been exactly that way on the surface. But open any cupboard, any closet, and liquor bottles would be concealed behind boxes of Rice Krispies, behind gallon jugs of 409, inside winter boots. That's why Tamara was here, pretending to be a carefree good girl instead of one who'd supported her mother by selling herself. No matter. She'd use this show as a stepping-stone to stardom.

Something was hidden here—she could sense it, like the rustle of deception in the dark of the night. What was it? How had Jocelyn gotten The Groom's attention?

She spotted another satchel under the high antique bed. It was black pigskin, expensive, with a huge lock, perforated sides, and a label: "CLEOPATRA."

Inside must be the secret to why Jocelyn fascinated men!

Tamara worked on the lock. Before she could open it, a laugh sounded in the hallway and the floorboards creaked as someone walked by. Better to work the lock in private than risk discovery. She opened the door and peeked out. No one. Grunting with effort, she dragged the case into her own suite.

The room was freezing cold. One of the heavy wooden shutters had been released from its latch by the howling wind. The window leaked damp like a pair of crotchless panties.

The hearth's fire blew out, but the flickering lamps on the nightstands bravely soldiered on as Tamara picked the lock.

Inside there was indeed a treasure trove that could account for Jocelyn's success—black kidskin fetish gear adorned with stainless-steel chains, a pair of thigh-high boots with platform soles, a ball-gag and riding crop. The oiled leather of the corset and boots whispered suggestively as she took them out.

Tamara held the outfit to her body and did half pirouettes. She slid out of her thong and stepped into the corset, wriggling it upward. Though barely able to breathe, she pulled the laces until the corset would get no tighter. Her gut rumbled in distress and her stomach felt as if it were dancing a tango with her spine. One glance in the mirror, however, told her it was worth the agony—her waist appeared all of twenty inches and the pressure had swollen her waxed pudenda until it bulged obscenely, reddened by the chill air. She turned this way and that, enchanted.

Would Jocelyn report her bag missing? The chance was slim as she'd have to report the contents and what good girl had the fetish equipment of a professional dominatrix?

* * *

Deep in the false bottom of the bag, Cleopatra stirred as a blast of frigid air awakened her from well-fed slumber—one moment, blissfully digesting defrosted rat, the next, chilled to her many, many rib bones. She poked her head up and found the weight keeping the lid on her compartment was gone. Her consciousness was dim, aware mostly of vibration and warmth, but the link between that warmth and human skin was strong. She began to move in an attempt to evade the frightening cold.

Outside the case, Cleopatra's poor vision blurred everything in the room. She flicked her tongue, sampling as she went, but found no taste of her owner, only the strong trace of another human. Being raised in captivity and handled with respect, she had little fear of people, and so she moved toward that warmth, hurrying before her muscles stiffened.

* * *

Tamara, enraptured at the thought that, if dominatrix was what The Groom wanted, she now had the goods, failed to notice the six-foot sinuous body moving across the shadowy floor. A touch at the back of her right leg alerted her. She looked down and gasped, clasping her hand over her mouth to keep the scream from rising in her throat. Fear froze her, open mouthed like a blow-up doll.

* * *

Cleopatra paused for a second as she slid over the corset, which tasted of her owner. But it was cold. Heat was what she wanted. Back home, she's been draped over Chablis' shoulders many times as her owner danced, adorned with her sinuous, sexy pet, but only for a single man at a time, so as to never startle the creature. And Chablis had been careful to beat her heels on the ground in a steady rhythm while her body moved with a mesmerizing fluidity. The beat reassured Cleopatra, who would have been grateful—if she possessed that emotion.

* * *

When the cool scales reached her upper back, Tamara began to thrash in an attempt to dislodge the heavy reptile, pulling at the dry, muscular body. Her desperate ragged gasps frightened Cleopatra. In response she looped herself around Tamara's neck and began to squeeze tighter and tighter until the hands ripping at her skin ceased their frenzy and the human's body slumped to the floor.

Cleopatra stayed with the corpse until it began to lose its warmth. Then she slithered toward another distantly perceived source of heat. The floor changed from soft wool in the bedroom to tile, harder and colder than the carpet. Distasteful. The forward movement was more difficult on the slick surface, but she continued on. Beneath a huge raised porcelain container was a hot water pipe piercing the floor. The access hole was big enough for her. She dropped down, her flickering tongue sensing a good supply of her favorite food squeaking as it ran in the manor house's ancient lath-and-plaster walls below.

* * *

Mabel, looked with distaste at the body. One really couldn't blame that beautiful 'boa for leaving. The dead creature was so *déclassé*. No snake would want to be caught dead on it.

She trailed behind Cleopatra, heading into the bathroom just as the snake's yellow body slithered into the hole beneath the tub. The pipes were no longer wide, no longer the real iron installed by Max when he'd brought modernity to the manor. They were now cheap plastic, like the new females. Like this cheap, bare-twatted thing lying dead.

But the snake? Mabel chuckled. The snake was a good thing. Entirely too many rats in the walls. Mabel planned to drop in beneath the plaster from time to time, to watch the hunt, but for now, she sped off, the merest hint of a shadow in the eye, checking on the intruders. Little Hortensia could help—it would cement their friendship.

CHAPTER NINE

Mabel poked her head through the floor, her neck growing longer and longer, until, with a snap, her body popped out into the room.

Hortensia, on a loveseat next to a plastic palm tree, was working on a filled croissant, her face smeared with chocolate. Mabel daintily sat her sequined rear on the couch's arm. "What to do, what to do?"

The croissant in the child's fat little mitt didn't look as good as Café du Dome's back in the '20s. But still good. Mabel's stomach rumbled with the memory of hunger. "It would be polite to offer me some."

"Would it just come out your bottom like croissant doody?" Hortensia dug a finger into the pastry, pulling out a big lump of Valrhona chocolate. Across the room, Isabella loitered near Suzanne, who was talking to a very, very delicious man. A Douglas Fairbanks-looking man, but with violet eyes. *Hubba-hubba!*

Mabel crossed one leg over the other, letting her skirt ride up.

"Good thing no one but me can see your undies," Hortensia said. She pointed that chocolatey finger at her own shirt, which was strangely lumpy. "Kimmie's underneath, keeping warm. 'What do you think,

Kimmie?'" She bent her head as if listening, then looked up at Mabel, "Kimmie says Isabella looks like a Barbie doll. We hate Barbies."

Mabel shifted her skirt a bit higher, batting her eyelashes at the man who, of course, didn't respond. "But you like croissants even though they're very fattening."

Gazing defiantly at Mabel, Hortensia pushed the rest of the pastry slowly into her mouth. Her tongue moved the wad from her left cheek to her right as she chewed. She looked like a chipmunk, but a lot less adorable. Had no one taught her manners? "You're a real little bearcat, ain't ya? Who's the fella?"

"That's the Groom. Looks like Ken, Barbie's boyfriend."

"A sheik doll to go with the slut doll?" Mabel flicked her foot up and down. "Not sure I approve. When I was a kid, we had nice baby dolls. We played 'mommy,' not 'madam.'"

"What's a madam? And what's a slut?"

"Never you mind."

Hortensia banged her heels against the edge of the couch, *thunk, thunk, thunk.* Across the room, Isabella glared, running a blood-red fingernail through her shiny black hair.

The little girl whispered, "More than Barbie, we hate Isabella. Kimmie and me hate her extra more than anything. She's mean to me and Suzanne."

Next to the exotic and erotic creation that was Isabella, Suzanne was a killjoy. A faucet with a slow drip. The homely girl in every makeover movie, except without a movie star's potential.

Hortensia's voice was hard. "Suzanne's the only one who cares about me here." Kiddo had some spunk to her.

"The only one?" Mabel pouted. The kid wasn't

much but she was Mabel's only living person, period.

Hortensia shot a quick glance at her. "Oh, come on. I mean the only not *dead* one. Suzanne's better than that Isabella. She's even better than my mommy."

"I'm shocked! That's not a nice thing to say about your mother."

Hortensia shrugged.

"Well, I gotta admit my own mom was no great shakes. Took all the money I made when I was little." Mabel paused to suck hard on her cigarette and looked across the room at the others. "You know, your Suzanne does nothing to fix herself up. Could pluck those eyebrows and apply some powder." The cigarette's tip glowed hot. "Maybe a little rouge on the cheeks and kneecaps. But don't you worry. We might be able to help. But first..." She stood, shook out her glittering gown, and floated to Isabella. She took a deep breath and blew a gust of air down the back of Isabella's blouse, puffing out the seat of her pants.

"Hey!" Isabella squealed, pulling at the cloth. She looked around, baffled. "Somebody goosed me!"

Mabel blew another breath. Isabella yelped and batted at her rump.

The Groom laughed. Hortensia jumped up, yelling a childishly fake laugh, "Ha, ha!"

"Why's that awful child here? Do your job. Send her away!" Isabella screamed at Suzanne.

With a thud, Kimmie slipped out from under Hort's tee shirt onto the floor.

"And get rid of her damned doll. It's as ugly as she is." Isabella stomped off.

Suzanne ran to Hort and hugged her. "Don't listen to her."

The Groom picked up Kimmie and handed her to Hortensia. "Bought my niece the same doll—it's real popular with the kids." He smiled down at the little girl.

"She's my favorite one."

"Ham it up!" Mabel ordered Hortensia. "You've got him in your corner."

Hiding a big grin by pressing close to Suzanne, Hortensia sniffled loudly.

"Don't cry," The Groom said.

"Lady's not nice." Hortensia's words were muffled.

"No, she's not," he said. "I don't like people who are nasty to kids. I love kids, especially my sister's kid. And I like women who are good with kids."

Suzanne hid her blush, bending down to Hortensia. "Why don't you go to the breakfast room and get another croissant?"

When Hortensia ran off with Kimmie, Mabel stayed behind to peer into The Groom's violet eyes and send a gentle gust to ruffle his dark hair, which hung over his brow. When had men stopped pomading, keeping their locks sleeked back?

The Groom brushed at his forehead as if shooing a fly, looking as confused at the *nothing there* as Isabella had been. "My niece is special needs, too," he said to Suzanne.

Special needs? Was that the latest term for "feeble-minded"? Good thing Hortensia wasn't close enough to hear. She might have bitten him. Maybe he wasn't the right guy for Suzanne.

* * *

That night was The First Date, when The Groom's initial pick would be alone with him. Traditionally, it resulted in emotional meltdowns by the other girls. The sarcasm, nastiness, and cat fights were ratings gold.

Irwin met with the contestants to whip up the rivalry, but their whining about the unfairness of this and the injustice of that wore his patience as thin as one of Brad's Trojan Bareskins.

Trapped inside by the storm, everyone had cabin fever. Everyone but little Hortensia. She spent her time hurtling along the manor's corridors and sliding down the staircase banisters, bellowing to an imaginary friend. Kid was weird—one moment Yoda, the next baby Yoda without the cuteness.

The wind and sleet made the roads impassable. The local farms had stopped supplying them with goods—thank God the manor house had a huge storehouse of wine! And if the generator crapped out, as it was threatening to do, they'd be in the dark. Worrisome as scarce food and precarious light were, they had a more pressing issue: dissention in the ranks. Blame directed at the executives. He and Brad, along with Suzanne, had gone to calm the waters. Despite their efforts, cries of "rigging the win" went up.

And then there *was* that little matter of the dead contestant. He kept seeing the body covered in old burlap sacks on the ancient table. Several of the contestants had asked where Hailey was. Irwin told them she'd left the competition just before the storm cut them off from the world. And really what harm did that lie do? In reality, she *had* left.

They were stuck here now, and no one could come to their rescue, so why alarm the girls? Why not continue as if everything was normal? There were twenty-one young women for whom they were responsible.

Twenty-one? No, subtracting the deceased meant they were down to twenty. Nineteen—but at last count there'd only been eighteen girls present. He grabbed his laptop and looked at their photos. The first one missing was a blonde named Diana. When was the last time he'd seen her? Had that been at casting in L.A.? His records showed she hadn't been on the plane. Had she ever arrived?

Curiosity tinged with worry drove him to her floor. Two maids were coming down the hallway, carrying linens.

"*Excusez-moi,*" he said, his terrible accent ringing in his ears.

When they answered him in French, he said, "In English, please."

They rolled their eyes at each other. One walked up to him and said, "Yes?"

"There's a young lady down the hall, a blonde lady, last room. Have you seen her? Her name is Diana and she's American. With our show."

The maid tossed her head in the general direction of Diana's room. "Yes, we have seen her. She refused to let us make up the room. She was very unpleasant."

Irwin went down the hall and saw the "*Ne pas deranger*" sign. He raised his hand to knock when the second maid said, "I saw her go down for breakfast."

"*Merci!*" He left the hall and hurried down the steps.

* * *

After the little American *homme gai* had disappeared from the floor, the younger maid turned to her friend and said, "You did not see her today! Should you not have told him that?"

The other turned to her with a loud sniff and said, "That whore was after your Lucien! Wherever she is and whatever she is doing, is of no interest to me."

* * *

The rain was coming down so heavy and hard, it was going sideways, sleet stinging anyone who ventured outside. The drive was flooded. But no matter, sooner or later the weather would break, and the police would come to investigate. They had to get this season in the digital can.

Irwin put thoughts of Diana on the back burner. It was more important to focus on the front-runners. Top of the heap was Isabella, that loathsome compilation of nips, tucks, Botox, and silicone. The most likely to succeed, by far the most beautiful, with her sharp cheekbones and full mouth, but a certifiably cold bitch. How would viewers react? He and Brad needed to cook up an angle that would be palatable.

He pulled out his pack of *Gauloises*. Though he'd promised his husband he'd quit tobacco, nothing cleared his mind—relaxed him, even—like smoking. He leaned back and lit up, imagining himself Jean Cocteau.

Eh, who was he kidding?

* * *

Mabel was surprised to see the director take out a cigarette. And a French one, no less. Most Americans who came to *Couvent de la Mer* were too cowed to smoke. They lacked the *je ne sais quoi*, the courage to live life at the border of death. The indefinable, mysterious quality of men like Valentino. Rudolph was a man whose glances sang verses of love. Both she and Max had been enamored of him.

She was more than surprised when homely little Irwin spoke aloud words of pure poetry: "Ahh, the delicious sensation of nicotine plumes curling into my lungs like a drag queen's marabou fan."

Marabou! She hadn't thought for years about those lovely feathers. Josephine Baker might have had her bananas, but Jazz Baby Mabel DeVine had danced naked as a jaybird with only a length of delicate white fluff guarding her modesty. Only at their private parties, of course. The hoi polloi *paid* to see her in the cinema.

He tilted his head, blew smoke upward and gave a deep sigh. "Face facts, Irwin boychik, you'll be a schlockmeister forever. Don't have the courage to make great virtual cinema."

Mabel drew so close her nose almost touched his. She yelled into his face, with as much force as she could, "Make it here! With me! I'm as virtual as you can get." Being a great actress had always been her goal.

Irwin didn't pay any attention to her, of course. Mabel paced, mixing her smoke with his. Here was the cure for her boring existence. An end to scaring the pantaloons off locals. Here was entrée into art, revenge on those who'd said that, despite being a star, she'd never be a *real* artist, courted by some of the greats for their projects!

Fritz Lang had offered her a part. A bit part only. But then he balked at her wardrobe demands. Expected her to play a peasant girl in rags. Have dirt smeared on her face! As if she couldn't act as if she were poor and filthy rather than actually *be* dirty. He didn't understand her, didn't take her seriously, didn't understand that a beauty needed to be...what was the word? Beautiful. No one really got her until Max de Summer, her adoring and adorable husband. "Oh, Max! It's you I wish were here. Forgive my silliness about Valentino. It's great love that makes a star, the love of great art and the love of a great man."

"My God, those ruins would make an incredible setting," Irwin said.

Yes! A serious production right in her own backyard. She had to find a way to communicate with him. A go-between.

There was only one person who could fit the bill.

* * *

The somber house staff moved about the corridors, their usual bustle muffled, their mien *triste*.

"It is understandable they are sad," the concierge told Irwin. "Their little villages of stone, they are built in shallow valleys, and the low areas now flood with the rains."

There was no let-up in sight. The two storms, one boiling up the English Channel and the other roaring down from the North Sea, had stalled each other off the Normandy coast. Luckily, the area had been evacuated, except for the manor house. The district authorities had forgotten—or ignored—the isolated mansion, which was full of non-French. The manor staff was irate at being included in the official lack of concern for foreigners. It was as if they, too, were being dismissed as Americans.

Things were growing more unpleasant every day. With the contestants at each other's throats, the dining room was like a cage of agitated parakeets. Good for business, yes. Great for viewership. But bad for his nerves.

And then, the Meat Packers...

"Hey, Irwin!" The Sausage King pulled him aside as he headed down the hall. "Come on, every party it's the same girls." He shrugged his great slouching shoulders and clapped one big hand against Irwin's back. "We're getting bored, all cooped up here."

That was it, just fault finding. No appreciation for all the work he'd done to make them happy. That was the way they were, men of privilege. Never satisfied. Thinking they can buy their way out of anything. Like his partner Brad, like Irwin's own father, never forthcoming with a word, a crumb of encouragement, a smidgeon of praise. He'd tried so hard to please, only to fall short time and time again.

His father's Lincoln Continental was what he pictured when the Meat Packers waxed effusive, lording it over him, promising to send a side of beef, a rack of ribs. He imagined his father, admiral of the open road in his land yacht, sitting on plush and shiny Majestic upholstery.

All those lonely, humid afternoons Irwin spent rubbing a chamois down nineteen feet of steel from the elaborate front grill to the bulging spare tire mount in back. All to get a high-gloss, highly desired "attaboy" from his dad.

His father, hands on the steering wheel—at ten and two, stogie in mouth, cruising to services on Saturday morning, when you weren't supposed to drive. His father had been a self-satisfied, self-made man, married to a woman who made sure that his stomach—and his conscience—were coddled in the creamiest of lies.

Irwin's gut boiled over at the injustice, the double standard.

When his father heard he'd corrupted Lanzo Greco, a God-fearing altar boy, with his sinful ways, the break was abrupt, the respect and love irrevocably lost before it was even gained. Irwin, aged seventeen, but still the size of a fourteen-year-old, had been kicked out of the house. And now, here Irwin was, in charge of the hottest online reality show.

If only he had someone fatherly in his life now. He needed a place safe from the demands of contestants and staff. A place safe from the assaults of Brad's testicles on the show's wallet.

CHAPTER TEN

CONTESTANT #4—GEORGINA

Georgina was considering swiping a bottle of champagne, one sweating appealingly in an ice bucket, ready to have its cork popped. It was Reveal Night and stealing that bottle would only be fair. The producer and director, with their little gaggle of investors, were guzzling a vintage Clos d'Ambonnay, whose bubbles danced with much more enticing vigor than the liquid in her own glass. They had cheaped out for the rest of the cast and crew.

She moved next to the goofy-looking technical director, the one who could make sure the camera angles were best. "So, have you spent much time in Britain? That's where I come from." She fluttered her eyelashes. "My parents own quite a large estate in Devon."

"Oh, yeah?" He didn't look down at her but, instead drifted away, a vague look on his face. Only the skunky scent of weed lingered behind.

Left alone, she stood shivering, her decolletage roughly handled by North Sea winds leaking through past the drapes. Georgina cursed the stupidity of locating the show on such a God-forsaken spot. Did they not know the record winds of Le Havre had once reached 180 kilometers per hour? The Beeb always had educational shows about wretched Channel weather, all the way back to the hoary old story of the hurricane sinking Henry VIII's *Mary Rose*. Didn't Yanks learn anything in school? Were they too stupid to have not noticed the wind farms?

Bored, she wandered the periphery of the room, inspecting the manor's paintings, obvious Victorian copies of French originals. The Americans, parvenus from a country with no history, ooh'ed and aah'd over them. The people in the portraits had faces like Shropshire sheep, all bulbous noses and blubbery lips over receding chins.

Another chill shot through her. God, there were enough drafty, uncomfortable heaps of stone in England; they might have picked one of those instead of luring her to this Frog-pile-by-the-sea.

Mummy had told her not to try out, saying it was mortifying to be on a reality show, but then, when Mummy brought up Georgina's sister, how she dated a prince and married a viscount, Georgina decided the die had been cast—she could no longer be bothered about her mother's feelings. How many eligible viscounts were there, anyway?

She looked toward the men clustered at the drafty room's far end. While The Groom was being introduced to the moneymen, he was obviously scanning the crowd. She put her shivering to good use, letting her (almost) natural blonde ringlets tumble over the peekaboo cleavage of her azure-blue gown. Looking down, she admired the tops of her breasts, their skin classic British rose. Bringing her gaze up, she realized The Groom was gone and she was standing alone.

After that, the only person who spoke to her was that smug bint, the horrid Isabella. "So, looks like you've been snubbed." The grin on her face made it obvious she was delighted as she snagged a glass of champagne from a passing waiter.

Georgina took one too, narrowing her eyes at the tall, dark haired beauty. A scene ensued. A minor one, worsening with each glass of bubbly imbibed, until that little Hebe director told them to knock it off—irritating Georgina no end.

She decided to head to her room. On the way, she did a theatrical dip and swiped the expensive champagne. She headed up the staircase. At the landing, the many panes of clear glass in the huge window rattled in their leading as the wind buffeted them. The noise made her heart pound beneath her push-up bra. Suddenly, journeying alone up the stairs seemed perilous.

Her room was cold, though the antiquated radiators were clanking for all they were worth. Here it was, late April—high spring, and the weather as miserable as winter. She lifted the bottle to her lips.

The wind howled, its dissonant Wagnerian bellows hiding the usual creaks and bangs, the ones the stupid girls thought were ghosts. She took another swig, letting drops hit her gown, puckering the material. That ugly midget of a wardrobe drone could press it later.

Another gulp and the room began to spin. The gale swirled in gusts down the chimney to the unlit fireplace. Ashes fanned out, blinding and unbalancing her. She leaned against the wall. The light flickered on and off. The electricity was a total load of tosh. If leaving wouldn't mean slinking home, tail tucked between legs, to Mummy's "I told you so," she'd be long gone.

She had to come out on top. The Groom had to be hers to reject.

Cheek against the wall, she drowsed in an alcohol haze, opening her eyes at a faint murmuring sounding far away and yet close. Two voices, a woman and a man.

Not just any man, The Groom's distinctive American voice. Not just any woman, but that vile Isabella!

Another flicker and then, with a pop, the light burned out. She ran her hands along the wall, feeling for the torch on the bedside table. Before reaching it, she came upon the waist-high wooden door she'd tried to open that morning—just out of curiosity—only to find it stuck badly. Bracing her feet against the wall, she pulled with all her might. Behind it was nothing but an air shaft, smelling closed-up for eons, strongly mildewed. She leaned into the darkness. The voices were louder. No mistaking the cooing; a seduction was going on somewhere above. She let go and the door swung shut.

She downed more champagne, staggered through the room. Found the torch where she'd left it. Now she'd be able to see inside that shaft.

She pulled and the door opened again. Casting the beam of light from side-to-side, she glimpsed a frayed rope disappearing into the darkness above. Below was a wooden platform attached to the rope. She pulled on the rough cord and, with a groan, the platform moved a little. A dumbwaiter! Just like the one in crusty old Aunt Maude's London townhouse.

She hiccoughed. Pressed her hand over her mouth to hide a giggle. The shaft in her room must lead to a room above her, one occupied by the two people she overheard. Stealth was needed. She moved her fingers from her mouth until only the index remained pressed against her lips. "Shhhh!" she said to herself, giggling again.

The voices were louder but still indistinct. "Bollocks!" she swore—a low-class word Mummy detested more than any other. Full laughter bubbled up in her chest but her compressed lips kept it from bursting forth. What if Mummy saw her now, drunk as a lord?

She had to hear more. Pulling on the rope did

little good at first. It stuck after a few centimeters. The pulley must have rusted, unoiled for half a century. Standards were never high in France, the whole bloody country rotting. She pulled again, leaning her weight into it. The rope gave a smidgeon, the platform moved with an uncanny shriek.

Georgina paused, fearing an alarm from above, but the murmuring of the couple continued. Perhaps the rising storm outside hid the noise.

The only way to hear more was to get closer. She pulled until the platform was at her level and the shelf on which food had been sent to the bedrooms was within reach. If the underfed, tubercular slatterns in Victorian kitchens could manage this device, she certainly could after those spinning classes with weights.

Below, however, was a disused French kitchen, most likely swarming with black beetles. Beetles unmolested by Pro-Active C cockroach killer. Shudder! But it was best to be brave. Winners never quit and quitters never win.

Wrapping the rope about the sturdy knob of the little door, she fetched a chair to squeeze through onto the platform. But splinters and an odd nail or two protruding from the frame caught her gown, holding her back.

No pain, no gain. Everything she had on needed to go to give the best chance. She shucked off the dress and her panties. Naked as the day she had both first met and first embarrassed Mummy—at a formal tea, no less—by abruptly coming out of her naughty bits, warm amniotic fluid drenching an eighteenth-century brocade chair, she tried again to enter the dumbwaiter. The same sharp protuberances snagged at her skin, but alcohol plus anger not only warm, they anesthetize. Not even when blood trickled down her flank did she quit. She tried straight in, on her side, and then on the diagonal. Still, no matter how she twisted and turned, the opening defeated her. She was just a smidge too wide to fit.

Bouncing back into the room, she stalked in high dudgeon. Thank goodness the accommodation had a private bath. At least the manse wasn't like the awful B&Bs to which her boyfriend—who Mummy dismissed as "that penniless Irish beggar"—had taken her. Her darling Seamus, deemed by Mummy to be unworthy of her daughter's hand in marriage.

She had to pee badly—all that champagne. She went in and sat on the loo, idly rifling through her toiletries case. It held a super-sized tube of personal lubricant. Its marbleized blue-gray box soothed her with memories of the lovely Seamus, his lovely Celtic penis—which, endearingly, he called his shillelagh. As if anyone bloody cared, so long as it was large and firm and annoying to one's mummy.

Her mother had gotten the trustee appointed by Georgina's dear departed Nana to keep any and all funds from her until she turned twenty-five. That ended her trips with Seamus. He had run out of funds.

"Oak club," was how Seamus, with a grunt, translated "shillelagh" from the Gaelic, rolling her over in the bed for another battering. No wonder she'd needed the lubricant, sore as she was.

Time to get going. The Groom represented enough prize money for her to live happily with Seamus' shillelagh until financial majority, two years away. She stood and faced the mirror. Christ, she looked like bloody hell.

She opened the tube and spread the gel on her torso first, and then her arms and shoulders. She continued down her legs and then slithered back to the room. With her skin slick and greasy, she was able to force her body into the orifice of the dumbwaiter. Pulling on the reluctant rope, she ascended just enough that her room was out of view. Light coming through a crack was visible above.

In her hands, the rope strands untwisted one by one. The harder she pulled, the higher she rose, the more the antique fibers frayed against the rusty iron pulley, squeaking and squealing softly above her.

She was alone and drunk. No one knew the peril she was in.

The storm intensified, the waves crashing more violently, drowning out everything else, obscuring the final *SNAP!* of the rope. Obscuring the echoes of her final screams as she plunged to the black beetles waiting in the abandoned kitchen below.

It had been decades since they'd had a good meal.

* * *

Hortensia was napping. Without her living companion, a bored Mabel floated down to the basement of the manor, looking for entertainment. No more shooting for her, no wolfhounds pursuing prey. Her thrills were now limited to being a voyeur, watching a snake slither within the hollow walls, hunting vermin.

But Cleopatra wasn't to be found anywhere behind the plaster. No chorus of frightened squeaks were to be heard, though droppings were everywhere. Had the snake already found success? Had she holed up to digest one of the manor's rodents?

Mabel entered the ancient kitchen, with its huge rusting stove and grease-covered walls. A black mound on the floor writhed with ecstatic energy, shimmering in the dim light from a filthy window. She moved closer. Disgusting—even to someone dead for nearly ninety years—closer inspection revealed it was a moving mass of black beetles, swarming on the body of a young woman.

Footsteps sounded on the stairs and two youths, the same two who'd found that blonde hussy gassed, entered the kitchen, smoking marijuana. Wrapping herself around them, trying to inhale their fumes, Mabel was envious. If only she'd stuck a muggle ciggie in her holder just before dying, she might be enjoying her time in purgatory.

"Lucien, stop!" One man put his hand against the other's chest. "Look on the floor!" He turned the beam of an old-fashioned torch—the sort doughboys had carried at the Maginot Line—on the beetles. "Yet another dead woman. We had better run!"

"No, do not run." The one named Lucien paused on the steps. "Let us think for a moment. It is true we were told not to smoke cannabis at work, not to hide from tasks, not to interfere with the guests, but no one said we could not come here."

"Well, then," the other worker said, "let us *fumer ce joint* and think for a moment about the beetles' dinner."

The two of them thinking would certainly be amusing. Mabel forgot her search for Cleopatra.

"*Maman* has told me, 'Lucien, lose another job and I will put you on the boat of your uncle Alphonse to fish for mackerel. You will stink like pussy and your girlfriend will drop you like a hot *patate*!' I cannot risk that, for I love my Agnes."

Mabel's laughter tinkled out, shattering like ghostly glass against the grimy walls. Frenchmen had scarcely changed in the past century. Agnes or not, this Lucien would gladly have taken his little *Popaul* to the circus with that blonde number.

The other worker relit the joint. "You know, Lucien, the Americans' *Grab le Groom* is a show for romance, not for horror. Perhaps it would be very hurtful to have the death be known. A person could do very well offering to keep this very, very quiet."

"Perhaps." Lucien stroked his chin as if he was old and wise. "Perhaps we missed the boat last time. We shall go carefully speak to the men in charge. You take one and I will take the other."

Mabel put aside any thought of frightening them. This was much more fun.

CHAPTER ELEVEN

In a potted palm nook off the ballroom, Irwin was setting out the necklace to be the night's prize, when Brad came in, long faced and dour.

"Another girl out of the picture. Another body to conceal. Oh, God!" Brad collapsed into a chair like a debutante with the vapors. "I paid the guys who found her five hundred Euros to keep their mouths shut. Or at least until we wrap."

"Shit, no! That's horrible, Brad. Where'd they find her?" Irwin asked.

"In the old basement kitchen. Doesn't seem like they know about the other body."

"Hailey."

"Yeah."

"Who was it this time?"

"The English girl, Georgiana something. Found just under the dumbwaiter shaft." Brad had developed an intermittent tic over the past two days, his left eyelid jumping and fluttering like a can-can dancer. France had really gotten to him.

"She fell down a dumbwaiter shaft? How could that even happen?"

"Who the hell knows? Maybe someone pushed

her. But what are we going to do?" Brad said.

"What can we do?"

"Maybe thirty reality shows have had someone die. Mostly no one found out, but we now have two dead girls. I'm worried this could shut us down before the police even arrive."

"We do have our contingency plans." Good thing they had takes showing each of the girls supposedly being bid adieu by The Groom, whose carefully scripted brush-off speech would be edited in later. The L.A. takes were just close-ups of the contestants, sniffling, tearing up with makeup running, looking devastated, along with sound bites of them describing him as "the sexiest—no, the sweetest man" she ever met.

Female viewers always sighed longingly at the word sweetest, casting irritated glances at their own men, who were busy dropping chips on battered leather sofas, hoping an Amber alert would interrupt transmission.

These bet-hedging shoots would keep the results as honest-seeming as possible. "We'll have to use the tape with her elimination. Have the others missed her?"

Brad shook his head.

"They're either glad she's disappeared or too self-centered to notice, I bet. Busy plotting and scheming."

"I'm worried about the concierge. He's been acting weird lately…"

"Hard to blame him." Irwin wiped a smudge from the necklace's biggest pearl until it shone brightly.

"I don't think he's spilled the *flageolets* but even the L.A. staff's starting to worry about ghosts. They've been talking with the Frogs-for-hire. They know something's up but not sure what."

Irwin raised one eyebrow. "Could it be that there really is a ghost?"

"Nah! Can the ghost crap." Brad stood. "If there was anything, literally anything, pointing to something ghostly, *Haunted Houses* or *Ghost Collectors* would have been here videoing doors shutting by themselves, wispy spirits like cheap homemade Halloween cutouts — audiences go crazy for that crap, even the 'just around the corner but never actually seen' shit." He put on his Brad-thinking-deeply expression. "It could be a killer with weird sexual cravings. Would explain why this one was naked and…well, if he'd been pissed off and chucked the first one off the balcony. You know, if he found out that she was a he...." He paused a second. "No offense."

Irwin sighed. "I'm ordinary, boring gay, not transsexual, but no offense taken." They were in this together. No sense being testy. "We don't need to jump to a sexual serial killer. You do an autopsy? A rape exam? Like I said, this isn't *CSI* or *Forensic Files*. We're just a dating show…"

"Before you sneer, she had K-Y smeared all over her. Body was shiny as shit."

"How the hell do you know what it was on her? You taste it?"

"Couple of empty K-Y tubes on her bathroom floor. I had her brought up from the cellar. She's in a small room off the lobby. Soon as we can do it discreetly, I'm having her put with the other one down in the old kitchen, where she can be kept cool. So no tell-tale odor."

"We should evacuate as soon as possible." Irwin was glum. "With the lack of food deliveries, the menu's getting pretty restricted for the ordinary folks, anyway."

"Are you kidding? Where would we go? The weather's too bad to leave. Besides, that would ruin this season financially! Absolutely ruin it!" Brad squeaked. "This isn't our fault."

Irwin reached up and put a hand on his shoulder. "It's okay, Brad. Relax, take some deep breaths. We can't get out now even if we want to."

Brad huffed like a teenage girl with a panic attack. And then he brightened up. "Well, at least let's shoot some extra footage. If we can ever use it, if we ever *have* to use it, we'll slant it toward sexual predator. Everyone loves serial killer stuff. Might just save our asses from being canceled."

Irwin couldn't help but shoot him a disapproving look.

"Hey, like I said, it's not our fault. How could we have even known there was any risk in this isolated place?"

The investors' group rounded the corner and came down the hall, having finished their sumptuous breakfast. Despite the growing shortages, the best had been put aside for the money men.

"Hey, fellas," Irwin called. "Having a good time?"

"We're gonna have a hot tub party with the reject girls tonight, right?" said the pork distributor from Mason City.

"Well…" Brad's voice had a weaselly edge to it.

Irwin hoped the investors wouldn't catch on. Georgina had been one of those slated for that event and he doubted they'd want her floating in the hot tub in her present condition. "Not exactly those girls, but some of the others would be glad to join you." In the corner of his eye, Irwin saw a man's silhouette, backlit by the storm's garish light. It was the concierge, hunched over, pulling a table on vintage cast-iron wheels from one doorway to another across the hall.

He poked Brad, who diverted the group's attention to a window displaying the English Channel. "That was some wild weather last night, right? The surf's still pretty impressive!"

*Squee, squee, squee…*The ancient iron wheels of the rolling table protested softly. Irwin felt the blood drain from his face. The table had a thick white tablecloth on it, covering something of suspiciously voluptuous shape. The other end of the table was pushed by another, similarly hunched-over, man. Irwin made a mental note to slip the extra man a tip.

"Holy crap! Look at that wave!" Brad yelled, pointing to the sea in all its frothy glory.

The cliff seemed to tremble at the massive upsurge, but it was only the rippled antique glass in the window shaking in the wind.

"Well, I'm glad to hear the party's coming off," the pig man said. "I was beginning to worry."

They had to have the party soon. If they lost any more girls, the Meat Packers would be in the steamy water, bobbing around alone.

* * *

Hortensia sat leaning forward, wheezing like an old man with emphysema. Aside from her nasal breathing, she was, for a brief and blessed time, still and silent. Her attention was on Suzanne, who sat at one of the makeup mirrors, plucking at the wandering part in her hair.

"I think I did okay coloring it at home. What do you think, Hort?"

Mabel rolled her eyes. Jeez Louise! Who dyed their hair mousy brown? "Tell her she needs a trim and a hot oil treatment. Don't think there's any chance she'll ever be pretty, a real tomato, but she'd look better with a marcel."

"Don't know what that means." Hortensia shot a wrinkle-nose look of puzzlement at Mabel.

"Finger waves." Mabel moved one finger in half-circles, while pointing to her own platinum bob.

"Who are you talking to, Hortensia? There's nobody here." Suzanne stopped pulling at her tangles.

Dammit! Mabel had told the little girl to listen but not look, though it was impressive how quickly that smart little tyke recovered. Hortensia held her doll up by one leg. "Kimmie. She knows more about makeup than me. She says you should get little curls."

Suzanne laughed in a "that's so adorable" way. It made Mabel feel all warm inside. Proud. Someone else appreciated Hortensia's smarts.

"Bet the hair lady will do it for you. And Kimmie says you should try a lipstick, too. But not too red." Hortensia pretend-walked the doll on the countertop. "Red looks cheap. Maybe pinkish brownish. You'll look pretty."

Suzanne's blush was sudden and fierce. "Where did you ever learn about looking cheap?" She turned back to the mirror and pulled out a tube of soft rose.

"Don't get your hopes up, my little friend," Mabel said. "Pretty may not be in the cards."

Hortensia stuck the tip of her tongue out at Mabel. She turned to Suzanne. "Do you think my daddy's pretty?"

The kid's wide stubby feet, free from their footie PJs, were in sneakers flashing indecipherable, random Morse code when she banged them together. The sound reverberated in Mabel's head. She longed to grab the kid's ankles and hold them still. If only she could grab something, anything.

"Yes, your daddy is pretty," Suzanne said after another moment. She was blushing.

"Even I would say that your daddy is a sheik," Mabel added. She leaned in through Suzanne to admire herself in the mirror. "I've watched him shower."

"Eww," Hortensia said.

"No, it's true. Very handsome." Suzanne

shivered. "Sure are some funny drafts around here."

Isabella walked in. From her cat-with-cream smile, it was obvious she'd overheard the discussion. "Making yourself over, Suzanne?" She placed her palms together and rolled her eyes heavenward. "St Jude! If anyone needs the saint of lost causes today, it's our Suzanne. This is *Grab the Groom*, not *The Miracle Worker*" She smiled at Hortensia and said, "Your dad's hot. Very, very good-looking."

Hortensia held up her weird, spidery-limbed doll. "Kimmie says you're wrong. Says Suzanne was always pretty. Still pretty now. Besides, my daddy's not pretty like The Groom, so you should like him instead."

Isabella let out a nasty witch's cackle. She put the back of her hand against her forehead and theatrically moaned, "God, I have hellacious dark circles under my eyes."

"Listen to the Discount Del Rio!" Mabel lit up again. "Those aren't dark circles. They're either her evil thoughts or her shit backing up!" Mabel yelled at the top of her voice, snorting with laughter.

The kid laughed, too, and repeated Mabel's last comment.

"Hortensia! That's rude!" Suzanne looked shocked. "Where did you ever learn to say such a thing?"

Isabella leaned in to adore her own reflection. "If that kid's the daughter of handsome Brad Hudson, DNA certainly is a crap shoot. She can't help being rude, looking like that. When I marry her daddy, I'll get him to send the little monster right back to her mommy." She turned to Suzanne and narrowed her eyes. "Lipstick's all smeared. Maybe I'll give you pointers some time." She pirouetted on her heels and left.

"I hate her. I hate her. I hate her!" Hortensia banged her feet harder, then clapped her hand against her lower belly. "She makes me have to go pee-pee." She slid to the ground and headed to the stairs.

Mabel lingered for a moment, floating back and forth, swinging her gold flapper chain like a lariat, contemplating Suzanne from all angles. The woman's gams weren't bad, but the rest of her was nothing to write home about. Skinny but with a small roll of flesh around her middle. Dull hair. If she was stuck on a gorgeous man, there was a lot of work to do. She shook her head, sighed, and headed to Hortensia's room.

The little girl stood next to her bed, her fists on her hips, looking for all the world like a miniature Mussolini, Mabel's least favorite dinner companion ever—as if anyone listened when that tinpot dictator went on and on about his crazy plans. Better things to do when there was hooch flowing free. "What are you all in a lather about? Isabella again?" She dug her fists into her own waist, imitating Hortensia. "Look, toots, nice of you to want something for Suzanne..."

"She takes care of me, like my *abuela*."

"But what's in it for you?"

Hortensia looked puzzled. "Don't know."

Mabel was pretty sure she did. "Well, that Isabella is a real female dog, if you know what I mean. It'd be my pleasure to take her down a notch, so here's what we'll do to help Suzanne..." She bent over the little girl to whisper in her ear, even though no one could overhear her.

It was too easy. The kid would do anything for Suzanne, it seemed. She didn't realize the plan had a lot to do with what the Divine DeVine craved. When Mabel was satisfied that Hortensia was on-board, she flew to the nuns. Perhaps their endless praying would help ease the strange feeling in her heart—empathy had ebbed away to be replaced by a twinge of something else, another thing she'd never felt before. Guilt.

* * *

"Just say what I tell you to," Mabel whispered as they approached the table in the dining room, where the executives—including Hortensia's father—sat having hors d'oeuvres and wine.

"Uncle Irwin?" Hortensia was being as slick as a five-year-old could be, her voice reminiscent of that old cure-all, cod liver oil, but poured over Grape Nuts.

Irwin glanced at the child with wary eyes. That gave Mabel a chuckle.

"Would you go on an adventure with me?" Hortensia said. She seemed to be doing a halfway decent imitation of winsome.

"Go on, Irwin, sounds interesting," Brad said. Their business meeting seemed over, now Isabella was sliding onto his lap, nestling her round behind deep in his crotch. "I'd really love it if you guys were friends."

Bullshit. Mabel steamed with anger. That bastard just wanted to tomcat around, starting with petting this Isabella. Hortensia deserved better than him. Better than her mother. Who leaves their kid with a lousy bum for a father and sails off to a Polynesian paradise?

"But I have so much work to do, Brad. Remember, things are in a bit of turmoil right now..." Irwin didn't look happy.

"Turmoil?" Isabella gasped. "None of the prizes are missing, are they?"

"No, no, relax. That's all fine. But I've had a bit of down time from headaches. And I really wish you'd get off him. Against the rules." Irwin glowered at the two of them.

Isabella merely laughed.

"Brad, weren't you going to read to Hortensia again? *Charlotte's Web* this time?" Suzanne's voice was stern. More than stern, frosty. Mabel was forced to admit, the girl had real guts. Only his assistant but she faced him down when needed. And it seemed her definition of "needed" was when Hortensia's happiness was on the line. Or maybe when Isabella was involved.

"Say it's okay," Mabel coached Hortensia. "You want to get to know Irwin."

The little girl whispered too softly for the others to hear. "But Isabella's on top my daddy. I need to go push her off."

Mabel shook her head and took another puff of her cigarette.

"What if her butt is so nice, it makes him want to marry her?"

"Won't happen," Mabel yelled. She curbed her temper when Hortensia looked as if she'd stubbornly dig in. "Now go on, I need Irwin to love the convent. We'll take care of Isabella later."

Hortensia gave her a grumpy look and said, "Suzanne, I want to go on an adventure with Uncle Irwin."

Mabel cleared her throat, warningly and Hortensia added, "Very, very much."

* * *

Irwin followed Hortensia down a dusty—and seemingly disused—hallway, their feet making impressions in the inch-deep dust.

"Where are we going?" he asked the kid, who had marched him along like a drill sergeant.

The dark end of the hall, a quarter-city-block from the entryway, was closed off by eight-foot-tall doors of desiccated wood with a rusted, ancient latch.

"What does that say?" Hortensia pointed at words scrawled on a piece of cardboard, which was nailed to the right-side door.

"*Entrée interdite! Hors limites! Privé!*" Irwin said.

She looked at him with scorn. "What does it really say?"

"Basically, 'stay out.'" He turned to go back, but a determined shove stopped him. Short as she was, once her feet were planted, Hortensia was solid as a fireplug.

"Okay, okay!" She had a point. *Grab the Groom* was paying oodles to rent this dump. They should have full use of it.

He jammed one shoulder against the door. Despite his musculature, which had in the past been likened to that of a plucked chicken, the latch tore out of the wood. The door creaked open, only to hang up on the uneven floor.

He pushed again and the door swung wide enough to pan his flashlight app inside. The corridor continued but, unlike in the renovated manor, the floor and walls were made of huge gray stone blocks. There was no light from windows or lamps, just the occasional flash of distant lightning through clerestory windows coated in cobwebs and filth.

The little girl scampered ahead, her rotund figure vanishing into the darkness. She was sure-footed and seemingly fearless, as if protected by a guardian angel.

His throat tightened as he followed into the chilly space. The air tasted of mummified decay—no one had disturbed it in years. Stained glass panels, loosely covered by boards, creaked and groaned with the wind.

He caught sight of Hortensia in his phone's beam. She sneezed over and over but kept trundling forward, her churning legs sending up more dust. She pointed at tapestries, grayed over, moldering on the walls. "Like in *Abuela's Iglesia*."

Outside, the wind was a rushing locomotive—the

noise echoing between the stones. Lightening cracked overhead and thunder boomed. A segment of blood-red glass crashed down and shattered at his feet.

An abrupt change in pressure stole his breath. The still air was sucked upward, swirling, as if by a giant celestial Hoover.

Chilly, fleshless hands touched the back of his neck. He turned, but no one was there. Lightening cracked again and icy winds from the broken pane surrounded his body, wailing as a supernatural force grabbed him.

A puddle had half-frozen on the stones below. He hydroplaned a few feet, his Brunello Cuchinelli-clad rear landing on a dry stone.

He shivered on the floor, not wanting to be the one to cry uncle, but that feeling of skeletal hands touching his neck had really creeped him out. Several rats dashed by. Two of the bigger rodents paused, turned on each other, and began to fight viciously, like rat stallions defending their herds. Their inch-long incisors gleamed yellow in the dim light. Some of the other rats turned their glittering beady eyes on the two human invaders.

"Maybe we should go and come again tomorrow," Irwin said, backing away from the rats. "The storm might die down a bit."

Hortensia turned back, pressed her lips together tight, and grumbled, "Get up, Uncle Irwin." His hesitation exasperated her even more. "Don't be a scaredy cat. I'm with you." Hortensia reached out her hand to pull him up.

There was no way to turn back in the face of so brave a child, but he didn't want to get up, not just yet. Afraid of another fall, he checked the extent of the puddle. Beneath the ice at one edge was an incised motto: *A fronte praecipitium, a tergo lupi*. He dredged his memory for the translation, sounding out each word softly. At last, the Latin he and Lanzo Greco took back in junior high, just to impress the handsome priest at Lanzo's church, had come in handy.

Shame, the priest hadn't been handy. If he'd had any vices, they had nothing to do with altar boys, least of all those found out to be Jewish and uninterested in converting. Irwin was kicked out of the altar boys and deprived of the surplice that had taken him weeks to save for, though he'd bought it at Deep Discount Catholic Supplies.

* * *

"In front, a precipice, behind, a wolf," Mabel repeated Irwin's translation. A great subtitle for her film, right after atmospheric shots of the convent! She hadn't known what the Latin motto meant, despite twisting an ankle on it back in '26 while leading a conga line to the cloister, sloshed out of her mind after an all-night bash. After the accident, Max sealed the doors to the convent. He was always so protective. A real gentleman!

She followed Irwin and Hortensia to the hall's end at the ancient church's nave.

"Wow!" Irwin tilted his head back to take in the balcony above the chantry. "This is epic, fucking amazing! Looks so real!"

Max had once arranged some great gatherings here. the long altar groaning under the weight of roast meats, lobsters, and salmon in aspic, pastries and fruits, the font flowing with bubbly. Mabel smiled at the memories. "It ain't Notre Dame," she said to Hortense, sighing fondly, "but it does okay."

Hortense parroted her words and expressions with only slight exaggeration.

Irwin looked at the kid with such an odd

expression that Mabel began to worry. She'd had little experience with ankle-biters back when she was among the living. Would a kid say something like that? Even a weird old-young kid like Hortensia? Was she over-playing her hand?

Achieving her goal might require restraint, never her strong suit.

The high arched ceiling seemed to make Irwin dizzy. He had to be kept from returning to the manor. He had to see the convent and the tower.

Mabel pointed out a door in the transept. The living went through the door, Hortensia first, while Mabel slipped between the masonry of the far wall.

CHAPTER TWELVE

CONTESTANT #5—PEARL

Tonight's prize was a fine two-strand pearl necklace. Pearl, like her name. How fitting. She slipped on her own pearl necklace, the one her father had given her. The natural drop lay warm beneath her high collar, nestled against her throat. Pearls brought luck, had the power to grant wishes. Especially a pearl like this one, born in the depths of the Persian Gulf, a rare and priceless antique for which he'd saved since she was born. She was his favorite child, and this deceptively simple ornament her most precious possession.

She waved her hands to dry their red nail polish. Her lipstick matched her nails, and, with her high-collared cheongsam, she was a knockout. The ruby color accentuated the paleness of her skin—so desirable a hue, so like a white peach, that she'd been picked as representative of L.A.'s Mid-Autumn Moon Festival. So much classier than these trashy girls with plunging necklines. Against the deep inky waterfall of her hair, the pale celadon gown would be stunning on television.

Perhaps she should hide the nail polish away—Christian Louboutin, costing fifty dollars a bottle. Thank goodness her mother wasn't here to get upset at that waste of money. But when Pearl won, the prize money would be more than enough to mollify the old dragon.

As for The Groom, well, a fool and his fiancée are soon parted. Pearl had already scored a high value, but undisclosed, fiancé. The CEO of an internet startup in Beijing that was going gangbusters—his parents had bankrolled it from Hong Kong. Pearl needed the prize money to pay for a wedding banquet that would put his family to shame. She'd get the cash, "regretfully" ditch The Groom, and fly the old folks in, first class. Lord knew her parents couldn't afford that!

The polish remover and a carafe of water were on the nightstand alongside an opened airplane bottle of whiskey. The first night on location, she'd sipped it, fearing she wouldn't get to sleep otherwise. Jet lag and beauty contests, which was what this was, didn't mix.

Opening the doors of the bedside table, she put the polish inside. She reached for the remover. It slipped from her hand, falling to the floor. The smell of acetone rose immediately, stinging her nostrils.

The wet container would damage the cabinet's wood if put inside. She'd be responsible for repairing it. Taking care to ensure her mani wasn't ruined, she poured the remaining contents into the carafe, replaced the lid, and hurried out of her room. The ceremony was starting.

As she'd anticipated, Pearl won the five-thousand-dollar double-strand necklace when The Groom selected her as his date for the evening.

* * *

Irwin stepped over a large tapestry fallen from the wall, where it had obviously covered a door. Maybe it had served to prevent mass exit if the sermon dragged on too long.

The door opened onto an open courtyard,

bounded on each side by walkways of worn gray stone. Arched columns on the garden side supported a roof. The storm's sleet kept the light dim. It was difficult to see any distance but when Irwin squinted, the tower was dimly visible, looming above the convent's ruins.

"Aren't you cold?" he asked Hortensia. The church had creeped him out and now, out here, driving sleet had become snow. It pelted down, rapidly covering the courtyard's weed-filled center. While he stumbled along the nearest wall, guiding himself with one hand on the ice-cold masonry, the child was sure-footed, bounding ahead like a musk ox calf. "Let's go back in. It's freezing."

As if she hadn't heard, Hortensia continued toward the tower, stubby legs churning through drifting snow, low-centered body like a bowling ball headed for a strike.

He slipped again, catching his balance on a downed statue. It might once have been a saint or even the Virgin Mary, but now lay scattered pieces on the ground. Chunks of marble were like a three-dimensional jigsaw puzzle, a hand here, a blank face there, all strewn about the walkway. He perched on the empty base, catching his breath.

Hortensia returned to stand just out of reach, kicking at a column as if she hoped to bring the place down. Even with her back turned, she radiated contempt.

The sky was solidly white, the sun obliterated, the snow hypnotizing masses of swirling flakes. Voices circled Irwin, dancing between the columns and whispering down the walk. They came from all directions, unintelligible but persistent, a chant, a *chanson*, a spectral lullaby, filling his mind, making his eyelids heavy, lulling him into nightmare-plagued sleep.

* * *

He jolted awake with a scream, shivering, his teeth clacking together like castanets. Someone stood before him, a squat little woman wearing the clothes of his overbearing Bolshevik great-grandmother, the one his father Morris called Gitta the Red. Fiery-tempered, believer in the evil eye, she had lived longer than seemed possible. Had she returned from the grave?

Oh, God, had she read his thoughts? Had she found out he'd been an altar boy in order to seduce a priest? Could his dead father have betrayed him? He willed himself upright and blinked. Gitta's figure wavered like a reflection in a pond and transformed from elderly woman into fat kindergartener. Hortensia. He must have awoken still in a dream state but could swear he'd heard, "You bum, do something to make me proud."

"Whoa, what the heck happened to me?" He rubbed his eyes and looked closely at her. "And what did you just say?"

"How 'bout a show with ghosts?" Her gleaming little eyes stared into his.

"Ghosts?"

"Everybody loves ghost stories, scary ones. That's what all the people say."

"That does sound like a comer, but we make a reality show. Anyway, your dad already said no. No ghosts." Sleep still shrouded his mind. "And right now, I can't think straight." Besides, his bladder was full. Painfully full.

* * *

"Why'd you want me to say that?" Hortensia asked. "Big people don't think ghosts are real."

You'd be surprised what people believe. Mabel didn't reply aloud. She was busy patting herself on the back for that "skeletal hands" bit, the sum of several little gusts of freezing air. How proud Max would be of her, able to solve problems all on her own. Max, who, if he hadn't gone to his eternal rest, was probably haunting the safari lodge in Africa. Her adorable, brave, manly—if balding—Max. How horrifying it had been when that huge dusty creature bore down upon him as his shot went wild? Yes, he was probably there, haunting the spot where the rhino bagged him, wondering why his darling Mabel wasn't there.

Now she needed someone to showcase her talents as history's greatest dramatic actress. Irwin could be that someone. And when they wanted to relax and be amused, what fun it would be motoring up to the Catskills, hunting Borscht Belt vaudeville. Those song and dance routines! The comedy, a laugh riot! Irwin was one of *those* people!

He might be her William Wyler, with little Hortensia as her transmitter and Hortensia's handsome father as partner selling the series.

Maybe—but maybe not. After all, the show he'd brought here was a real turkey. She felt movement near her and looked down. "Huh?"

Hortensia repeated the question.

"I'm teaching you to sell. You have to *act*, not just say the lines. You need to be convincing."

"Your movies didn't have talking. Movies need talking."

Mabel tossed her head to dismiss the idea. Obviously, Hortensia didn't understand great cinema, which *Grab the Groom* would never be. "I didn't have to speak. My eyes, my smile, my body communicate for me. For example, in *Flapping Flannels*, to show wanton seduction, I did this..." She let her eyes roll slowly beneath lowered lids. Her mouth opened slightly. She emitted a silent moan. "See? To be an actress, the first person you have to sell to is yourself!"

Hortensia had lost interest. She was already headed back to Irwin. Mabel *tsked* in annoyance and followed.

As they approached, he scuttled by, legs pressed tight together. "We've got to go back. They'll be worried. Just stay there a moment." He yelled over his shoulder at Hortensia, "Don't follow."

He hadn't told Mabel not to follow, so she raced after him as he darted out into the snowy garden. He went beyond the little girl's sight, desperately unzipping his fly. When he let loose, with an audible "Ahh!", she sent a strong breeze blowing across his nether region. The pattern of a spiderweb was rapidly traced in yellow on the white snow. In the center, the words "SOME LOCATION!" were prominently featured.

It was derivative, straight from the book she'd seen in Hortensia's room, but then everything in Hollywood was, and had always been, derivative. Hopefully, this would get his attention. Hopefully, this would do the trick.

* * *

CONTESTANT #6—ADDIE LYNN

Trying to ignore the wailing of the wind, the contestants digested the tough *filet de bœuf en croute*. But not Addie Lynn, Georgia's contribution to Grab the Groom. She was tiptoeing along the corridor on the second floor.

As she eased open the door to that bitch Pearl's room, Addie Lynn's face was burning—the flush rose from the waist-deep décolletage of her gold-lame gown. The heat from her anger might melt the glue that kept her breasts from popping out like fresh buttermilk biscuits.

"Wow," that Isabella had said. "She's a foreigner, even if she was born in America. Wearing a neck high, slutty-tight dress. No cleavage! Imagine that! How could they pick her over me?"

Isabella just stood there as if she was the only one who deserved to be chosen. Like Addie Lynn was trailer trash. Well, Addie Lynn begged to disagree. Only Southern girls should win. They had the edge, the blonde all-American, Original Barbie, wholesome cheerleader-next-door bounciness. And she was a prime example of a Southern belle. She was the only one who deserved to have the damn-fine-looking The Groom slip the damn-expensive-looking pearl necklace about her throat while he kept a hand on her tight little ass.

That winning bitch Pearl went up to her room after the ceremony and, when she came back down, she'd forgotten to lock up—probably so over the moon from winning. She'd pulled off that slinky dress and changed into a flowing robe over her bathing suit, most likely a one-piece, granny sort, since she had no tits. Should have bought herself a pair, like half the other contestants had. But no, she was so skinny she had no shadow!

The necklace had to be here somewhere, just out of sight. She pawed through an open case on the dressing-bench at the foot of the bed. Not there. She sighed and plunked down on the bed.

A necklace was on the nightstand—not the fancy prize, but a pathetic single drop, the one Pearl always wore, as if her name wasn't enough of a joke. This necklace would have gone much better with the high-collared, overly modest dress that, Addie Lynn grudgingly admitted, showed off the slender figure, elegant because of its very lack of voluptuousness. It must have been removed when she went out in her swimsuit, showing off the prize strands. Stupid to risk them in the chlorine water and protect this one. Besides, nice jewelry looks silly with a bathing suit.

The pearl was warm when she picked it up, almost as if it were alive, and larger than she'd first believed. She rolled it between her fingers and had a sudden irresistible yen to make it her own. The bitch would never miss it, not with winning that prize strand of many pearls.

God, she was thirsty. The chefs had over-salted the beef, if that chewy slab wasn't from a horse. They stuck everything in a crust, probably to hide mystery meat. So inferior to a nice char-grilled American steak, served naked except for a scoop of herb butter. How the hell did French models stay so thin, eating carbs all the time?

Next to the necklace stood a carafe and an airplane bottle of hooch. Several of the other girls had already made fools of themselves getting plastered. Not her! No siree! She wasn't going to get caught out like that! She'd just have some water.

She removed the carafe's lid. Fumes assaulted her nostrils. What was that smell? Bad enough to knock a dog off a gut wagon! Polish remover. Chuckling, she realized someone else must have wanted Pearl poisoned. Probably that she-devil Isabella, who'd had words with everyone, twice with Addie Lynn. There was the snide stuff she'd said tonight and before, by the ladies' no less, banging on the door while Addie Lynn was changing a tampon.

Waving the fumes away with her left hand, she replaced the lid and slid the pearl necklace down the front of her dress into her Two-Timing Firm Control Open-Bust camisole. Thank the Lord for Spanx! You could hide anything under them. Invented in Georgia!

She inhaled deeply, letting the pearl and its chain find a comfy spot where the lump wouldn't be seen through the skin-tight sheath. The Lycra keeping her belly flat made it hard to breathe. It wasn't her fault she loved food. It was her daddy's fault, always taking her for rides to Jim's Smokin' Q up in Blairsville. And now her father was gone, having drag-raced Dead Man's Curve for the last time.

Her still grieving mother would admire the understated little necklace when Addie Lynn gave it to her. First piece of real gold she'd own, though the woman really loved her Walmart jewelry collection!

Instantly, she felt guilty for dissing Walmart, where she bought her own clothes. Thank goodness this production—unlike the other one—supplied dresses for the parties, as well as hairstyling and makeup. Otherwise, she couldn't compete. Guess the other show thought only rich girls deserved a chance at love. Or prizes.

Sleet, wailing down from the Arctic on the eighty-mile-per-hour wind, hit the window like death knocking. Addie Lynn shivered in the drafts sneaking past the shutters. It was too cold to go out to the hallway, even to the conservatory housing the hot tub, but she had to be brave. The old wreck of a mansion leaked like a hair net. She headed back to her room. So far, there'd been enough hot water, though it took like an hour for it to reach her bath, but no sense pushing her luck. Not on a night like this. Tomorrow was another day! Another chance at winning.

Once safe in her room, she disrobed and dragged the coverlet off the bed, wrapping it around her for warmth. The white enameled taps for the bathtub faucet were the cute Frenchy-kind, one saying CHAUD, the other FROID. It was hard to understand why they didn't have a single one that let you pick the temperature you wanted and just let it run. Instead, you had to keep dipping your hand in to check. It was so much more primitive than in America.

When the tub was full enough, she checked the water one last time. Too cool. She bent over and grabbed the CHAUD. As she did, the forgotten necklace fell out from beneath her left breast and hit the floor. Ducking to pick it up, a sudden movement caught her eye. Something small, yellow, with two prongs like the head of a big snail. In another second, she realized that this was no snail's head, but a tongue, flicking back and forth. She was face to face with a creature whose unblinking eyes and sinuous body decidedly read "snake."

Addie Lynn's scream went unheard in the simultaneous crash as something slid from the ancient roof, hitting the bathroom's shutter on the way down. Drawing back in horror, slipping on the rolling pearl of the necklace, she lurched forward, grabbing the rim of the tub for balance. Her hand slid off the wet porcelain and she was falling, falling, falling. She didn't fight the water entering her nose and lungs—the blow to her forehead from the tub's enamel edge had knocked what little thought she had right out of her.

Over the night and long into the next day, the water in the tub cooled as Addie Lynn's red hair fanned out like river weeds.

* * *

Cleopatra would have luxuriated in the heat beneath the full tub, but the splash of the human's body flooded the floor, setting up vibrations that matched and heightened those of another crash outside. Primordial memories of trees falling in a monsoon cyclone stirred terror in her tiny brain. She hastened away from the bright light of the bathroom, her coils contracting and extending across the tile and the old splintery wood of the bedroom floor, up the half-fallen sheet, across the bed

—depositing a slick trail of stinking excrement designed to discourage large predators—and then down under the door. She disappeared into one of the convenient rodent holes in the ancient baseboards of the corridor.

CHAPTER THIRTEEN

"Brad, have you seen that girl from Georgia?" Suzanne had a habit of interrupting him when he was settled into work, and right now, he was comfortably settled at a dining room table, reading scripts.

Brad shook his head, took a sip of his espresso, and continued leafing through the pages. Everything now seemed like a burden. He sighed deeply. "They all blend together after a while."

Hearing his own words aloud stopped him for a moment. What the fuck was wrong with him? None of this year's crop had given him a boner. If these beautiful, voluptuous women failed to turn him on, something must be wrong with his plumbing. Why? Overwork? A latent effect from the steroids he'd tried in high school? The contestants were all pretty, but aside from Isabella, not one of them seemed remotely sexy to him, not one face was one he'd like to wake up to. There was that Pearl, but she seemed cold as ice and, anyway, what tiny breasts she had! Aside from her, they all had the same eyes, same nose job, same inflated tits and lips. All swirled together like the oil slick on his espresso.

Only Isabella was intriguing. She was gorgeous, yes, but it was her wild meanness that made him sit up and take note. Making love to her would be like having sex with a rabid cougar. But when he moved discreetly in his seat, it was easy to feel what wasn't happening at the thought of her: no wood.

"Not interested in any of the girls?" Suzanne said with a tiny smile. "Maybe you're just getting old."

There was a depressing thought. Should he borrow a Viagra from the Sausage King and test it out? He tilted his cup, took a last sip, and motioned the waiter to bring another double shot.

"Addie Lynn, the redhead who wore that bright green dress. You know. Can't find her."

"Oh, yeah, the one whose head looked like a cherry tomato on the vine." He tried hard not to look concerned, but with two girls already found dead, that was an uphill struggle. Could it be that another was missing?

"Besides Addie Lynn, I can't find Irwin or Hortensia." Suzanne plopped her iPad on the table and her butt on a chair.

Was she really not wearing a bra beneath her buttoned Oxford shirt? The sway of her modest-sized, actually small, but disturbingly real, breasts captured his attention. He wanted to press his hands against them and see how soft they were. Geez, they would rest in his palms, softly spread out if she lay back instead of straining upward like they were trying to escape. And dainty nipples seemed a certainty. Pale, unused pink.

She gnawed a fingernail. "I'm worried."

He suppressed the amorphous arousal stirring like an amoeba in the primordial stew of his mind. She was his assistant. And for sure not a beauty queen. "Hmm, they're not around? Where could they have gone?"

"Brad! You were sitting right here when Hortensia asked 'Uncle' Irwin to go on an adventure. Don't you remember?"

He searched his memory but came up blank. Anyway, he wasn't worried. Unlike the missing contestants, all stunning adult women, his partner and the kid would show up sooner or later. Alive.

"It's been hours. It's almost dinner time. You should go look." She tapped her foot on the floor. "Be like a father."

What? The not-so-subtle expressions of impatience were bad enough. His back stiffened at her words, her condemnation. He swung his legs off the chair supporting them. He *was* a father, whether he'd signed on for it or not. But should he be concerned now? Even worried? "You think Irwin's a pedo?"

"For Christ's sake, Brad! No, that's not what I'm saying at all. But people are missing around here and Hortensia's just a kid and kids need to be watched over and Irwin has no experience." She was getting overwrought, her voice rising into a wail like the wind outside. "I checked, thinking maybe she'd gone for a nap, but she wasn't in her bed or anywhere else..."

He used his little espresso spoon's handle to lift the edge of the paper and take a peek. Page seven. He was only on page seven. So many more to go. He sighed and slid the spoon back out.

Susanne apparently failed to notice his furtive movement, but she scowled at his sigh.

"I'm sure they'll turn up soon, none the worse for wear." He smiled reassuringly. It was cute that she worried about his kid. More than her mother did.

The Groom entered the dining room and, prowling with the grace of a leopard, headed to their table. He smiled and nodded hello to them. The black curl that drove the ladies wild adorned his forehead. His biceps rolled beneath his jersey. Brad felt a surge of unreasonable hate. Especially unreasonable because he'd been the one to hire the guy.

The Groom leaned over Suzanne. Was he looking down her shirt? "Where's our little girl?" he asked.

Brad's head shot up as if it had a will of its own. *Our little girl?* Hortensia wasn't The Groom's kid and The Groom certainly wasn't a couple with Suzanne. He better not try to steal *Grab the Groom's* best employee. Or Brad's child!

"That's what we were just wondering," Suzanne said to the handsome interloper. "She went off exploring this place with Irwin and they haven't returned. Maybe *you'll* help me look." The emphasis on the "you'll" was gratuitous.

"For sure," The Groom said.

Suzanne took her iPad under her arm and stood, ready to leave, when Hortensia ran in, followed by Irwin. She flung herself into Suzanne's arms.

"Sweetie-pie, where have you been? I was so worried!" Suzanne kissed the top of Hort's head.

"Yes, baby, *we* have been so worried." Brad stood, ignoring the script pages fluttering to the floor. Conflicting thoughts swirled in his mind. It was heartwarming to see his daughter and Suzanne hugging. The kid was still homely as a mud fence, but she was his. Somehow, in some strange way, that made her almost loveable. And Suzanne was such a good caretaker.

"We been exploring. It was fun." Hortensia grinned, her little teeth like sugar-corn kernels.

Several contestants filtered in. Brad jerked his thumb toward them and narrowed his eyes at The Groom. "Duty calls."

The Groom backed reluctantly away as he went to join the women, glad-handing in response to their coos of welcome. Several grabbed onto him like remoras on a sleek shark.

Brad, Suzanne, and Hortensia watched from across the room until Brad broke the spell by raising his voice and calling, "Come give your daddy a hug."

Suzanne gave her a push, and Hortensia, with seeming reluctance, went to him. She even let him put his arms around her. "But where did you go?" he asked. "We looked everywhere."

"Oh..." Irwin answered him, signaling for a coffee. "Here and there. I'd bet when you looked here, we were there and when you looked there, well, we were here."

Suzanne scratched her head. "Did you run across Addie Lynn? Tamara's been missing, too, come to think of it. Last I saw her she was talking to Isabella. Maybe yesterday? Seemed to be in a heated discussion about something or other."

Irwin blew out a breath. "Georgina also had words with Isabella, but who the fuck hasn't argued with her?"

Brad shot a meaningful glance at Hortensia and Suzanne and, through clenched teeth, said to Irwin, "Not in front of."

"Sorry. Slip of the tongue."

Suzanne rubbed her cheek with her iPad stylus and shook her head slowly as if she was puzzled. "Come to think of it, there are some others I haven't seen around. Tonight, when we tape, I'll call names and do a proper head count." She shook her head. "Where could they have gone? The roads are flooded and it's too nasty to set foot outside."

"Maybe sulking in their rooms because they didn't win a prize?" Brad slid his eyes toward Irwin. "Have the other girls said anything, Suzanne?"

"If they even noticed, they were probably glad. Some of them are real killers when it comes to competition. Like Isabella. I know I shouldn't say anything, but she's positively poison."

Brad stifled a laugh that bubbled up in his throat

like a sip of the bubbly. Come to think of it, had the concierge complained that a bottle of expensive champagne was missing?

Suzanne stabbed the stylus through the hair behind her right ear. "We can't just twiddle our thumbs. We've got to do something, so let's split up and look for them. I'll go with Hortensia."

"I'll come with you two," Brad said, glaring at The Groom at the other table, "to make sure it's safe."

* * *

"Things are really looking up. Got a fish on the line." Mabel curved her index finger—the one without the cigarette—into a hook and put the tip in her mouth, distending her cheek. She pulled her finger out with a loud pop. An old vaudeville routine.

The nuns, continuing their low susurration, failed to find her antics amusing.

Mabel ignored their ignoring, her enthusiasm undimmed. She waved her arms widely to take in the entire place. "This convent is the ideal place for a series. Gothic, mysterious, full of spirits, and with oodles of inspiring stories, I'm sure."

Did their veil-hidden heads dip lower over their breviaries? Were they trying to deny her existence in a more deliberate way than usual? No matter. She soldiered on. "Stories like yours. Get this, ladies—I want to make a series about you."

Any sensible group of women would jump at the chance to have their moment in the spotlight, especially if portrayed by a great actress—and let's face it—great beauty like Mabel DeVine. But the nuns chanted on without stopping.

Ten minutes more of calling "Yoo-hoo" into what

she assumed were their ears, of waving her hands between the openings of their hooded veils and their little prayer books, and Mabel was ready to leave. She drifted slowly along the cloister walk, holding her hands in front of her eyes, the way she'd seen directors do, thumb tips together, fingers up, framing the scenery.

Before she reached the church door, a soft voice called out. She turned. Floating slightly above the ground, one of the nuns was following her. Mabel was elated. Acknowledgement at last!

Wait a minute! Elation turned to resentment. If they could hear her now, that meant they'd been aware of her all along, just pretending not to be. As if she was unworthy of their holy attention, annoying as a gnat.

She stopped in her tracks to consider. Perhaps they were jealous? Reasonable. She was, after all, a real dish, one whose husband never ditched her. Still desirable, even after death.

But weren't nuns above that, what with the "being brides of Christ" and all? Maybe they thought she was a floozy, a low-class broad.

With a renewed sense of indignation, she faced her pursuer, her penciled eyebrows arched. "What's up, toots? Bumming a ciggie?"

The face inside the veil's hood was nothing but mist, the mouth a hollow black hole in which a disembodied tongue waggled like a clot of blood. Stock horror movie tricks. Boring stuff. Nothing to give anyone the heebie-jeebies.

The nun's voice was hollow, echoing. "We are intrigued with your request."

Aha! She knew they'd come around! A dame is a dame, and a dame is vain, dead or not. *Play it cool, Mabel DeVine... you need them more than they need you.*

She blew two casual smoke streams from her nostrils. "What's the next step, doll-face?"

“Come.” The wraith turned and headed toward the tower. Mabel followed, though the theatrical holier-than-thou air of mystery annoyed her. Maybe she wasn’t one of them, Sister Mabel of the Holy Horsefeathers, but weren’t they really sisters-in-death? Shouldn’t they be sharing every secret?

Once inside the cold stone walls of the tower, the two drifted down the circular stairway, ignoring its broken steps, down further than Mabel had ever been. The breath of decay rose up to meet them. The nun’s long skirt billowed up with the tower’s sigh to reveal she lacked feet as well as a face. Sad, really. No wonder they wore such drab getups.

Unlike the nun, Mabel’s legs were silk-clad, gleaming in the pallid light. Her feet were encased in chic silvery satin t-straps. Sporting a stylish Louis heel and generous buckle. What girl wouldn’t want to be so hosed and so shod?

On second thought, the poor thing would be forced into oxfords if she had feet. Or into those oh-so-sad Jesus sandals, for extra suffering in winter snow.

At last, they reached the bottom. A studded wooden door barred the way, its huge lock adorned with a snarling Devil’s face crafted of bronze. The sister stopped dead and bowed her head in prayer.

Mabel puffed impatiently on her cigarette. She didn’t want to wait centuries for the nun to finish. Hadn’t there already been enough chanting out in the cloister?

Since she could easily pass through the hardest granite, why wait? Confident in the rules of her haunting, Mabel walked swiftly into the door. And was thrown back, landing halfway through the opposite wall. Her dainty nose was bruised from hitting the Devil’s teeth.

Was there the ghost of a snicker behind her? She couldn’t be sure.

The nun finished mumbling her prayer and said,

"Before entering, we must genuflect and request permission." She dropped to the floor in obeisance and said, "Reverend Mother, we beseech an audience with you."

Mabel hesitated for a moment before grumbling, "Oh, okay," and bending her own knee. Hopefully, her stockings wouldn't ladder. They were the only pair she had.

The groaning and creaking of the door as it opened was straight out of central casting. Mabel smiled to herself—if the sisters could be persuaded to buy in, a fortune would be saved in sound effects. That was a great selling point.

The chamber within was small and dark, save for an unearthly glow coming from a niche in the wall. Or rather, from the contents: a hideous carved head. The nun glided toward it with Mabel in her wake.

They were directly in front of the carving. With a *SNAP!* the head's eyes opened, dark and brooding but, unlike the rest of the face, alive.

"Holy crap!" Mabel exclaimed. This was no block of wood shaped by human hands, but the desiccated head of a woman, cheeks sunken, lips shriveled, neck hung with shreds of nun jerky. Hideous but–on further reflection—probably not attractive from the get-go.

"Reverend Mother...." The nun's cowled head remained bent.

The head cut her off. "You bring a sinner before me? A creature of Satan who brought screeching imps to our place of peace? Interrupted the silence in which we pray? Where..."

"Can it, Sister." Mabel almost drew a line across her throat to show she had enough but thought better. "I got nothing to do with all that. Hate the whole reality show shebang as much as you do."

The ghost nun beside her fairly vibrated with agitation. "Silence! This is no ordinary convent dweller, but our Reverend Mother, the Prioress!"

Maybe being called a sinner hurt her feelings, though in life she'd been a proud modern girl, Martini-swilling, rouged-kneecap jazz baby, at least until Max ignored the rumors and made an honest countess of her. Or maybe it was her fondness for vaudeville wisecracks, but before Mabel could stop herself, she blurted out, "So, Reverend Mother, are you *head* of the convent?"

Her nun escort gasped, exploded in smoke the sickly color of dung, and disappeared. On the other hand, the Prioress let loose a deep rich and rolling belly laugh. Without a belly that was a miracle, as Mabel had to admit.

"Thank you," Reverend Mother said. "It has been centuries since someone jested with me. The downside of being a Holy Relic, I guess. Five hundred years I've been down here, drying up, endlessly reciting the Pater Noster. A bit of levity wouldn't hurt. It gets so lonely." Her eyes welled with tears that trickled down the dehydrated ravines of her cheeks.

Mabel took the scented hanky she carried in her little mesh purse and dabbed at the Mother Prioress's face.

"Been eons since someone touched me. Would running a feather duster over my face every century or so be so hard?"

"There, there. Of course not." Mabel added a few cooing sounds for effect and dabbed some more.

The head sniffled and jerked away. "Tis enough already. Now say why you want the stories of the sisters buried here."

Mabel hadn't had much need to persuade anyone, ever. Everything had just fallen into her lap, so to speak, especially Max de Summer. Max had sat next to her on a swing at a drunken garden party. He'd fallen over, snoring, and when he awoke face down, centered on her beaded skirt, he realized he wanted to stay there forever and proposed on the spot. So, feeling the need for some preparation prior to selling the nuns on a show, Mabel had listened in on the contestants. Though they flung their coochies about like hors 'd oeuvres at a cocktail party, they believed themselves modern, independent feminists. Believed they were right to be indignant about the way men treated them.

She had their litany down pat, ready for this very moment. Taking a deep breath, she launched the spiel. "Your stories are the universal stories of women, from Eve to Helen of Troy to Mae West. Women controlled, women blamed for the behavior of men, women left to pick up the pieces of a world ruined by men. All women over the ages, especially those discarded by wellborn husbands yearning for younger flesh. Or bigger estates."

The head seemed lost in contemplation. "The things you say are true. Once I was a queen, the mother of two boys. In a warmer clime, too, not freezing my haunches in this miserable spot. Told that suffering made one holy." Her eyes filled again.

Oh, brother! Gotta keep a straight face, no matter how maudlin this gets. I've seen worse—think Mary Pickford as the heroine in "Tess of the Storm Country". Now, that honey could jerk a few tears!

"My children ripped from my arms. I was exiled, locked away to spend my time in prayer and contemplation. My husband, on the other hand, remarried the daughter of a rich count."

A little flattery never hurt. "And still you made lemonade out of those lemons, right?" Mabel would have given a friendly poke if she could. A little "us girls are all in it together," poke. Never mind that her life had been endless partying. And Max had adored her until his untimely end. "It continues to this day."

"The injustice?"

"Well, things do seem to be a bit better now." Mabel leaned closer to the niche and dropped her voice. "I heard in L.A. the wife gets almost everything when the husband's screwing the nanny. Even if she's secretly been Barney muggin' the pool boy."

CHAPTER FOURTEEN

Brad and Suzanne, with Hortensia in tow, checked the English girl's room first. It was empty, seemingly abandoned in haste. Makeup lay scattered on the dressing table, clothes crumpled on the floor by the bed. The covers hadn't been turned down by the maids and the pillows showed no indent from a sleeping head. An open bottle of the most expensive champagne they'd bought, the vintage Clos d'Ambonnay, lay tossed into a corner, leaving a puddle on the floor. There was a distinct odor of harder alcohol lingering in the air like a wanton kiss.

Brad stepped into the bathroom as if he thought Georgina could be found soaking in the tub. His feet slid from under him and he would have fallen, had he not grabbed the doorframe.

He wiped his shoes on the bedroom's carpet. "The floor in there's covered with goo. Seems to be..." He held up a nearly empty tube of K-Y gel.

Suzanne's eyes widened with shock. "Oh, my goodness!" She walked with endearing care to inspect the tiled floor.

The K-Y really was disturbing. Was Irwin right? Had something really kinky gone down? Were they facing a sexual serial killer who lubed up his victims?

"She doesn't seem very neat." Suzanne wandered back through the maze of items on the floor. She pointed to an opening in the wall, its door ajar and asked, "What's that?"

Brad shrugged. "Don't know." He peered inside. "Hmm, seems to be a laundry chute. Or an old dumbwaiter to send food up from the kitchen."

Suzanne examined the wall around the dumbwaiter's door. "Look, scratches in the plaster! And here's a bit of silk snagged on a nail." She stopped to pick up a negligee from the floor. "See, the fabric matches." She stood again and peered inside the shaft. "I see rope. Looks broken. But that's all."

"I wanna see!" Hortensia pushed Suzanne with both hands. Instead of stepping to the side, Suzanne tottered toward the opening.

"Hortensia!" Brad yelled, grabbing Suzanne around her waist. "We don't push people." He held on to her, to the tiny, soft roll of flesh concealed beneath her utilitarian shirt.

"You can let me go now." Suzanne, blushing, firmly in his grasp. "I wouldn't fit through the hole, anyway."

He dropped his hands. "Well, this gives us no clue as to where Georgina went. All we know is she's not here. It's a mystery."

"One we have to solve." She tucked her shirt back into her skirt, her face still blazing red and turned away from him. "We need to check Addie Lynn's room next, so let's go." She started down the hall. He had no choice but to follow.

The hall outside the bedroom was quiet as a coffin. At least until Hortensia stopped to bang on a table holding a porcelain vase, which tinkled musically as it fell to the floor. Brad decided to ignore the damage.

They came to Addie Lynn's door. Suzanne

knocked, but there was no answer. They called her name and knocked again without response.

"Well, nobody there, door's locked, can't get in, let's go," Brad said in a single rapid breath.

Suzanne held up a master key, let it dangle for a moment, and undid the lock.

One of the maids appeared in the hall, carrying rolls of lurid pink, scratchy, non-absorbent French toilet paper. "Everything is all right, *oui*?"

"We're checking on the girl in this room. She seems to be missing. Have you seen her at all today?" Suzanne asked.

The maid shook her head. "*Non, mademoiselle.* And I would remember, for she is, how you say it in English, a real bitch! Just to the staff, maybe, because we are nobodies." She leaned conspiratorially toward them with her hand cupped over her mouth. "Also, we think she steals from the others."

"Might be better to get Irwin before we look around anymore." Brad said. "We're entering Addie Lynn's room without her permission. We'd be responsible to her for any claims…" He turned to the maid. "Please go find *Monsieur* Irwin."

"*Monsieur* Irwin the little *Juif*?" When they nodded, she thrust her hands under her apron and scurried away, crossing herself and muttering just loud enough to be heard, "*Mon Dieu*, make these TV people be gone *vite*!"

A moment after the maid disappeared down the steps, Irwin arrived. "You sent for me?" He asked, flustered and breathing hard from the stairs.

Brad nodded. His tic had returned, his lower eyelid jumping. He rubbed the eye with a fierce and desperate vigor.

"Okay to look around?" Suzanne asked. Without waiting for a reply, she walked into the bathroom.

"Addie Lynn!"

At Suzanne's scream and the thud that followed, Brad rushed in, his heart pounding, Irwin close behind.

Suzanne lay crumpled on the bright yellow bathmat like a used tissue. A body, a very naked and very feminine body, hung draped over the edge of the tub, half-submerged in the water. For a second they all stayed still as the faucet dripped *plink, plink, plink.*

"Oh, shit!" Recovering from the shock, Brad and Irwin exclaimed in chorus.

Suzanne groaned and began to sit up just as Hortensia came into the bathroom. "Wow," she said. "What's that lady doing?"

Brad put his arm about his daughter and turned her away from the body. "Aww, honey, she's just sleeping."

"In the water?"

"Well," Irwin said, "maybe she got thirsty."

Hortensia shook her head. "Looks like my goldfish Frederick." She paused after each syllable, Fred-er-ick, which added ironic flair. The expression on her face was doubting and yet full of sarcastic cunning, like that of a half-grown raccoon. "Mommy said he was sleeping. But really Frederick was dead."

She already knew about death? Brad gave her an extra squeeze, amazed that she was so precocious. Made a dad proud. He kissed the top of her head.

As soon as he let her go, Hortensia bent and snatched up something from the floor. It dangled, glittering, in his little girl's fist for a moment before she shoved it into the pocket of her little overalls.

The theft left his mind completely when Suzanne attempted to rise. In her struggle, she bumped into the right leg of the drowned girl. The contact jostled Addie Lynn's corpse. The dead woman's head moved up and down in the water as if bobbing for apples.

"Should we…" Brad pointed to the bathtub's grisly contents.

"Best not to move the evidence," Irwin said. "Not until the *flics* come."

Brad pulled Suzanne up into his arms and carried her. with Hortensia in tow, out of the bathroom and down the hall to their rooms. His daughter didn't seem in the least disturbed by what she'd seen, but, still, a good father believes some things in life really should be rated R!

* * *

Mabel black-bottomed into the bathroom, really feeling her oats, the best she'd felt in a long, long time. In fact, since the day she realized her fate was to eternally haunt the manor.

Irwin stood next to the tub, scratching his head and looking at the redheaded corpse. He seemed quite distressed, talking to himself, saying, "Show or not, I'm going to the concierge to demand he get the police ASAP."

"Oh, buck up, buttercup! I've got great news. Found everything, storyline, setting, and more." As if he could hear her, the excitement bubbled out as Mabel went on with her plans.

He was immobile, frozen in place, his eyes on the russet strands fanned out in the cold water.

"Yoo-hoo!" She waved her hand in front of his eyes. He shivered but, as usual, made no connection. *Dammit!* Appealing to the Reverend Prioress hadn't improved her status among the living one jot. She still needed her little transmitter. Now where was the child?

* * *

Irwin retired to the only private place he could find, his own bathroom. A quiet bathroom, without that awful floating hair. Funny, those dyed tresses were worse than the body. They almost seemed to still be alive, moving like seaweed in a gentle tidal pool. He'd half expected to see crabs crawling in and out of them. Crabs ate the eyes out of corpses.

It must have been what caused him to feel that hideous, uncanny chill.

He wanted all the shit to be over. Enough of complaining contestants, technical issues, lack of communication with the outside world, Brad, Hortensia, the boring food now that fresh supplies were no longer coming in, money and rating worries, cabin fever from the storm still raging outside... Not to mention dead girls.

He wanted to be home in L.A. With his husband, Guglielmo.

There was no solution to any of that, not yet. He needed to concentrate, move on, focus on his dream. He'd yet to come up with a plot or even a theme for his art movie. He burned with desire to create something deep and lasting, but time was going by and he wasn't getting any younger. All those parties in L.A., with Guglielmo being introduced as "the noted physician and humanitarian" and Irwin, to the amusement of everyone, as "the guy inflicting *Grab the Groom* on America." As if America sinking ever deeper into the shallow pool of anti-intellectual trivia was his fault. There it was, the cultural pool, another "in the water" metaphor!

Everyone at the parties laughed, all except his husband, who said, "Pay them no mind, *amore.* They all envied the money you make." Maybe, but they still cracked jokes at his expense.

When an indie producer became a critical

success, even without making one thin dime, the chatter stopped and sycophants rallied around, longing to bask in reflected elitist glory.

It was imperative that he come up with a smashing, brilliant, meaningful topic and make it entertaining on a low budget. Fantastic amounts of money going out might bring more money in but wouldn't win over the intelligentsia. To get their attention, you had to suffer. Sacrifice. Appear poor, even if you aren't.

Money aside, he *was* impoverished, his early dreams of creativity starved to death and buried in the great garbage heap of mainstream entertainment. And now, the lowest of the low. Reality.

What if Guglielmo tired of being with a *schlockmeister*?

"A great series," a voice whispered, echoing in his head. "I will give you the stories for a masterpiece!"

He was hearing things again. The stress of this season was driving him crazy.

"Shame there are no longer any great stars." The voice sighed melodramatically. "What you need is a collaboration with someone fresh, new—or at least recycled—and untainted. Someone with real acting chops. Not to mention beautiful and exceptionally well dressed!"

It must be another aura, heralding a new and particularly punishing migraine. Not just an aura of sound, but of smell—that heavy narcissus perfume again. He shook his head to clear his mind and looked in the mirror, hazy with the coastal moisture. An image formed, an ethereal mist in the vague and wavering shape of a woman's face. *Visual hallucinations too! A cluster headache trifecta!* Soon would come the zig-zag lines that preceded a wave, no, a tsunami, of nausea. He sat on the edge of the tub to wait.

A minute later, words appeared in the fog on the mirror: SOME ACTRESS!

They faded, only to be replaced with: MABEL DEVINE. What or who the hell was that?

EVERYONE LOVES A GHOST STORY!

The letters filled in before he could make sure they were real.

* * *

CONTESTANT #7—ROSITA

What was she doing here? These weren't her kind of people, no matter how hard they tried. Oh, and they tried, all those bitches, imitating the way they thought she should speak. Saying "y'all" every few seconds, even when just talking to her. Calling her *chiquita* and *mija*. Combining a hellacious Texan accent with garbled Spanish.

"'Y'all' is plural and all y'all are ignorant. I'm black and Native mix from Oklahoma," she wanted to tell them. "My name's the only Mexican thing about me." But no sense making enemies. She already had enough of those.

Friendly was okay, but in-your-face stupid was not. She'd gone through the same tryouts for the show as they had, she looked great in her gown—better than they did, but they still obviously thought she had no chance of winning.

Deep down, Rosita didn't care what they thought, as she'd never see a one of them again. She desperately wanted to win, to come strutting home like the cheerleader she hadn't gotten to be, trailing a gorgeous man, waving a diamond ring bigger than she'd ever seen, and flashing all that prize money. In her ex-boyfriend Jake's face.

And The Groom was a stone-cold fox, for sure. First time she saw him, she felt lightning-struck, as if she'd been out dancing around her grandpa's ranch house during a prairie storm. The famous storms that generated twisters, produced mammoth hail, and electrocuted the odd steer.

The Groom made her palms—and her other parts—sweat. He would be the perfect revenge on that son-of-a-bitch Jake. It had been a long dry spell.

Rosita always did like a guy with muscles. She prided herself on being a gym rat since moving to Tulsa from the ranch outside of Boley. Went to Planet Fitness every day, with Jake when he had a day off work.

Just yesterday, she'd watched The Groom working out in the little gym they set up on location. She'd come to show what she could do. And see what she could see. Even through his wife-beater, The Groom's abdominal muscles rippled and bulged with each breath, but when he stripped off his tee and hoisted himself on the pull bar, she whistled quietly and spoke softly to herself, "Oh, wow! The legendary, rarely seen eight-pack."

He might have heard the whistle, as he grinned at her and pulled himself up on the chin-up bar to do one rep after another. Up and down. Up and down. Up and down.

"Doing those reps for my benefit?" Rosita cocked one hip as she leaned against the elliptical and looked up at him.

He grinned again and shook his head. "Who says I'm trying to impress you? Keeping fit and looking good is in my contract." Dang, he was cute *and* flirty.

Jake had great abs. But not as great as this. No more than maybe a six-pack.

At the Planet Fitness, Rosita had been single-minded when working out, striving to be trim and shapely, but all Jake did was look around for the next available slut. Especially after he realized she trusted him and wasn't paying attention. That's where he met Donna Sue Holcslaw, head cheerleader at one of the local high schools.

He'd been athletic in a small-town rodeo way, so gentle with horses that the calmness of those he broke was legendary—a child could ride them. Rosita and Jake were supposed to get married, take over her grandpa's ranch, make a business out of training horses.

Jake, that bastard, had quit riding horses for a weekend to ride Donna Sue Holcslaw, right into a bouncing baby girl. To put the cherry on the betrayal sundae, after he told her about the upcoming blessed event, Jake had looked at Rosita like a calf mooning after its mother. Pulled her to his chest, saying, "I still love you. We can still meet up, right?" That memory made her want to weep on someone's shoulder.

Rosita's second biggest mistake, after taking up with a bronc rider, was opening up to that black-haired witch. Sat up one night with her, drinking wine like two girlfriends, looking at the photo album she'd brought from home. Showed Jake lounging on a bale of hay they were about to roll in. Told her about Donna Sue and little Mariposa Lily. Told how glad she was Donna Sue was now fat.

Last night, Isabella must have tip-toed into the gym. "You look at him like a starving dog eyeing a big, greasy knucklebone. Looks so *dang* much like Jake, doesn't he?" she'd purred in Rosita's ear. Her breath was hot with betrayal as Jake's cock had been. "Jake, your totally unreliable, cheerleader-screwing ex-." As if Rosita needed to be reminded. "Story you told me sounds like y'all would have been a hit on *Jerry Springer*!" She laughed. "Too late now."

Isabella had been *such* a good listener.

Rosita wanted to kill her, especially since she followed with, "That 'y'all' was right, right, since it would be the three of you? Still, so sad you're gonna lose again."

The Groom wasn't black, but he did look a lot like Jake. Same strong jaw, same sleepy bedroom eyes. No, not the same eyes. The Groom's were more honest. Jake had snake eyes, a snaky pecker, too. In fact, he *was* a snake!

The Groom was better in every way. And with the prize money, she'd be far richer than Jake and his Donna Sue, with her upturned piggy nose and thin dishwater blonde hair. That baby mama had no pride—she'd stuck with Jake, even when Rosita had a mutual girlfriend divulge the real reason that he'd been so late to the delivery room. It wasn't a flat tire. It was Rosita fucking him in Donna Sue's own bed. After just two goes, he'd looked at the clock and said, "Only one more time. My baby's coming!"

At that, she'd kneed him in the very nuts that had seeded Donna Sue's womb, ran home and packed her bags. Drove due west, with plans to become a movie star. Or maybe, she'd thought, staring out the window of a Raising Cane's Chicken Fingers outside Phoenix, contemplating the traffic streaming by, an online makeup influencer for black skin and hair. The possibilities were endless.

Her life was in L.A. now, among the swimming pools and palm trees, no longer in flat, boring Oklahoma. It wasn't like she ran *away*, more like she ran *to*. That was why she had to win. Show Jake that Donna Sue was nothing. Show Jake *he* meant nothing to her. Nothing to the fabulous Hollywood couple of Rosita and Her Groom.

To get herself a winning edge, Rosita had listened in on conversations, watched hairstyling sessions, and observed every flirtatious moment. She noted where eyes went and how the corners of mouths moved into smiles and grimaces. She knew which contestant was seriously taken with The Groom, and which one was more seriously taken with one of the other girls. Or a cast member, like Isabella was with the handsome producer. You never knew where such knowledge could take you. Where tidbits of gossip to the right person could lead.

It was the pursuit of information that led her down the basement stairs and out to the storerooms. Two local workmen, young and attractive but no Jakes, passed by her in the early evening. It was after dinner and the other girls were preparing for the night's shoot. Busy getting made-up, gossiping and complaining like a group of turkey buzzards picking over a dead mule.

Rosita had no idea what these two French guys were talking about, but the way they furtively moved, their hushed voices, made her wonder if they were meeting up with a contestant. Maybe even for a three-way. Rosita had heard rumors that Diana, a girl from L.A. had been sent home for something like that, before shooting had even begun. And a teacher, no less. Disgraceful.

If Diana did reappear, that tidbit of information would really be useful, and God only knew what info the cute Frenchies might drop about other competitors. She followed them down the hall and to a service stairwell.

The ancient wooden stairs to the lower level were creaky, but the two men quit whispering. They spoke aloud once they'd gone halfway down, their boisterous voices covering what little noise she made, If she stayed to the side by the wall.

They entered a dark and foul-smelling corridor, stopped outside a door, looked at each other meaningfully, shuddered, and moved on. At last, they came to a large room open to the outside. Firewood was piled against the walls on either side. She ducked behind a pile and listened, but they had fallen silent, except for grunts as each took an armload of logs. There was nothing else to see or hear. Disappointing.

When they left, going back the way they'd come, she walked to look out at the sea. The waves were still high, splashing brownish foam up over the cliff's edge, but the weather had subsided a bit.

Movement on the ground caught her eye. A serpent, colored bright yellow in a hypnotizing pattern, was headed toward her. It looked fearsome, thicker than the rattlers and cottonmouths she was used to. She stepped slowly away, keeping a wary eye on the reptile, muttering, "I hate snakes, you goddamn sumbitch!"

Backed into the wall, hands stretched out to either side for balance, the snake still approaching, she came upon the wooden handles of several axes, all worn with long use. She grabbed one and advanced on the critter, planning to split its head down the middle.

In her single-minded concentration on the snake, she missed a huge rat, grown fat on the kitchen's black beetles, as it sniffed its way through the wood pile. Untold generations of its ancestors had taken advantage of the pig and sheep carcasses brought to the manor and, before that, the convent, for food.

Something spooked the rat, and, in panic, it did something foolish: it ran toward the human.

Alas! The ax Rosita selected was the most ancient of the tools, one nearly three centuries old. As she raised it overhead and began the downward swing, the snake suddenly darted away. Rosita stumbled on the rat and fainted, just as the head broke from the rotted handle. Her unconscious fall moved her from beneath the blade. She missed the loud squeal that came just after the ax head fell.

* * *

Sudden movement, and something large falling to the ground, stopped Cleopatra. She recoiled, her head rising up to taste the air. The hot, iron tang of blood came toward her like a shock wave. She pursued it to the source and discovered a huge and nearly bisected rat. Her flickering tongue explored the body.

Cleopatra had grown unused to having her food provided, but this was too tempting. Despite the lack of movement, she struck with violent force. Momentum allowed her muscular coils to wrap about the furry body until, at last, it lay safely still and warm in her hold.

Pleasurable feelings swept through her. She rested from the effort for a moment. And then she unhinged her jaws, opening wide to swallow it headfirst, more and more of him disappearing with each gulp.

It was chilly by the woodpiles, the sea breeze entering easily. She decided to leave. Ascending back to the warmer part of the building was laborious because of the bulge in her belly, but she longed for a cozy spot to digest her meal. The tip of the rat's naked tail still protruded from her mouth, and that was most annoying. It tickled her throat, and, not possessing a diaphragm, she lacked the ability to cough.

CHAPTER FIFTEEN

Mabel wanted to find Cleopatra before the contestant named Jocelyn did. The cheap skirt believed she owned the snake, as if anyone could *own* such a magnificent creature.

To find a snake, you need to think like a snake! Mabel put on her thinking tiara and imagined herself a cold-blooded reptile, wriggling like an ectoplasmic serpent through walls. As such, she traveled up and over lath, past ancient, crumbling, horsehair-shedding plaster. She searched the storerooms where rats and black beetles looked for food, traveled to the basement to check the deliciously overheated furnace room, and slid between the logs in the woodpiles. In the wood storage she saw the girl, clutching an old axe handle. And that darling snake in peril.

The issue, of course, was how to save Cleopatra.

Oh, well, she would ponder that later. She headed back to the space between the walls, still seeking Cleopatra. Finally, the creature could be seen, coiled like a beautiful yellow and white turban. Under a radiator, fast asleep.

Making herself as two-dimensional as a fallen leaf, Mabel slid beneath the clanking iron radiator to lie beside the slumbering serpent.

A loud *hiss!* caused Mabel to pause—for a second the noise seemed to be steam escaping a valve. Then the triangular head rose above the muscular body and turned, golden eyes glittering. Cleopatra opened her mouth wide, her forked tongue darting in and out, and hissed again, more loudly than before.

The snake shot out from under the radiator, across the hall, into a hole in the baseboard—pulling hard to get her bulging middle through with an audible *POP*—and disappeared.

The vehement sound knocked Mabel on her ass, her head a disc between the radiator loops, reflexively avoiding the decades of dust rabbits hidden there. She didn't need any more filth in her brain!

Shocking! The snake had seen or tasted her!

A cackling chuckle harshly shattered the air, clanging on the radiator's metal, echoing in the hall. Had the sound been her imagination? Was it real?

"You are not the first disbeliever when it cometh to miracles!" The Reverend Prioress' voice rang in her ears, all the way up from her basement crypt. It could only be her doing! Mabel zoomed out of the manor, still serpentine in shape, headed to the chamber below the convent's tower.

* * *

Hortensia seemed unfazed by the dead girl in the tub, but Brad wasn't taking any chances. He put booking a child therapist in L.A. on his to-do list and prepared to give her some down time.

"I think you need a nap, Hortensia, honey," he told her.

"Don't want none." She bounced higher, her sneakers flashing as they indented her bed's coverlet.

"Wanna go see dead lady again." Her breath was short with the effort of bounding upward, chanting, "Dead lady, dead lady, floatin' in a tub! Dead lady, dead lady, *glub, glub, glub*!"

"Hortensia! Your mom wouldn't like that." Suzanne's eyes were wide with shock.

"My mommy's not here! I'm Daddy's problem now!" Hortensia bounded upward again and again, first on her right foot, then her left, repeating the words at the top of her voice.

"You need a nap," Brad said with parental firmness. He turned to Suzanne. "Think maybe you do, too. Been a stressful day and you look really dragged out."

Suzanne looked down at herself and frowned. Perhaps his words had been poorly thought out. Better to follow the caring route. "How about you and Hortensia curl up together? You can lock the door from the inside."

Hortensia shook her head. "Don't..." Left foot. "Want..." Right foot. "Nap!" Left again and again.

Brad didn't let himself be triggered. He had planned for resistance from the kid. "How about some milk and cookies?"

Hortensia had never turned down anything edible. It occurred to him in a flash that as eager as she was for food, she might have an eating disorder. Another thing a therapist could deal with! He silently congratulated himself for thinking of that. Paying for a therapist was what a good father would do.

He couldn't let her suffer the kind of teasing he and his friends had inflicted on fat kids. The thought of his own flesh and blood being tormented by heckling pre-teen boys made him feel awful, as if something had curled up inside him and died. Such teasing could make her believe she'd be a loser at life.

If he had to, he'd even go with her to Overeaters

Anonymous. There was probably a kid's version.

At the mention of cookies, Hortensia took one last high jump and executed a perfect two-point landing on the bed. She jammed her fists where a waist should be, elbows jutting out and said, "Sablés? Dipped in chocolate?"

Spoiled by the food in France, a mini gourmet in addition to being a glutton. Bad—more evidence of food obsession. But, also good—his milk and cookie offer was part of a devious plan. He needed her to stay in bed, or at least in the room, while he and Irwin handled "the situation," as he'd decided to call the rash of death that had broken out among the contestants.

"Chocolate sablés it is!" Brad chirped. "I'll bring a tray myself." He turned his attention to Suzanne, so fetchingly rumpled and bedheaded. "And tea for you." He headed to the dining room, with a quick diversion to his suite and its bottle of Smirnoff. Hard to taste even a bit of that smooth alcohol, especially when you were downing it in warmed milk and eating chocolatey, buttery cookies. That ought to keep his daughter quiet for the afternoon. For Suzanne, he added half a tranquilizer.

* * *

"Irwin? You done?" Brad called, knocking on the bathroom door.

Goddamn him, demanding babysitting even while Irwin was presumably on the toilet. And not even to care for Hortensia, his scary little girl, but just for himself.

Tempting to say, "If I was done, Brad, I'd be out there," but that wasn't true. He didn't want to be "out there" and wouldn't be, if he could help it. Still, duty called—if Brad was so anxious, there must be another crisis. Hopefully that didn't mean yet another body.

Sooner or later, no matter what excuses he gave, the girls still in play would notice their numbers dwindling. Something fishy about the disappearances foisted on them as "losers leaving the show." That would mean leaving a place no one could flee.

He stood, reeling from the pain of his migraine-plagued head, and flushed the empty bowl. "Coming," he yelled. To continue the ruse, he paused to wash his hands though they'd only helped him perch on the tub's rim.

Within a few minutes, Brad, Irwin, the concierge, and the rusty iron cart were all squeaking their way toward Addie Lynn's room.

* * *

Mabel stood before the relic's niche. "You can make me visible to the living? Let them hear me?"

"If you believe, my child." The Reverend Mother's lips pursed piously. "If you open your heart to the Lord and believe." She sighed, looked down. Then her eyes moved slyly toward Mabel's hair. "And also give me that crown on your head."

Mabel's hands flew protectively to the ornament on her platinum-blonde marcel. "You want my tiara?" She lifted it from her head. The diamonds sparkled seductively in the dim light. "But my husband, Count Max de Summer, gave it to me when he made me a countess."

"You may have been a countess, but if you remember, I was a queen." The Reverend Prioress spent a moment reveling in what seemed suspiciously like "see you and raise you one" smugness, somehow giving the impression of shrugging, despite having no shoulders.

"Didn't you take a vow of poverty and all? And I thought it was important for your stories to be told and your sacrifices remembered.'"'

The Reverend Prioress' features rearranged into a parody of disinterest. "Suit thyself. Then leave as I have some praying to do."

Mabel touched the center diamond. No one had admired or even seen the ornament in nearly a hundred years. Maybe she'd had it long enough. Maybe it was time to pass it on. The Reverend Prioress, poor shriveled thing, might look ridiculous with a tiara, but, hell's bells, why should dismemberment stop a girl from longing to look good?

And why should a present from a dead husband stop Mabel from longing for another shot at stardom? "Oh, what the heck!" She said, lifting the glittering bauble. She placed it with both hands on the dry, matted hair. "But no pool boy."

"What the devil would I do with one of those?" The head cackled with laughter. "My vow of chastity is easy to keep these days! Now, what is it you want again?"

"The only person who can see and hear me is a little girl. I need someone else, a certain grownup. A person in position to help me. He's here now..." She sighed with longing. "...the rarest and most valuable asset on Earth, a high-placed contact in show business."

"The man known as Irwin? He has already begun to see and hear you, something you would know if you paid attention. As a wise man said, 'It is a sign of greed to do all the talking and never listen.'"

"That a Jesus quote?"

"Have you ever read the Holy Scriptures? No, that was Democritus, the ancient Greek philosopher. We in the monasteries and convents kept culture alive throughout the Dark Ages." Despite not having a neck the Prioress shook her head. "Perhaps we need to do it again."

"I never learned much in school. Not much of a scholar," Mabel admitted.

"Could have fooled me. Yet, still, I grow fonder of you with every visit and am glad we let you stay."

"What do you mean, 'let me stay'?"

The head ignored the question. "We have prayed, the Lord has answered. We are already free of the most recent dead, those without souls, those with evil in their hearts. They have met their just rewards."

"The reality bitches?"

"Indeed, those are the ones."

Mabel was elated. No more fears of having to put up with them through eternity.

"They are either destined for Hell or back from whence they came, whichever may be worse. As for you, having only superficiality and a desire for wanton fun, you did not deserve to be the Devil's prey. The state of your soul is the fault of your times more than your sinfulness. Though when you owned the manor, your drunken parties did keep us up at night." The Reverend Prioress scowled at the memory. "Sister Antonia was driven to cursing one summer by the raucous revelry. She had to use the scourge on herself for hours."

"Give me a break! It was just after the greatest war the world will ever see. We were letting off steam, celebrating the end of the carnage. So what if we got drunk? We knew how to have fun. Nothing wrong with that."

"Fun? Is that a degenerate modern concept?"

"No! I'll show you the meaning of fun!" Mabel launched into her repertoire of songs, starting with "If You Knew Susie" followed by "When the Red, Red Robin Comes Bob-Bob-Bobbin' Along" and "California, Here I Come." She lifted the sides of her skirt to keep her heels from catching in the beaded fringe and danced a few steps of a graceful foxtrot, fearing the Charleston would make the head explode.

Drawn by the strangeness of the music, the sisters filtered in one by one, first just listening, then *boop-boop-a-dooping* along to "I Wanna Be Loved by You." When she closed with "Mammy," there wasn't a dry eye-socket in the house.

* * *

With Suzanne and Hortensia deep in their drug slumber, Brad mulled over their options, what with contestants dying, disappearing, and generally dropping like flies.

Irwin was nowhere to be seen. Again. God only knew where he was—probably hiding in his bathroom again.

The Meat Men and the remaining contestants were enjoying cocktails and hors d' oeuvres in the hall. As Brad made his way through the throng, he smiled, nodded, and fist-bumped or high-fived everyone in his path, even those who hadn't seen him coming and so jumped when he touched them. He checked the mood of the crowd. The investors appeared happy. They headed with their prey to the dining room for dinner, leaving the unchosen women to mill about alone.

"*Monsieur le Producteur*!" a man's voice rang out.

Now what? Brad turned to see who was calling him. There were only women nearby. He looked at each of them suspiciously. After Hailey, he couldn't be sure that someone hadn't tripped up, spoken in a natural voice. *Damn Irwin!* If he hadn't been so strict about Brad having sex with the contestants, there'd be at least a few whose bodies he was sure of. He turned around again.

"*Monsieur Grab le Groom*!"

The speaker was one of the local workers,

overlooked before, as manor staff should be invisible. "You talking to *moi*?" Brad pointed to his own chest to make sure the young French guy understood.

"It is perhaps possible to have a talk to you? A very small talk?"

"What for? I'm very busy."

"Just for a moment, *s'il vous plait*." The youth took off his cap, held it in front of him. "I am Lucien."

"That's so nice. Good for you." Brad patted the kid's shoulder. "Got a lot to do, sorry." He took a rapid step away, shaking his head while grinning madly to show he wasn't an elitist. He screeched to a halt when he heard, though just barely, Lucien whisper, "*Monsieur*, I know about the girl in the kitchen."

Fresh beads of sweat popped out on Brad's forehead. He stood for a moment, steadying his breath with his back to the young man, and said, "Follow me."

He led the way to his suite. Shut the door. "Okay, shoot."

Lucien scratched his head. His hand still held his cap, which flapped up and down with the vigor of his scratching. "Shoot? I do not have a gun. And why would I want for you to be shooted dead?"

"Your boss said he already paid you. How much more to keep things hush-hush?"

Lucien looked confused. "*Oui, Monsieur*, our boss he pays us every week, but this is not about the work here in the manor. I am not asking you for money."

Brad snorted. Everyone always wanted money. "What the hell do you want then? What'll it take to keep your yap shut?"

"If you please, *Monsieur*, hear me out. What I would like is one time to be The Groom. The first The Groom from France, in France."

Brad looked closely at the boy. Beneath a really atrocious haircut, looking as if styled with a scythe, and several unartistic but natural-looking smears of dirt was a rather presentable young man. Handsome possibly. He was tall enough, too, and women did swoon over that accent. They even thought that the garbled grammar was cute. It might just work and was certainly cheaper than paying blackmail.

The young man flushed, and Brad's heart sank. It seemed there was more.

"There is more," the lad said. "I have promised to marry a girl, who like me is a worker here, a *femme de menage*—how you say it, a maid? She could, perhaps be the one to win me?"

Brad raised an eyebrow with his best approximation of Gallic skepticism.

Lucien's speech was more pressured now, taking more concentration to understand. "My Agnes is *une belle demoiselle*. The equal of any you have brought from America. And we are truly in love!"

Huh, true love. Irwin, that little romantic, would adore the storyline, *Maid Wins the Groom*. And it would save money if they used the same location, maybe during better weather.

He could see it now: Ceremony out on the cliff. Trellis covered in those over-stuffed, smelly French roses. Maybe spring for celebrity chef catering.

"Please, *Monsieur*, I have not enough funds for the dream wedding of my Agnes. Every day, she is watching *Say Yes to Le Dress* on streaming. One dress she loved was more than poor Lucien earns in a year. It is your fault that ordinary girls have such expectations, spreading these reality show poisons throughout the world. But you can make amends! If she wins me, you make the wedding and buy the fancy gown." He looked puzzled for a moment and then said, "*When* she wins me."

Brad considered this boy Lucien's proposal.

There was a certain audience-pleasing logic to what he was saying, but, though Americans love true love stories, they prefer their love stories to be about the wealthy. Especially European aristocrats.

It was rumored a French nobleman had owned this estate, just a century ago. But what was his name? Brad clapped the heel of his hand against his temple, trying to jar loose the memory.

All that sprang to mind was the guy's fate—sometime back in the '20s, he'd been trampled to death on safari. By an elephant. Or maybe a hippo?

He had a great story prior to his demise, however. He'd married some American silent film star and made her a countess—an intriguing bit of zest added to the storyline.

He looked Lucien over one more time. Work had given him muscles that showed even through his rough work shirt. His lips were full and sensual, his skin basically zit-free and appealingly tanned, his eyes deep brown with flecks of green. Even close-up, he'd pass as a winner in next season's show.

All they'd have to do is claim Lucien was a descendant of the dead count who owned the place—an unclaimed bastard child, say—but didn't know it. Yes! An extra twist to be revealed in the final episode, just before the wedding. Rags to riches, a classic Cinderella story! Recycling old stories, from fairytales to comics was all the rage now. Returning to the tried-and-true, the easy to adapt. Brad pursed his lips, tight, deep in thought. He nodded in appreciation.

Lucien seemed to take that as meaning his chances were improving. "And I will not say a thing." He bent closer to whisper, "My lips will be zips!"

"You'll have to sign a contract for the whole season. Think your fiancée will go along with the plan?"

Lucien's blush deepened. "Fortunately, there will

then be the money for a honeymoon to the Maldives. My Agnes is *pragmatique*, she would understand if I must romance the American ladies with their giant bouncing breasts. Sex with them will mean nothing. Just the work I do for love of her."

CHAPTER SIXTEEN

When she woke up, Hortensia's head seemed to be stuffed with underbed dust balls and her mouth tasted like sour milk. She lolled on her bed, fighting her eyelids' downward drift. Sleep could mean missing something important.

Suzanne had been taking care of her, making her feel loved, making her feel safe, like nobody had ever done before. It was a shame Daddy liked the contestants so much, shame he wasn't always so nice. Hortensia had another plan. Suzanne just had to take the deal.

Hortensia held Kimmie up to her face. The doll would do the talking for her—it felt a lot less scary that way—who could say no to a doll? In a squeaky voice she said to Suzanne, "Hort's daddy's not pretty as The Groom."

Suzanne laughed, though her eyes squinted as though that hurt. "Both of them are handsome, Kimmie." Her face got that serious look big people liked to use. "But why are you talking about that again?"

Suzanne was nice to pretend she believed Kimmie was really the one speaking, but Hortensia wasn't fooled. Instead of answering the question, Kimmie said, "You was always bee-u-ti-ful. Bee-u-tifuller now."

"Hmm," Suzanne laughed. "Maybe I'll have the makeup girl do the full job on me and then I'll be gorgeous. What do you think?"

"Contestant makeup on you?" Hortensia pooched her lower lip out behind the doll's head, making it shake "no," though maybe a little makeup would be nice. "Uh, uh, you got to stay *you*. Not become one of *them*." Hortensia forgot to have Kimmie speak. "If you don't like my daddy, maybe you could marry The Groom. He likes you a lot, I think. He's real nice." Her eyes were suddenly itchy. She wiped them with the backs of her hands. "And maybe you and The Groom could be Hort's mommy and daddy, and…"

Suzanne didn't answer, which made Hortensia so sad, she dropped Kimmie. "No?" she asked with a little sniffle.

"You have a daddy. And a mommy."

"Daddy only wants me because you make him. Mommy doesn't want me at all. Too ugly."

"Oh, Hort, you are not ugly!"

Hortensia was tired of big people saying dumb stuff to her, like she'd believe lies just because she was little. She'd been to school, heard what the other kids said about her. Bashed them for it and gotten into trouble. And they didn't even matter. Not to her. "Mommy says 'Hortensia, shame you're not pretty.'"

"Oh, no." Suzanne shook her head. "Your mommy couldn't mean that."

Sometimes grownups just really, really wanted to be stupid. "I heard her. Told her boyfriend she was stuck with me."

"Aw, that can't be true." Suzanne held out her arms.

Hortensia didn't run to her. She stood firm. If Suzanne needed to be taught the truth, she was going to be the teacher. "Mommy's gone off with her boyfriend and Hort's not on the boat, is she?"

* * *

The latest dead contestant had been safely squirreled away, reducing Irwin's angst. He felt a strange, irresistible urge to explore the convent and its church. Somehow, braving it seemed important, something that might be the making of him. He had to go alone, without that scary little girl muddling his thoughts. He was still leery of her potential for aggression, not to mention her sneering, which seemed uncannily accurate.

Amazing that a kid held such power. He was more afraid of her than he was of the mysterious writing in the snow, which had given him a weird tingling at the tip of his dick, a lot less painful than the time he'd had chlamydia. That was before Guglielmo, of course.

All he'd wanted in the cloister was to take a leak, not get a message from the beyond. The whole thing had scared the bejesus out of him. But it hadn't scared Hortensia. Amazing the kid was so unaffected.

If only his husband was here, just for reassurance. "My little worry wart," was what Guglielmo called him. He'd always been plagued by worry. More than worry, fear, especially fear of failing.

"I fear you anticipate failure," Guglielmo said. "Anticipate it. Savor it, like I savor wild boar prosciutto, trichinosis and all, smuggled from my family's estate, right under the noses of the FDA. Just like that you savor failure. You're relieved when it comes, exhale with a giant *'phew'* and wipe your brow, no longer free-falling but landing safely in the realm of destiny fulfilled." He'd smiled fondly. "Your father made you this way, while my father taught me to hunt those boars."

If Irwin wasn't so besotted with Guglielmo, he'd have simply replied, "Shut the fuck up." Instead, he remained silent, studying the depth of his spouse's dark eyes.

"But, unlike your father," Guglielmo said, "I'll be right here loving you when you take another brave step into the void."

For Guglielmo, he'd take that brave step and go for gold.

He set out for the corridor leading to the church, taking just a few cookies for sustenance. All was quiet as a bated breath. Not even the rats appeared. Faint light filtered in muted jewel tones through the clerestory windows. The gaping hole made by the hail revealed a sullen gray sky, dully gleaming like a worn aluminum pot, but no precipitation. He stood, looking up through the gap. It seemed as if the storm might be over.

Moving down the nave to the cloister door, Irwin tread carefully on the stones. The ice patches had begun to melt and the skim of water made them even more treacherous. The water had washed away some of the dust and he could just make out a crude stone mosaic of Jonah surrounded by fantastical sea monsters—bulging eyes and upturned snouts. He reached the high threshold into the courtyard, stepped through.

Outside there was a fresh sea breeze, tangy as pickle juice. Brisk but far less so than the strong gusts of the previous day. It was cold though more pleasant without sleet falling.

Irwin stopped beneath one of the arches and looked about. A faint noise reached his ears, and a chill stirred the hairs on his neck. Something was surrounding him, an uncanny presence. Uneasy thoughts danced through his mind. He took a deep breath and tried to relax his shoulders.

But what if there really is a ghost? That

apparition in the bathroom had been mighty realistic. True, it had been playful, but hadn't the creepy clown in Stephen King's *It* been playful just before killing people?

The huge, tattered spiderwebs hanging from the roof held black beetles, mere shells now, sucked dry. They swayed in the breeze, clacking against the wall. They sounded almost like the utterances of the dead. A subterranean muttering.

"The cries of the women—highborn ladies and peasant virgins—who were locked up here…" a voice said, echoing against the stones. "They want—nay, they need..." *Hack! Hack! Hack!* The voice paused for a tortured cough. "...someone to speak for them."

Looking around revealed nothing stirring. All that could be seen were the sullen pewter-colored clouds, behind which the sun was slyly peeking. A general air of ancient gloom pervaded the dimmed rays.

"They need us."

He stayed quiet, hoping to see nothing.

The voice grew increasingly impatient. Did he imagine that its next words, spoken sotto voce, were "Oh, for Christ's sake!"?

A wispy outline appeared and then slowly filled in to reveal a translucent woman. The slowly developing image was reminiscent of the magic of Polaroid which, as a kid, he'd always thought captured ghosts. She wore a low-waisted, sparkling dress with fringed hem that trailed on the ground, and a long string of beads.

Now more defined, the shadowy woman coalesced and dissolved again, over and over. Shit! Fernand had warned them that the dead haunted this place. How he regretted laughing while Brad made fun of Fernand, imitating his accent, walking with his slouching, French lounge lizard stroll.

He tried to inch back toward the door, but the figure moved, floated in front of him, still in womanly form. She waved toward the tower, and Irwin's gaze involuntarily followed her middle finger. It sported a lit cigarette in a wire gizmo, like some weird Etsy find.

Whatever she was, he relaxed. She no longer frightened him. It felt as if he'd been waiting for her all his life.

The main building loomed ahead, grim and gray, its gothic, crenellated tower crumbling in a manner both foreboding and romantic. He'd been told that it was formerly a convent, but it looked more like a prison, all windows facing the wild sea.

Irwin stumbled to the broken statue and once again perched on the base. The ghostly image materialized further, floating before his eyes.

"You need to explore it all," said the figment of his imagination, for that's what he decided she was. "See the nuns' dark cells. Visit the cramped chapel where they recited the daily prayers, since the big church was only for the priest's mass." The ghost sounded like an old-time carnie working a peepshow, the kind no one would be interested in, now that limitless porn was online.

Irwin turned back toward the manor. Why had he felt drawn to this place? It was a dump.

"Open your mind! Imagine this convent being a budget-friendly setting for a sexy series on the sisters who lived here."

Ridiculous! "Sexy series? About a bunch of women who spent their lives praying? Romance with God? You really think that would get us subscribers?"

"Oh, for..." The ghost stamped her foot, which went through a chunk of the statue like a hot knife through butter. "It's all in their backstories! Every nun has her own tale. Seduction, lust, rape, abandonment, all ending up confined here." Her voice dropped to a whisper and her wispy upper body inclined toward him. "Picture the frustrated women locked away, the 'special' friendships. The late-night visits to each other's chambers. The flagellation rooms. Something for everyone."

Irwin leaned toward her. "Go on, I'm listening."

"Imagine, a beautiful young virgin in her father's castle, served by her ladies in waiting. Costume: demure dress except for bosom pushed high by tight-laced corsets. Breasts bulging, trembling like aspic with each breath. Alone with her ladies all day and all night. Nothing to end the boredom but sewing and leaning out the window to sigh as they watch knights ride off." The ghost held up see-through hands which moved slowly apart, fingers spread wide, expanding the imagined scene. "And then her father, the duke, engaged in arranging a marriage for her, one that will bring income to his coffers, makes a fatal mistake. He lets a handsome young troubadour into the castle to amuse everyone."

The ghost paused and seemed to consider Irwin more closely. "Maybe even thinks the singer, strumming his lute, is really a pansy, safe to entertain among young women. But that is just an illusion of his slender, boyish physique—he has another instrument at the ready. Opportunity for many scenes of the two becoming friends first and then, with being closeted together in her wardrobe... Her father discovers them in flagrante delicto and plans to immure her in the convent. Pause for many intertitles..."

"We don't use intertitles much anymore," Irwin said, wondering if he should have been offended by the antiquated gay slurs. "We tend to use sound."

"Sorry. Forgot everyone now has talkies."

Now he realized why the specter looked so familiar. She looked like Generic Flapper #3 from any movie set in the Jazz Age. "Weren't you in *Our Dancing Daughters*? I think you're the girl who asks Ben, 'Wouldst fling a hoof with me?'"

"No! That was Joan Crawford. She didn't hold a candle to me."

"*ZaZa*?"

"Gloria Swanson, and again, no." The specter now seemed a bit more steam than mist.

There ensued a pregnant pause, during which Irwin realized he was expected to make an accurate guess. He racked his brain but came up empty. She puffed angrily on her cigarette. "Why even the child, Hortensia, knows me! I'm the great Mabel DeVine, Countess de Summer!"

He recovered adroitly. "Mabel DeVine! Son of a gun! Cannot believe it. You were my favorite." He still hadn't the faintest. "But what are you doing here?"

"I first came here in '25, to help Max scout locations. We landed in France, but not aiming to see Paris. Too cliché. Everyone had done Paris—Jean Renoir, Rigo, Clair. But Normandy? No one knew Normandy. It was untouched. I fell in love with this place. The ruined church, the convent…exquisite!" She paused for a moment.

That made sense in a weird way. The convent was a derelict mess but by then, the nuns had been gone for two hundred years. "So did you make a film here?"

"Never got the chance before Max died on safari. When I lost him, I returned to Europe, to France, the scene of our early, passionate love. It's great love that makes a star, the love of great art and the love of a great man."

"I can get behind that," Irwin said. "Why are you still here, though?"

"Accident in the driveway. Absinthe party the night before. Still hungover. That damn stone wall ruined my Sport Phantom and trapped me here. This is my purgatory."

"Didn't get to Heaven?"

She chuckled. “Lucky it wasn’t the other place. Heaven, though, would be so boring.”

If this is your imagination, Irwin, you’re a genius. Go for it! “I have to say, the concept is most intriguing. Feminism and religious stuff juxtaposed, the opportunity for all sorts of sex scenes. Something for everyone, indeed.” Maybe even a handsome young priest and a possibly age-appropriate altar boy. Audiences were ready for that.

“So, a take-off on the show?” His eyebrows were raised so high they hurt. It was a delightful idea, at once skewering the crass way he was making money, pleasing the critics of commercialism, and making money off the immense popularity of *Grab the Groom*. The intellectual snobs would love it! Metacinema to the max!

His mind was roiling, turning over scene after scene. He could begin shooting here in France, have a good bit wrapped up before going home. Maybe even convince some of the staff and contestants to act in it. Back home in Hollywood, the design of the sets would be easy, all green screen and CGI, copying the old manor, wedded to this creepy ruin of a convent.

And then he remembered the dead girls. They could screw up everything. Or would they? As he had told Brad, audiences loved murder, especially of pretty girls. “We could have the contestants start disappearing…dying…”

The specter gave him an irritated glance. “Not an ordinary horror flick, but a metaphor for the position of aging women since time immemorial. Have the supernatural in it, of course, but maybe only to show how the emphasis on beauty and youth destroys women, sidelines them at the whim of men.”

Irwin nodded. Not bad, not bad at all. “Show the vicious treatment of women as they lose their looks. That would draw in the angry feminist crowd.”

"Actors with plummy English accents, even though it takes place here in France. English accents make everything seem classy."

He bookmarked the design of the sun-lit tower in his head. Better than the Paramount logo, for sure. He smiled at the change in the cloister. Things were rapidly warming up. The stones, glistening with melting snow, looked freshly washed. Icicles hung from the walkway's roof and the tower sparkled like a fairytale dream. None of the snow had become dirty despite turning to slush. He started back to the manor, his head full of dreams.

Behind him, the misty form of Mabel DeVine leaned against a pillar, smiling as she screwed another cigarette into her ring's little wire cage.

* * *

Brad's thoughts were whirling as he made his way down the stairs. Another dead girl! Still, he had to admire how tough a little kid he had. Straight out of *Charlotte's Web*. Some pig indeed! He imagined Wilbur's hyper-literate spider watching over them all, weaving their praises. What a shame she wasn't watching the contestants.

He went to the concierge's office. Stood outside for a moment, sighed, and knocked.

"*Mon Dieu*!" the man exclaimed as soon as Brad entered, "I worry that the storeroom is running out of space!"

"Yeah," Brad said, "that's my worry, too." As if that was the main concern—Irwin would have a field day with the concept. But speaking of Irwin, where was he? Never around when needed.

Brad wasn't sure he could handle "the situation," as he'd begun to think of the bodies. Things had gone way too far to worry about costs mounting up. "How about we try the police again?"

"But of course," the concierge said, doing the Gallic face twist: purse lips to the side, eyebrows up as if he'd just tasted a bad *escargot*. "But, alas, they don't speak too much English. I hope that the telephone is no more *cassé*—how you and the *Boche* say it? Kaput." He lifted the receiver. "Ah, the dial tone!" He smiled as if to reassure Brad help was on the way, though he hadn't yet spoken to the *Gendarmerie*. After a friendly greeting, the concierge began a rapid-fire conversation, then silence, punctuated by three or four exclamations of *oui!,* each accompanied by a snappy nod of the head. At that, the conversation seemed to be over. He gently replaced the receiver with an expression of regret, as if a good friend had died.

"I regret, *Monsieur*, that the many lines out of Normandy are still down. And the *Gendarmerie* is very, very busy right now. Many, many incidents due to *La Tempête du Siècle*, as they are calling it. The Storm of the Century. So, you are all to remain in place…" He looked extra-regretful at that. "…until they can send the *Général de division*, who, most fortunately, speaks excellent English. They must do…" He paused, scratched his head. Obviously searching for a word. "…a preliminary inquiry. They will, when possible, have someone notify the American Embassy that there is this little difficulty. We shall see what they say. But no doubt soon you will be able to speak to them on your cell phone, when those are again working, and we are connected to the capital."

Where, oh where was Irwin? No way Brad was calling the embassy in Paris without his partner's advice. He wiped his forehead. Sweating was becoming a bad, unattractive, habit. The sweat presaged full-blown panic. Three girls had died and now that he thought about it, a few more were missing. How legally responsible was the production company? Insurance should cover most things, but that wouldn't protect him, personally, from criminal charges, even though he hadn't killed anyone. What were French jails like?

The saving grace was the weather. There really had been no way they could have gotten the police to come, not with the phone lines out and escape cut off. That would be their defense against liability—if any—for failure to report the deaths. But would the investors be freaked? And could they get the season wrapped in time?

"So," the concierge went on. "We have the newly dead American *mademoiselle* in the bathtub, the dead English lady already in the storage room with the dead… what is the correct term in English? We French, we do not like to offend! The one who is not quite a lady but not yet a *gentilhomme*!" He shrugged his Gallic shrug.

Brad got up to leave, unwilling to admit that there were more girls missing. He had begun to sweat anew.

"*Excusez moi!*" The concierge held up an officious index finger. "Just one more little reminder. Please do not attempt leaving the manor. The *Gendarmerie* was very specific."

CHAPTER SEVENTEEN

Hortensia's head felt worse, even though she'd been up for a while, and her belly felt worse, too. Like back on that stinky bus after eating the Three Musketeers bars.

"I feel kind of sick, too." Suzanne put her hand on Hortensia's forehead and smiled. "No fever." She took her hand away. "Hope we're not coming down with anything. You rest some more, and I'll rustle up some tummy and headache cures." She stood next to the bed, swaying slightly, turned to leave, and let out a deep *urrrrp*!

For the first time, Hortensia didn't laugh at the sound. Instead, she sank back under the covers as Suzanne left to get the medicine.

There was a loud pop. Peering from under the stiffly starched and ironed sheet, she found Mabel sitting on the bed, one leg crossed over the other, her foot jiggling up and down. "Hey, Toot-toot-tootsie!" Mabel smiled a jolly smile. "Guess what?"

"I don't know what," Hort said. "And I don't even care." She wanted to tell Mabel *Stop fidgeting*!—as that's what her mama said when she swung her feet or banged them against her chair to make her sneakers blink. No one told her to keep still here—the adults were all too scared to tell her to quit it. Even her funny tummy felt better, thinking of that.

But maybe they just didn't care enough to tell her how to behave.

"That's not very nice, but I'll tell you anyway. That Irwin can see and hear me now. I just had a very good meeting with him in the convent."

Hortensia sat up. "Didn't wait for me?"

Mabel stopped jiggling her foot. "You were napping, baby. Thought you'd be glad you didn't have to be the go-between. You could get to be just a little kid."

"Who said I wanted to be just a little kid? Not me, not ever." Little kids had no say in things, like being left behind.

* * *

CONTESTANT #8—ISABELLA

It wasn't easy to embarrass Isabella, but her mother had managed to do so many times. Gwendolyn had starred in a few movies in the late '70s, titles best forgotten. Her claim to almost-fame came from her standing in for Farah Fawcett, the star she'd idolized for so long—she'd spent her pre-teen years glued to the screen of the old TV in a pine-paneled basement, watching *Charlie's Angels.*

Her resemblance to Farrah was part genetic and part deliberate—she copied Farrah's wide smile and breezy, all-American charm and her face-framing hairdo. She didn't date in high school. Flint, Michigan, was not where she wanted to end up, married, fading away, with four tow-headed rugrats hanging from plus sized culottes. Instead, she packed a few things in her old plaid suitcase and went to Hollywood to seek success.

Back then she'd been prettier than Farrah, her lips fuller, more luscious, her facial structure a bit softer.

Agents, both real and come-on artists, approached her whenever she walked down the street or entered a store. She got many screen tests but, somehow, the camera just hadn't loved Gwendolyn as it did the luminous Farrah.

Gwendolyn had to settle for being Fawcett's stand-in several times before launching her "career" as an occasional B-movie actress. "Not much to be said about her performance," and "She was okay," constituted the best reviews in her scrapbook. Big names wouldn't hire her, and it was only her scream queen roles which kept her in the far-peripheral vision of the movie-going public.

At sixty-five, her hair was still very, very blonde. Feathered out seven inches from her head. She still favored the same clothes as back then… Actually, they *were* the same clothes as back then: lavender polyester jumpsuit leaving her skinny shoulders bare but covering her feet, sweeping the dusty floor with the hems of its wide, flowing legs. Her face was technicolored with bright blue eyeshadow and frosty-pink lipstick. With that enormous hair—adorned with a pink camellia above her left ear—and her pastel-painted, withered face, she looked like a Halloween version of the movie star she emulated.

Isabella thought her mother was grotesque, but Gwendolyn didn't suffer from such qualms about her own appearance. She'd always been willing to do anything, really anything, to get back in front of the camera. For more than thirty years, years that blighted her daughter's childhood memories, nothing worked. It was too late and Gwendolyn had too little talent to be a candidate for stardom, so she'd put all her hopes in one basket: her only child. Isabella had to make it big.

This season's prizes, the money and The Groom, wouldn't gain her mother's respect. It was a one-off win, "Not a winning streak," as Gwendolyn said, slamming the liquor cabinet door shut. "A daughter of mine should be famous. I have great genes and you got my looks. Don't aim low.

"The producer of that show's rich. He's single again. With a contact like that, you'd be my ticket back to Hollywood. Oh, just to be in front of the camera again..."

Gwendolyn was thirty pounds underweight, existing on cigarettes and dirty gin martinis. "Don't call me 'Mom,'" she said when Isabella dropped by before leaving for France. "Makes me sound old." Her lips produced a loud *POP* as she pulled on her smoke.

Isabella put the bag of groceries she'd bought on a chair, since all the other surfaces were cluttered with old dishes, take-out containers, newspapers, and discarded food. Something beneath the litter lifted one of the paper plates and shifted toward her, rustling ominously.

Rustling more ominously was the sheet wrapped about the man who slouched into the kitchen, a bulky, hairy, muscular man of indeterminate age. Another of her mother's "boyfriends."

Her mother patted one of his sad, sagging, nipple-topped mounds. "Darling, this is Babar."

"Babar? Like the elephant in the kiddy books?"

The aging hunk beside her dropped the sheet clutched in his free hand, showing Isabella just how he'd gotten the nickname.

"Jesus Christ!" she yelled but her mother had only laughed.

Babar looked down and rearranged the sheet. "I'll go get decent."

"Good idea. I'm out of smokes. Get me some at the market, would ya?" Gwendolyn rifled through her purse and put a ten-dollar bill in Babar's outstretched hand. He went down the hall.

When Babar reappeared, he was dressed in a black tee and jeans belted below his gut. "Menthol!" Gwendolyn yelled as he went past on the way to the door.

"How about I take you out for dinner, after I put the food away?" Inside the refrigerator was nothing but moldy Chinese takeout, an ossified lemon, and bottles of cheap Chardonnay.

"We could just order in when Babar comes back, but he'll just want pizza. Grab me the bottle of wine, will ya?" Gwendolyn tilted a chair, dumping its contents on the floor, and sat. "Just you, me, and Babar."

"Stop calling him by that ridiculous nickname. Are you supporting him? On what I give you?"

"I have Social Security, too." Gwendolyn leaned her head over the chair's back. Sighed deeply, the familiar dramatic routine. "Just helping him out until he's back on his feet. Got a bad ticker, you know."

"He tell you that?"

Her mother looked offended. "They stuck that tube up in his heart but said they couldn't fix it permanent-like and he'd have to be on medication."

Babar walked in with a carton of Newports. "Here you go, babe. Light me one."

"My kid's here. It's like a party. Let me take a shower and get all gussied up." Gwendolyn left her daughter and her boyfriend alone in the kitchen.

"I want you out," Isabella said. "That's my money you're grifting."

"Now, now," Babar replied, drawing deeply on the cigarette Gwendolyn had left with him. "If you cared about your mother, you'd realize how much the love of a good man means to her."

"Oh? Who does she get that from?"

"I'm very understanding. A woman like your mother—a woman with aspirations but no talent or charisma—needs validation. Especially when they got old."

She pointed at the smoke. "I thought you had a heart condition."

"Oh, I do." He fished around in the pocket of his jeans, making the impressive bulge in the crotch move as if it was independent of the rest of him.

Just another bit of vermin in this kitchen.

He pulled a vial from his pocket and put it on the table. She picked it up. Nitroglycerin, prescribed by some free clinic or other.

"I get pains," His hands roamed over the expanse of muscle and fat which lay in the general area of his heart. "...happens sometimes during sex. I pop one of these babies under my tongue."

She rolled the medication vial between her palms, listening to the tiny tablets rattle. *How could sex be risky with a fragile bag of bones like my mother?*

"Anybody tell you you're more gorgeous than Gwendolyn ever was?" The rat in his pants stirred, pointed in her direction.

Isabella laughed. "You've got a lot of nerve, what with her in the bathroom right down the hall."

"She takes an eternity to get all fixed up, but at her age, it's necessary."

He was repulsive but sometimes sacrifices had to be made. She dropped her eyelids in a parody of sensual submissiveness.

"Come here." Babar's breath was coming hard.

She swung her hips suggestively as she approached him. Climbed onto his lap and began to slide back and forth on his erection, still entombed in those tight jeans.

He put his hands on her breasts. "Mmmm... Big change from what I'm used to!" She would have stopped to slap the smirk from his mouth had she not been on a mission. She rocked faster and faster, hoping it would soon be enough.

It was. Babar's face grew red, then bluish, and finally an astonishing purple. Choking noises gurgled in his throat. He dropped his hands from her breasts and reached toward the little pill bottle.

She got there first. Flicking her index finger, she sent that vial careening into the tower of takeout refuse, which cascaded to the floor. She swung her right leg off his lap and stood.

His bulging eyes pleaded; his fat slug tongue protruded from his swelling lips. Bubbles from his mouth popped in the dry air. He uttered one single, drawn out "*arrrgh!*" and slid from the chair to lie, face up and still on the filthy linoleum floor.

"Babar? Isabella? What happened" Gwendolyn came running down the hall in her robe, pulling a flowered shower cap from her hair. "What was that thud?"

"I'm afraid it's Babar, Mommy. He seems to be unwell."

"Oh, my God! Babar, your nitro!" Gwendolyn dropped to her knees and patted his pants' pockets. Her eyes were wild and, with her hair frizzing from the residual shower damp, she looked demented, ancient. "Isabella, where's his medicine?"

"Medication?" Isabella leaned her hip against the counter. "For what?"

"His heart! I told you he had a bad heart."

Isabella shrugged. "I didn't see any medicine."

Gwendolyn pushed up the sleeves of her robe, put her hands on the black-clad chest and began to pump. Her scrawny arm muscles bunched like little potatoes under her sagging skin but were too feeble to accomplish anything. She screamed, "Call 911! Help me!"

"Probably too late, but I'll try." Isabella poked the

emergency number into her cellphone and asked for an ambulance. She flung a chair cushion onto the floor, knelt on the other side of the body from her mother and began pressing.

Babar's face was fading from purple to gray and a tiny stream of bile came from between his lips.

Isabella shook her head. "I'm not doing mouth-to-mouth on him."

Ten minutes later, sirens sounded in the distance. Gasping with fear, Gwendolyn ran outside to make sure they knew the house.

Alone with Babar, Isabella saw a slight rise of his chest, pulled the cushion from under her knees and pressed it on his face until she heard her mother screaming, "Here! Here!"

A moment later, three EMTs rushed in, carrying equipment. They waved Gwendolyn and Isabella aside and got to work. From the far end of the room, Gwendolyn clung to her daughter, sobbing. Isabella gently moved her mother's head to the side so she could watch the action.

Alas! The EMTs' intervention did no good. Babar was really dead, really most sincerely dead.

"What am I going to do without him? I'll be so lonely," Gwendolyn sobbed.

"Mother," Isabella said, "you're too old for that foolishness, anyway. Act your age. Start with cleaning up this mess."

CHAPTER EIGHTEEN

The concierge had the maids come to his office.

"We found her on the floor, dead, *monsieur*," said one. "She was wearing a very strange clothes, one I only see before in…" She turned to the concierge. "*Comment dites-vous en anglais 'les images sales'?"*

"Dirty pictures." He turned to Brad and said, "It is most upsetting. Agnes here must lie down and have her fiancé come to comfort her. Difficult as we are very short on the staff."

Agnes. Lucien's Agnes.

"You may go, Agnes," the concierge said.

The dead girl was Tamara. Dead in fetish gear, naked from the waist down. Already moved to lie with her rivals.

"You may go, also." The concierge was abrupt, addressing Brad. "Please to make sure there are no more bodies."

* * *

When Irwin entered their suite's living room, Brad leaped up from the couch, shaking. "Where the fuck you been? I needed you!"

Irwin looked unusually chipper, and Brad's reaction to his arrival didn't seem to bother him. "I was just outside sitting and thinking. The storm seems over, the sun's out…"

"And the birdies are chirping. Fuck them and fuck the sun. There's been another one." Brad kept his voice level, despite his agitation. One of the staff just might be eavesdropping at the door.

"Another dead girl?" Irwin's mouth dropped open. "That makes three, right?"

"Four—Hailey, Georgina, Addie Lynn, and now Tamara. And one or two missing. It was a search for the missing ones that netted us Addie Lynn."

Irwin massaged his jaw joints and finally got them to unlock from the shock. "This is getting serious. Someone is killing these girls, so we can't go on like nothing's happening, not anymore. And we can't handle this shit ourselves. We need the cops."

"Already went to the concierge. He called the local *gendarmerie* but they're not rushing to help us. We're on the list for a visit once more important French incidents are looked into."

"That's unbelievable! What could possibly be more important than dead Americans? Not to mention an English girl?"

"Lost sheep, trucks stuck in the mud, crops drowned, who knows what other possible mayhem the French got up to in the storm," Brad said.

"Yeah, who the hell knows. How about considering they're doing their best?" Irwin said. "Can't be easy, with no supplies coming in."

Brad reached for the remaining bit of vodka.

The door flew open, and Suzanne entered, slamming the door behind her. "We're going to get some food," she said. "Hortensia felt a little ill for a while after waking up but now she's hungry. And at first, I was fuzzy in my head, like I'd been drugged."

"Are you okay?" Brad asked.

"Better now. Must have been the shock of finding Addie Lynn." She looked from one to the other and frowned. "Before we eat, I want to know what's going on."

"What's going on? What do you mean?" Irwin's face was a mask of innocence.

"Tell me." Suzanne demanded, hands on her temples, hair fetchingly tendrilled by her ears. "Where's Hailey? Where's the English girl?"

Brad looked at Irwin. Irwin looked at Brad. Both squirmed but neither said a word.

Suzanne sighed. "I take it something happened to her too. Have you even counted to see how many are still alive? And, oh, my God, are we all in danger?"

They kept silent.

She shook her head, an expression of disgust on her face. "The phone lines are back up. Did you call our embassy? No? I didn't think so." She crossed her arms over her chest. "For Christ's sake, the two of you need to tell me the truth. It's my job to take care of things and keep everyone safe, especially Hort. You assigned me to be her nanny and I've become dreadfully fond of her."

Nanny! Brad felt a tingle at the magic word and an overwhelming desire to stay in her good graces, to be judged a good boy. A pang of guilt smote his breast for spiking the tea, but only for a second. It had been necessary. What the heck? He might as well spill the beans. The police would be coming sooner or later—it was not as if the secret would keep. "Georgina seems to have fallen down that dumbwaiter shaft in her room. She's dead."

"Oh, my God! How horrible." She narrowed her eyes and stared into his. "That's why we didn't see any sign of her..."

"And Hailey—you know, the one who had a wardrobe malfunction at the Reveal—appears to have fallen off her balcony during the storm."

"Fallen?"

He swallowed hard. "Or been pushed."

Suzanne slumped into an armchair and covered her face with her hands. "You've got to be kidding," she said. "You never said anything to me. No warning. Those poor girls." She sat upright. "The crew! Are they alright? All accounted for?"

"Relax, they're all okay. The crew seems not to have been the target."

"Target?" Suzanne asked in a small voice.

"Uh, we don't really know..." Brad pulled his collar out. It had gotten tight.

"We're not sure if there's someone..." Irwin sputtered. "But we couldn't get the police here, anyway."

"You two..." Suzanne's face tightened with exasperation tinged with fury. "I hope that's all."

Chastised, Brad nodded, hoping to calm her.

Irwin cleared his throat. "Well," he chimed in, "maybe that's not entirely all. Seems that Tamara was most likely…how should I put it…strangled."

"I don't really think that adds anything." Brad shot Irwin a look.

"Brad! How could you!" Suzanne cried in a voice that made Brad think he was in for a spanking. The change in her manner, from obsequious to commanding, was turning him on as even the finest silicone implants couldn't.

"We tried calling the police," Irwin said, "but the phone lines were down. And we couldn't evacuate because…"

Suzanne stood firm. "You could have at least warned everyone! You just kept the cameras rolling."

"What good would a warning have done?' Brad

said. "Whatever was happening, happened when people were alone. No one told us they saw anything."

"Well," Irwin scratched his chin, "we didn't want people to freak out. This kind of thing is upsetting."

"Especially when you're trapped," Brad added. "Filming kept everyone distracted."

The door opened again, and Hortensia marched in. "I'm hungry!" Her voice was like the rumbling of machinery in a distant gravel pit. "So, so hungry!"

Suzanne rose and Brad noticed, with a little uptick—just an itch, really—in penile perception, that she had somehow become intriguing. Even arousing, if not quite hot. Had she dyed her hair? Put on makeup? Borrowed someone's clothes?

She turned to leave, saying in a stern voice, "Join us in the dining room as soon as you can. Hortensia should have her father's undivided attention after what she saw in that bathtub." She went, holding his daughter firmly by the hand, slamming the door behind them. It was getting to be a pattern, a brand-new pattern.

Brad murmured, "What a woman!"

"Oh, for Christ's sake, Brad!" Irwin exclaimed. "Fucking focus! This isn't some kind of rom-com where you fall for the homely girl, she gets a little makeover and suddenly turns gorgeous."

"You're just upset that your little scheme to keep me celibate has stopped working."

Irwin slapped his own head in disgust. "We're in the midst of a real murder spree that could ruin us."

Brad thought for a moment. "You know, you're right."

"This can't be hushed up forever. Self-absorbed as the contestants may be, the drop in competition will become noticeable. Let's get everyone back to work." Irwin looked at Brad and managed a small wink. "Just imagine when this all hits the internet. And it will."

"We'll get viewers coming out the wazoo, just out of curiosity!"

* * *

The sparkling bubbles Mabel made in the air turned dull gray and burst one after the other. Her elation fizzled out as the wonderful news of her meeting with Irwin fell flat. She wasn't experienced with kids, but obviously—even to her—little Hortensia was upset. Shame. She was fond of the ballsy little tyke. A rascal, homely, but, in her own way, still cute as a Bakelite button. Reminded her of the Our Gang cast, always getting into funny scrapes.

Could there be a role for Hortensia? The future is female, the new generation said, and a five-year-old could certainly be seen as the future. The important thing was getting a project nailed down, and that meant getting Irwin securely onboard. And that meant stories from the sisters, with the help of the Reverend Prioress.

She went down the tower's steps once more.

The same nun who had brought Mabel to the relic now blocked the door. "You cannot see the Reverend Prioress. She is at rest."

Mabel cleared her throat. "Sleeping? When does she wake up?"

"Sometimes she slumbers for a day, and sometimes for a century. But until she summons us, no one may enter her chamber. In the meantime, she has given permission for us to pray for God's forgiveness."

"That's it? Just go on as usual?"

The sister didn't reply.

"Okey-dokey, then. Who all wants to tell her story? Help the world see that the suffering of women is eternal and universal? Have her tale be known to the world?"

Beneath her white wimple, set off by the black veil atop it, the nun's face of roiling smoke turned blush rose, like a spray of watery blood. "We obey the direction of the Reverend Prioress. Without her approval, nothing can go forward." The wraith was obviously disappointed. Her color faded to dark and sooty.

"Hey, hey," Mabel said in as soothing a manner as she could, though soothing wasn't something she enjoyed. "You and me have a special working relationship, and you're the Reverend Mother's right-hand girl. I'm sure we can convince her."

The veiled head bowed.

"Say, by any chance, would you like to meet a kid?" Mabel kept her voice spritely.

"Is it the one who visited the cloister?"

Mabel nodded, doing her best to look enthusiastic. "Think so. She's a real peach!"

"She scared us. We stayed in for a whole day afterwards." The nun moved back to her spot, once again guarding the door.

CHAPTER NINETEEN

Brad found it unnerving that Lucien waited on them in the dining room. Now the storm had ended, some of the staff had bolted to check on their farms and their families, and workers unaccustomed to pampering guests had been pressed into filling their *sabots*.

The concierge had begged forgiveness in advance for any irregularities in the service, but Brad worried that such irregularities could include Lucien making assumptions. Acting as if a deal had been struck, that he was The Groom's heir apparent. Brad hadn't discussed the arrangement with Irwin yet. Or even with Suzanne. A big part of the value of unusual casting was the surprise of it all, which, if Lucien blabbed, would no longer be a bombshell. Their thunder would be stolen, and properly timed thunder meant increased audience share.

Meanwhile, Hortensia gnawed on a slice of brioche, shaping it into a pistol. She aimed across the room at Isabella's heart with a big smile and a cheerful, "Bang! Bang! She's dead."

Suzanne pulled her arm down. "That's not nice, honey."

Hortensia only snickered and rolled some chewed bits into bullets.

Brad wasn't sure if Isabella noticed his daughter's

hostility, but almost immediately, the black-haired beauty unfolded her long legs and moved to their table. She squeezed in next to him.

"So, Suzanne," Isabella said in an unnervingly pleasant tone, "how long have you worked for *Grab the Groom* and the amazing and sexy Brad Hudson?"

Lucien interrupted, the white serviette on his arm fluttering close to her French-twisted hair. "Pardon, mademoiselle, we are running very low on the milk, so the au lait you ordered is not possible."

"How the hell can a French kitchen be low on dairy?" Isabella asked.

Lucien bent closer to her ear. "The *vaches*, they have left the farms. They cannot swim. It is simple, no *vaches*, no *lait*. Perhaps mademoiselle knows where the *lait* comes from and so would accept an espresso?" He looked down at her chest and his eyebrows wiggled suggestively.

"Perhaps you would like to be fired for being forward with the guests? And, no, I'm not drinking that axle grease."

Rude? The kid was downright cocky. Brad caught his eye, smiled, and said, "Remember, we give good tips when lips are zips."

Lucien got his drift and moved away, but still had an overly jaunty bounce to his step. He'd have to be watched closely, at least until arrangements were settled.

Isabella might be mean, but Brad had long realized she wasn't stupid. She barely missed a beat before patting Hortensia's head, cooing, "Adorable!" while his kid glowered beneath her hand. After a few beats, she added, "Just like your daddy!" She leaned toward him with an innocent smile, like a lover coming in for a kiss, stopping just inches away.

Then she looked into Suzanne's face without blinking for longer than seemed normal, her steady gaze like a snake's challenging stare.

He looked at each of them in turn until, out of the corner of one eye, he saw Hortensia stealthily slipping her hand into the pocket of her overalls. His attention was momentarily diverted. Was she hoarding pastry? Getting that therapist might be an emergency.

Isabella rose with languid grace, ran her palm over Brad's cheek and headed back to the table she'd occupied before joining them. To his surprise, Hortensia slid from her chair and followed, tapping on Isabella's hip to get her attention.

The beauty looked down with a plastic smile widening her fuchsia-painted lips, glanced back at their table, winked—at him or at Suzanne, he wasn't sure—and crouched down to his daughter's level. Impressive, squatting in six-inch heels, without wobbling.

Isabella and Hortensia talked intently for a moment, back and forth, seemingly engaged in a hard-bargained negotiation. Finally, Hortensia pulled something shiny from her pocket. It dangled in the fat little fist for a moment. She looked at it longingly, stroked it with her other hand as if it was a small, furry pet, and handed it to Isabella, who grabbed it immediately.

Huh? What could his kid possibly have that Isabella would want? He dithered for a moment, wondering if he should investigate, but It was much safer to stay put.

He turned to Suzanne. "I think maybe she's right. Isabella, I mean. Maybe I should monitor Hortensia's diet. Food seems way too important to her."

"Oh, Brad! For God's sake, have a heart." Suzanne's whisper was forced and high-pitched. "Food's been the only comfort in her life. Don't say or do anything about her eating until she feels secure."

"Secure?" He had trouble thinking of Hortensia

as anything but.

"That you care for her."

"Of course, I do!"

Brad was about to say more when she grabbed his cheek, between two pinching fingers. Added, "And I never want you to use the words 'Isabella' and 'right' in the same sentence again."

Just then, Irwin appeared. Like a runaway locomotive, Brad's thoughts raced back to the disappearance—in fact the deaths—of the absent girls. The police would want to talk with everyone, and that could take days or weeks, as nothing happened very fast around there. Nothing except bribe-taking.

What would happen to the show? Would they all have to pack up and go? How much would the cops want to let them finish filming?

And who had bumped off so many, right under their noses? One of the contestants? The crew or the manor staff? An outsider who'd somehow managed the wretched weather and impassable roads?

Brad scanned the room. The killer would most probably be a man. Few women would be strong enough to hoist Hailey over the balcony or stuff Georgina in that little opening. Plus, there was that KY jelly bit. He couldn't see a woman thinking of that—unless it was a ruse to throw them off her scent.

Let's see, if I were a Netflix exec, who would I want cast in the role of a serial killer?

Every female was picking at her food, while the men were chowing down with gusto. Odd, but he felt a touch of disappointment that they all looked so mundane. No one seemed evil, competent, or even interesting, enough to be a murderer. There were the cameramen, of course, and the other crew, but he knew them too well. It was doubtful that a murder spree would be undertaken by someone whose main goal in life was to lie about, constantly stoned, only working when the bud jar was empty. Murders in a crowded place like this would take scheming.

Brad barely knew the manor's French staff. Could it be one of them? The concierge? The handyman—plots often had a brooding handyman as the killer! He eyed the nearest waiter, who happened to be Lucien, but somehow couldn't buy him as a murderer. A lady-killer, *oui*. A lady-murderer, *non*.

Oh, my God! What if the killer's an important investor? Would that freeze his funds? Aghast, he looked at the Meat Men, all responsible for the slaughter of so many cows and pigs. None of them would shy away from death. *Did I invite a beast into our midst?*

Irwin had slipped into a seat and quietly ordered food. "I think we need to say something, Brad. Before the *gendarmerie* drops in for a visit. We have to look like we're on top of things."

Relieved that his partner was present, Brad nodded and rose. "May I have your attention, ladies, gentlemen…" Even to his own ears he sounded like the barker at a freak show. "As you might have noticed, the weather has broken, and the sun is shining down on us." He paused to smile, noticing his voice shift, become unctuous, go from barker to snake-oil peddler. See? Irwin was wrong about his acting potential. He didn't need instructions or faking to be believable.

"Ahem," Irwin cleared his throat to speak from his seat and still be heard, clearly reminding Brad that the case for no accountability had to be made. "Yes, the weather's better but the roads are still closed," he said to the assembled girls, crew and investors. "And due to a few unfortunate accidents…" He left off, "resulting in the regrettable demise of …," sympathetic pause, "some of our contestants unfortunately will not be continuing." The remaining women looked about the room. One or two raised an index finger and were obviously counting their remaining competitors.

"Who's missing?" one asked, turning to the girl beside her.

"I think Megan is," the other said. "But I get her confused with Stacey."

"Hey! I'm Megan!" the first said, her voice rising in indignation. "Stacey is a friggin' heifer!"

Isabella stood, instantly commanding attention. 'The show is continuing, right? We each invested a lot, gave up a lot, to come all the way here!"

Irwin cleared his throat again. His speech wasn't over. "While steps will be made to ensure everyone's safety, we will not be immediately leaving for home and our loved ones." The heaviest of the heavy-duty investors grinned at the idea of putting off the return to his aging wife.

Brad interrupted. "We deeply regret the loss of our valued cast members and will understand if any of you need grief counseling and/or time to regain your bearings. The local police have asked us to remain in place pending the necessary investigation, of course, but we hope to make arrangements for as little disruption as possible. We'll be getting you home as soon as we can."

A soft whispered female voice—too soft to be localized—said, "Police? Investigation? Were they *murdered*? If we're in danger, I want to get out of here!"

It was immediately countered by a louder whisper, "Are you nuts? Our odds of winning are better now!"

The first speaker responded with, "Well, the prizes are still going to be awarded, aren't they…? And nothing happened to The Groom, right? I mean, 'cause he's not here."

One of the investors raised his hand. "Will the show continue?"

Brad stuttered, "Uh-uh-uh, yeah. the show must go on." He cleared his throat and regained his composure. "Of course, it will go on, no matter what the reasons for the disturbances. We'll know more, once the police come."

It was a difficult situation, soft-pedaling the deaths. Brad's sweating had started again, his forehead prickling with dampness and his armpits swampy.

He really needed some support if he was to handle this delicate situation and prevent mutiny once the police arrived. More than support. He cleared his throat and dumped it all on Suzanne, introducing her with, "All of you know my lovely assistant…"

Suzanne raised her head with an astonished expression and her cheeks tinted a becoming and delicate tea-rose pink. He wondered why she seemed so shocked. She'd handled many touchy things for him in the past.

"…as she's taken such good care of all details addressing your needs. I'm going to ask her to come up here and explain the circumstances." He swung his arm, an open-door invitation for her to join him.

"Lovely?" Suzanne whisper-squeaked just loud enough for Brad to hear. "You've never—no one's ever—called me lovely before." She pushed her chair back to stand.

Brad held out his hand to her. "Lovely inside and out."

Suzanne stood to join Brad, and Hortensia hopped up to take hold of his hand. All eyes were on them, the widest, most piercing eyes were Isabella's. When Brad slid an arm about Suzanne's waist, those eyes narrowed and the beautiful face darkened, its buttressing cheekbones blazing.

"I was just doing my job," Suzanne began to say but her head turned as a sudden movement distracted her.

Isabella, even more stunning in a state of fury,

approached them. She confronted Suzanne, who took an involuntary step backward. Isabella moved into the vacated space and turned on her widest beauty contest winner smile. Clutching Brad's arm, which she'd removed from its place around Suzanne, gushed, "Giving credit to an assistant? Isn't he wonderful, everyone? I want to thank Brad Hudson for the opportunity to be on the show. Also, for being my personal hero, keeping us safe. I'm sure no matter what has been going on, he'll help us weather the storm."

Hortensia tore her hand away from her father's. She whirled about, her eyes bulging from the fat pockets of her cheeks. "We had a deal, you cheater, so stay away!" She flapped her stubby arms wildly, as if shooing Isabella off. "No good ugly lady! You got what you wanted, so don't you touch my daddy!" She stomped her foot and her rear vibrated rapidly side-to-side like The Tasmanian Devil revving for a run. Then she took off.

Everyone's attention locked onto her small, stocky figure and her rapidly pumping limbs. Irwin yelled, "Hey!" as she defied gravity with the same graceful, leaping kick used on the plane on the back of the Sausage King's seat. She planted her foot in Isabella's crotch with an audible *THUD*! swiveling in mid-air, landing square and racing away. Isabella had let out a loud *OOF!* and was left doubled over, hanging on to Brad for support, the wind knocked out of her. He tried to pull away, but she was even stronger than she looked, and struggling failed to free him.

Time slowed, jelled as if the moment was preserved in aspic. Stunned silence filled the room, only to be followed by a chorus of snaps as dropped jaws closed again and time once again became fluid.

Irwin muttered, "Kid should be in the Olympics!"

Isabella, her face now grotesque with rage, dropped Brad's arm and set off in hot pursuit of

Hortensia. For someone with a groin injury, the woman was amazingly fast. Especially on her high, high heels. The assembled group followed as one, a mob jostling and pushing down the corridor, past the couches and the potted plants, out toward the lobby. Brad was at the front, fear making him fleet. What would Isabella do to his kid if she caught her?

Irwin was pacing him as if they were marathon winners in a dead heat. Shocking! He'd never seen Irwin do more than a gentle lope, and even that winded him.

They reached the lobby. There Hortensia stood, wildly turning her head and gasping like a mouse caught in a spring-loaded trap. When Isabella lunged at her, she pivoted again, remaining just out of reach, and darted down another hall, raising a cloud of dust.

At the end of the hall, a rotted door stood ajar. Hortensia slipped through. Pushing the door open further slowed Isabella but she gamely plunged on with the horde close behind, coughing in the dusty air. Where the hell were they headed?

CHAPTER TWENTY

Irwin ran recklessly, intoxicated by the thrill of the chase. Perhaps it was the exertion, but he was much warmer in the church than he had been before. The ice had melted. Sunlight lavishly poured through the stained glass of the clerestory windows, kaleidoscoping the nave as he ran. footfalls pounded behind him.

He imagined the pack racing behind him, tongues hanging, slavering for the kill. When he turned around, he saw what he imagined was real. Everyone from the show—and even the manor staff—was baying at Isabella's heels, yelling, "Get the bitch!" in English and in French. Logical, as she had treated nearly every one of them like crap. But this vigorous pursuit by the mob of workers, normally so laidback as to be practically comatose, and self-absorbed, disinterested beauty queens? All surreal as a hit of acid. He laughed aloud, triggering a few excited, howling guffaws behind him.

Up ahead, Hortensia leaped through the open door to the cloister just ahead of Isabella, who paused to duck to avoid the low stone transom.

* * *

Brad outran Irwin in the church's nave. He was

driven to push himself on, harder and harder, couldn't think straight—the rapid pace, the desperate breathing made him lightheaded. His heart hurt, hammering against his breastbone. Hortensia was a part of him. Nothing and no one had ever been so before. The only time he glanced back was to see if Suzanne was behind.

What the hell was this place? The cross at the end meant it was a church, an ancient one at that, but if ever there was a building grim and foreboding, this was it. He exited the church going full bore, right leg outstretched like a hurdler, passing through the low door and landing out in blinding sunlight.

A short distance away, Hortensia ran across a muddy, neglected garden, Isabella only a few steps behind.

Brad stumbled slightly and slowed, looked back once more. The assembled cast and crew of *Grab the Groom* caught up to him as he swung his head round again to see his daughter clamber up onto a rough-cut stone, fallen from a tower looming over the courtyard.

Brad started across the weedy patch, still icy in spots. His heart, firmly lodged at his larynx, cut off his wind, but he kept going.

Fathers don't need oxygen when their child is in danger.

* * *

High atop the tower, peering through the embrasure between two merlons, Mabel saw tiny figures racing below, two ahead of the others, the first small and squat, the second much taller. They were pursued by what looked like an army of ants.

She watched idly for a few seconds, still planning the nuns' interviews in her mind, until she realized that the first ant was her own Hortensia and the second, Isabella. She shot down through the air, forgetting the pretense of using the remaining stairs as if she were a solid, living human.

Hovering over Hortensia, Mabel yelled, "Climb, climb!"

If Irwin had been able to see and hear her, maybe she had a chance of being perceived by others, of diverting that black-haired she-devil. She circled Isabella, let out her fiercest banshee wail, dropping the temperature by twenty degrees and fogging the air, but the bitch kept coming. Mabel reached out again and again to claw at that raven hair, to trip her feet, but Isabella moved right through her as if she were as insubstantial as a dream.

All that was left for Mabel was the role of cheerleader, egging Hortensia on as the tyke climbed higher and higher onto the stone pile. "Faster, faster! Reach high, climb! Save yourself!"

* * *

Ahead of Brad, that she-devil Isabella howled, her face a mask of rage. His kid, for once, was silent, nodding at something unseen as she focused on scaling the tower's crumbling wall. She clambered over lichen-covered stones, clutching at small cuts in the limestone, jamming the toes of her sneakers into ancient cracks.

Her climb was halted by a massive stone so smooth her feet scrabbled against the surface helplessly. Her arms were extended as far as they could go, hands locked on the closest corner above her.

"Daddy's coming," Brad yelled, forcing the words from his parched throat. He ran on, doubled over by a stitch in his side.

Isabella had come up close behind Hortensia. She reached for one dangling LED-lit foot. The other sneaker, sparkling in the light, kicked alternately at Isabella and at the stones to find a niche.

A thick vine clung tenaciously to the tower's wall, its leaves wintered dry and brown, fluttering in the salty wind. It seemed just beyond Hortensia's stubby fingers as she reached desperately above her head.

Brad could swear that someone or something shadowy, something made of smoke, helped Hortensia extend her body, almost *stretching* her like a rubber band up, up, and out as far as possible. He stopped, rubbed his eyes with disbelief, as she grabbed the thick vine and pulled herself up out of Isabella's grasp.

Brad was still back fifteen feet when a low-pitched, ominous rumble brought him up short. Isabelle's cried out as a precariously balanced stone shifted and began to fall, dislodged by the desperation—and bulk—of his daughter as she swung away from the wall. With a drawn-out shriek, the huge block of granite moved from its place, scraping against the rough wall as it tumbled down.

Ignoring the risk of the unstable structure, Brad pressed on to the base of the tower. He held his arms out for Hortensia. For a moment, she looked at him with distrust, then her eyes widened as the gray haze surrounding her transformed into a mass of fireflies, glittering, widening to envelope him. It almost seemed as if the shining swarm smiled.

Hortensia launched herself into the open space below, landing in his arms. Her leap knocked Brad to the ground. From that vantage point he saw a fuchsia-nailed hand stretched out from under the fallen stone. The hand clutched a pastel sneaker whose LED lights coyly winked at him.

He struggled to stand with the weight of

Hortensia, who wrapped her arms around his neck. "Daddy, you saved me," she cried, snuggling into his neck. His heart was warmed. It only cooled the teensiest bit when she added, "Get my shoe!"

He obeyed, half-expecting the dead woman's outstretched hand to turn to dust.

As he carried her back across the wintry garden of the cloister toward the safety of the manor house, she clung to him like a baby gorilla, heavy and dense, but he forgot his aching back when she relaxed trustingly against his chest.

Brad looked for Suzanne, but she wasn't in the convent's garden. He found her in the church's nave, watching them, leaning against a pew. The Groom stood next to her, looking worryingly handsome, and supporting her *by holding her waist*. Genuine caring shone from his chiseled face. Icy fear froze Brad's heart.

Suzanne shook off The Groom's arms without glancing up at him. "Thank God you're okay," she said when Brad and Hortensia grew close. "I twisted my ankle. This is as far as I got."

"Daddy, put me down and help Suzanne!" Hortensia released her grip on Brad's neck and slid to the stone floor. She looked up at The Groom and said, "I don't need you anymore."

With Suzanne leaning on Brad, Hortensia on the other side of her like a squat but sturdy crutch, they made their way back to the manor house. It was deserted as the others hadn't returned from the chase.

"Sad, though. You missed the best part," Brad said to Suzanne when she was safe on a couch. "The denouement, the ending, the last of Isabella. The part where the screen reads 'FIN.'"

* * *

Irwin was delighted and couldn't wait to tell Brad the good news. Their ace cameraman had run, professional to the last, filming the entire scene.

Most of the crew clustered around them in the manor's hallway, gesticulating while watching the recording. There was an occasional snorting laugh. Voices rang out.

"For a fat kid, that little bugger sure can run!"

"Go, girl, go!"

"Damn, we should have been betting," was followed by someone else saying, "It's always money with you. Ever get lost in the moment?"

And at last, with much wincing and intaking of breath, a few "Ouches! " and one cry of "Whoa! That's gotta smart!" they viewed the crushing blow.

"Okay, that's enough," Irwin said when he reached them. He was always conscious of how attitudes would play, especially in delicate situations. "You get it all?"

The cameraman nodded.

"The race, the stones falling, Isabella...?" Not only was it evidence of everyone's belief in Isabella's evil, with, perhaps, the worst part—her demise—edited out, it would make great cinema.

At the cameraman's, "Sure did," Irwin said, "Great. We'll review it later tonight." With this footage, the show would be a definite hit. Reality at its realest, completely raw and unscripted.

Schlock though it might be, this season's *Grab the Groom*, with its smash ending, could ensure funding of his magnum opus. The most important thing was to keep this spectacular development—with its shock value —under wraps, leaking only teeny bits, an excerpt, a created meme on the internet. Viewership would skyrocket.

He walked slowly back to the manor, thinking things over. The Death, as he thought of it, was a great climax, but the season needed an ending, a bride for The Groom. Isabella had been the one slated to win. But she had been taken out of the running.

Delicate handling was needed, so he'd keep Brad out of it as much as possible. Right now, after the difficult day they just had, he wanted a nice cup of coffee with, perhaps, a baguette. And then, if he could get through, a call to his husband back in L.A.

CHAPTER TWENTY-ONE

With the roads drying out and pressing local business resolved—missing farm animals located, vehicles freed from tenacious muck, looters roughed up, the inspector from the *Gendarmerie Nationale* finally arrived at the manor to deal with the less important problem of dead Americans. Irwin knew that he had been urged on by the concierge's wish that the bodies, and the *Grab the Groom* crew, be removed from his property posthaste.

Irwin waited with Brad in the office. Through the closed door to the concierge's private rooms, they overheard the clink of a bottle on a glass rim, followed by the concierge's voice. "*Cousin, ces Américains! Ce sont doulors dans mon cul!*"

"That fucking French twerp! Did you hear that?" Irwin murmured, though the only French words Brad knew were for food. Irwin understood a lot more than he could speak or than he let on, so eavesdropping proved useful. "He said we were pains in the ass."

"After all the generous tips we gave him?" Brad's angry reply was a stage whisper.

Irwin put one finger over his lips. "Remember, those were hush money. I doubt he'll disclose them to the cops. But whoever's in there is apparently his cousin."

"I heard the word, *cousin*, Irwin!" Brad snapped.

His tone softened as they heard "*...mais les filles sexy*!" "What now?" he asked. "Did he say 'sexy'?"

Irwin nodded as the door opened and the concierge exited, followed by a middle-aged man, somber and slim. He was not in a uniform but in a marginally out-of-style gray suit, a bit rumpled. The kind of suit a man of importance might wear if he had been operating in a provincial city since the '90s.

Irwin was disappointed. He had been mentally casting the role of inspector and this guy looked nothing like what he'd envisioned. He was even more disappointed when the inspector spoke. "Good day. I am Inspector Durand of the *Gendarmerie Nationale*." Durand's British English had almost no trace of an amusing French accent. He was far from a farcical, audience pleasing Clouseau, pompously spouting Gallic gibberish, far even from an updated version of the comic character in a deconstructed trench coat. No, instead of a highly marketable adversary of the Pink Panther, he was a stodgy, boring Gallic Inspector Morse. The whole schtick would be box-office sludge. It would have to be re-imagined and cast, possibly with a high-cost actor.

At Irwin's unhappy look, the concierge hastened to say, "With the Inspector, you will have no trouble with the English. He lived a long time in the *Angleterre* when a young man. That is why he speak so well. But he is *un inspecteur francaise extraordinaire*! *Absolument incorruptible*!"

"We're certain he's honest and has solved many crimes," Irwin said, "and we look forward to his solving our little problem." He made sure nothing more registered on his face, though such a character would need lots of work to bring to life. And such a character—incorruptible—would be tough to bribe, should that be needed.

Brad jumped in with, "I'm delighted! That'll

make our interaction so much easier."

Irwin sighed. No one owed them ratings success, but it was so much better if success was provided gratis by a real-life person who still managed to look straight out of central casting. Comical French *flics* might be stereotypical but, well, he'd already emphasized to Brad that they had to provide what the public expected. Would the Kardashians have ever become popular if they didn't provide the obvious?

"My men are securing the establishment and searching the rooms. The bodies are being examined. It's a shame they were moved from the scene of their deaths. The wrong thing when murder is a possibility."

"I apologize, Cousin. But with the terrible storm, I was afraid of the… the… *comment tu dis en pourriture*?"

"'Rotting.' But better 'decomposition.' More respectful."

"We had no idea when you would be able to come," Brad interrupted. "And we have a lot of impressionable, delicate young ladies here…"

"I understand," the inspector said. "And I or one of my investigators will be speaking to each and every one of them. By the way, we have been in contact with your embassy. They are overwhelmed with requests from your fellow citizens but will get someone here as soon as possible. Perhaps in a day or two?"

Irwin wondered why the inspector had made that statement a question. Brad had probably forgotten to make an ego-stroking courtesy call to the U.S. embassy, who responded more quickly to celebrities than ordinary Americans. Good thing everyone would assume a lack of support was due to the unusual weather of the past week.

* * *

Irwin, Brad, Suzanne, and even Hortensia were confined to their rooms until the interrogation was over. Hortensia would be assigned a female officer to interview her.

Brad protested. "You're not talking to my daughter alone! In the United States, such a small child would never be interrogated without a parent present!"

That gave Irwin an idea. "It would be good to have a lawyer present during questioning of any suspect, right?"

The inspector's expression soured but Irwin persisted. "I mean, I love French culture and I know your devotion to the ideals of *liberté, égalité, fraternité*." Irwin couldn't keep a small smile from creeping onto his face. "If I remember correctly, the right to counsel is part of the Napoleonic Code. In place since 1808."

The concierge exclaimed, "That is true! I remember from learning in the *ecole*! Perhaps since you attended abroad, *cousin*…"

If official looks could kill, the concierge would have dropped on the spot. "I know the law, *cousin*!" the inspector snapped, his face choleric. "It may take quite a while for a lawyer to be available. Many people have had property destroyed. Crimes were committed under the cover of foul weather…"

"Well, I am an American attorney," Irwin said, lying through his teeth. "I'd bet our embassy would object if I couldn't attend. And that way, we wouldn't give the wrong impression of your country to our international viewing audience, the impression of the police intimidating a little child."

Brad's look of astonishment might have cost Irwin the gig, if anyone was paying attention to him, which they weren't. Instead, the two Frenchmen exchanged rapid-fire comments of heated debate. Irwin didn't catch every word, but it seemed both were anxious to get the show on the road.

"You can question me alone," Irwin generously offered. "I waive my right to counsel. In fact, why don't you interrogate me first?"

While the inspector's men searched the rooms, finding one more corpse—that of Diana, dead for days of uncertain cause—the cast and crew of *Grab the Groom* were sent to the dining hall, with English-speaking gendarmes posted to make sure they didn't discuss the murders. The manor staff were also sent to wait in the dining hall. "We must prevent any possibility of collusion when it comes to inventing alibis. Anyone stepping out of line will be chastised," declared Inspector Durand. As he said to the concierge, American criminals often had "*une histoire à dormir debout.*"

Hustled into his bedroom, Brad had no time to ask Irwin what the French phrase meant. Good thing, as Irwin needed to use his secret weapon—a Merriam-Webster French-English dictionary, conveniently stored on his newly charged Kindle. He swiped through the pages while orders were being given. Most of the translations felt flat, but he ultimately settled on "a cock-and-bull story."

Once down in the manor office, Irwin faced Durand alone.

"So, *Monsieur*…" the inspector began.

"Call me Irwin!" It didn't hurt to be friendly, a bumptious American, naïvely acting as if they were equals. Better than seeming cringing, conniving, and therefore suspect.

"So, *Monsieur* Irwin, where were you…"

Irwin detailed his location and activities during the window of time of each death, though no one could be sure of the exact hour they took place. "All we know is the last anyone can remember seeing them. Each woman had her own bedroom. Came and went as they pleased. We treat our contestants like royalty. Private en suite baths." He took a sip of Perrier. "I am certain that my partner and I were together with a large group the night the first victim went off her balcony." He paused in thought. "And the one who was strangled…she didn't show up the night she died. It seems like she disappeared during the day when we were entertaining our investors…"

The corner of Durand's lips twitched upward. He pursed his mouth, hiding a possible unprofessional smile. "The one wearing the sexy outfit?"

Irwin nodded. Perhaps the inspector hadn't learned fetish words in his British school, odd as that seemed.

"Do you have any idea what was the funny smell in room of the one in the tub? Seemed to be on the bed. There was something smeared on the coverlet, but it had dried. Perhaps caca?"

"No idea. It was really awful, fouler than anything human. Foul as snake shit." Irwin leaned closer, playing the role of conspirator. "But tell you what—we videoed every show, every gathering…"

"Ahh, good!" exclaimed the inspector. "Shame you didn't video in the bedrooms like the Big Brother show. All that footage would be most interesting! However, we shall watch what you have and see who is there and who is not. And to whom people talk!" His posture changed as if he remembered that they were not colleagues but instead interrogator and suspect. "Did you have romantic interest in any of the deceased?"

"Good Lord, no. I'm married," Irwin said. When the inspector let out an "as if that meant anything" snicker, Irwin opened his wallet and showed a photo of himself and his husband.

"Oh, well, that leaves only the one who fell off the cliff, the one with… the necessary equipment…."

His conjecture was enough to piss off the Pope, but it was best to keep cool. "No. No! I had no idea she wasn't all she appeared to be. We wouldn't have selected her if we'd known. At least not without the agreement of The Groom, the man who was to pick one of the contestants and marry her. If he took the surprise poorly, we'd be in trouble. Everything is so politically correct these days."

"What about your business partner? There are many articles about him. Research reveals at least two ex-wives and children. He seems to be a serial seducer. And what with the many lovely ladies you have brought...."

"Oh, *Monsieur Inspector*! You're too smart to fall for the American media's tendency to make up stories. Brad Hudson was just as foolish as any Frenchman, a patsy for manipulative women, especially those who are beautiful, and he is always surrounded by the beautiful. But even the most idiotic skirt chaser can be reformed by a good woman, right?"

A typical Gallic shrug broke through the expressionlessness taught to British schoolboys.

"Brad has fallen for his assistant, Suzanne. He is in love." For the first time Irwin realized the truth of that statement. He was pretty sure that idiot Brad had yet to do so.

"His assistant? He picked her, what with all those other women? But she is so..."

"Isn't it always like that? It's the plain, quiet ones who sneak in and grab you."

Another shrug. "Perhaps you are right. It is like enjoying a simple filet after too much rich food. The heartburn goes away." Durand leaned forward conspiratorially. "And it doesn't matter in the end.

Madame Durand started out a vixen and now... She is like an old bear, with a hairy mole on her chin."

Irwin nodded. "Brad's so smitten with the plain one that he didn't even notice when another of the girls put the moves on him." He wanted to add that the girl was the odious Isabella. Why speak ill of the dead? "Besides, he and Suzanne have been caring for his little girl, Hortensia. That has drawn them close, like family. No time for the others."

Durand kept his counsel, shuffling a few folders he'd put on the concierge's desk. After a pause he said, "A few of the young ladies have already been interviewed by my junior officers. Oddly, not one had ever heard there was an American attorney here. But they feel they have nothing to hide and wish only to say what little they know. I will now interview those who have, by a first pass interrogation, something to add. You will be silent, please, during this time."

The first girl to come in was Jocelyn, whose pert triangular face, with its little pointed chin and big, innocent eyes beneath a heavy black fringe of hair, made her look like a pedophile's dream. She sat across from Durand, who was busy shuffling the papers in front of him. As she waited, she raised a trembling hand to rub her cheek.

"You seem nervous, Mademoiselle," the inspector said. "Is something in particular troubling you?"

"Is Tamara really dead?"

"She is," Irwin said.

"Please be silent!" Durand snapped. "Yes, unfortunately, the young lady is deceased. How well did you know her?"

"Not well, not well at all." Jocelyn seemed even more nervous, but the Frenchman didn't address her anxiety further. "I just met her for the first time a week ago."

"Did you and she have any disagreements?"

"No…" Jocelyn sat forward with an abrupt movement. "But I did see Isabella get angry—blow up, really—when The Groom left her to take up with Tamara."

"Isabella, the young lady who…"

"Yes, the one who was smashed by the boulder." Jocelyn broke out in sobs with even deeper breaths, her breasts rising like helium-filled balloons. "What a way to die!" Her eyelashes lowered as if she blinked back tears. "It was awful. She wasn't very nice to anyone, but still…"

"Did you know if this Isabella became angry or had altercations with anyone else?" Durand continued.

"Oh, yes, some of the other girls complained about her. She wasn't nice to us, or to the stylists and the wardrobe people. Or even the cameramen, come to think of it. She was downright awful to the manor staff." Jocelyn wiped her eyes with her hands and sniffled. The inspector offered her his handkerchief. When she composed herself, she smiled at him sweetly and said, "Actually, she was a hateful bitch! And dishonest. Someone went through my stuff and I think it was her."

The Frenchman leaned toward her "Are some things missing?"

To Irwin's eyes, Jocelyn's expression grew shifty. "Yes, maybe, this and that. What with all that went on, I haven't looked through things carefully yet."

"Well, you may go," the inspector said, tapping his pen on the desk. "If you remember anything else or discover what is missing, let one of my officers know."

The next four girls all had similar tales. Isabella seemed to have quarreled with every single one of them. One contestant said, "She had a big fight with Hailey the night of the Reveal."

"The Reveal?"

"When The Groom is introduced. Hailey threatened to expose Isabella as a total phony, pretending to be exotic, Italian. And now Hailey's dead." She broke down in tears and for a moment, couldn't say another thing. When she recovered, she had apparently remembered something. "Brittney Woodcock! That was Isabella's real name. And she was more than just a bitch, she was a racist. She said Pearl didn't have the right to compete because she was Asian." She furrowed her brow for a moment, then corrected herself. "Asian-American."

Durand asked to speak to Pearl next. "Yes," she confirmed, "Isabella said some nasty things to me about being Chinese. She was really angry when I won the first night. After that, a necklace of mine disappeared. Quite expensive but very un-showy. Only a single natural pearl and very precious to me—a gift from my father. It was my good luck charm. I questioned the maids and went to the manager, but no one had found it. Of course, I suspected Isabella."

Durand nodded and motioned the *gendarme* to escort Pearl from the office. He called in another of the officers. This young man had a discussion with the inspector, speaking in low tones and too rapid fire for Irwin to understand. All he heard clearly was "pearl."

Once the *gendarme* had gone and they were alone again, Irwin said, "Inspector Durand, we'd really appreciate it if you didn't mention anything about the contestant named Hailey. It's a matter of sensitivity. She went to a lot of trouble to hide her identity and keep things secret and I'd hate for her family to find out when they've just learned she was killed." Perhaps that didn't make much sense. Her family had to be told Hailey was dead, and whatever her real name was, her family would know she'd been born a boy. They might have known she was now a woman and even gone along with her plan of non-disclosure, just for the prize. But what difference did that make now? Better to err on the side of caution, protect Hailey's family and save the show.

He rephrased his argument. "They may want it all to be kept hush-hush until they're ready. They may not even have known she was here, in France, as a contestant. And though this is a very forward-thinking and cultured country, parts of America are quite backward." He looked down modestly. "My parents didn't accept that I was gay."

A show featuring Irwin and Brad gently breaking the news to Hailey's family would be in dubious taste. But, of course, "dubious taste" was the best kind of taste in the reality ratings competition. He swallowed his qualms for later, when Brad's enthusiasm would override any reservations he had.

Durand contemplated Irwin's words. "Perhaps you are right." He stood to leave but, as he ushered Irwin toward the door, he turned and dropped his voice. "Have you considered including this entire investigation in the show?"

Irwin shrugged. It was intriguing but he'd have to run it by the legal team in L.A. and they already would have a lot to consider.

"I have often thought of being a consultant on French productions, but they seem to want only Parisians."

"Shame," Irwin said. "Parisians are so full of themselves."

Durand took another step. "Or even being in front of the camera. In school we often performed plays. I was noted to be quite dramatic. Not the leading man type, of course."

"Uh-huh."

"As a professional in the business. What advice would you give someone like me, who wanted to get onto a show? Say one like yours?"

"I'd say to approach someone in the business, a professional, and show what you have to offer. How you'd make life easier for the production and its staff. Not to mention your understanding of costs and deadlines. The need to get things moving along."

"Ahh, I understand. Delays cost money. Of course, my experience in solving crimes would benefit any show with mysterious occurrences. Should I have a spot offered, I would do my utmost to ensure that things went smoothly and quickly."

Irwin put out his hand. "Welcome to *Grab the Groom.*" He wanted to shake on the deal before the inspector angled for a monetary bribe.

"As we are in agreement," the inspector said, accepting the handshake, "I have no reason to disclose the information about the victim named Hailey. France is not like your Texas. We will mention this to no one." He opened his laptop and clicked multiple times. "And to interview the child in her own room. You may sit behind her to keep her calm but no prompting. And, of course, not a word to anyone about what she says."

* * *

"That was very interesting." The nun was perched atop one of the tooth-like crenellations of the tower, where Mabel had left her. "Very noble of you to save that little girl."

"All in a day's work. There's lots you can do out there in the world to have an impact." Mabel didn't want to let up the pressure until the show was in the can. The sisters might get cold feet, so to speak. Still, subtlety was needed. The Reverend Prioress was no pushover, and it was pretty obvious she was overseeing things from her stationary niche. "Besides, I'm very fond of the little darling."

"The concept of instructing through un-real reality is interesting and, in a strange way, amusing," the nun went on.

Mabel was a newcomer to the concept, but she couldn't let that stop her. "That's what these shows do. They teach you something you didn't know about people and the world but make it fun."

"Don't they rot your brain and doom you to Hell?" The nun leaned farther over the parapet, looking disappointed that there was nothing going on below.

* * *

At supper time, a uniformed police officer brought cheese, fruit, and baguette slices to the suite. He also had wine for the adults, milk for Hortensia, and another warning against discussing the deaths.

"*Merci beaucoup,*" Brad said, remembering Irwin's insistence he appear grateful. The officer bowed slightly as he left.

Topping a piece of bread with cheese, Brad chewed slowly, pondering what Irwin might have said, trying to figure out how to exactly mirror his story when in front of the inspector. He hoped the French wouldn't be as crafty in questioning as the actors on CSI.

As they finished their food, their guard sent them to their bedrooms for the night.

Breakfast was similar, with the addition of some delicious poached eggs and fresh brioche toast. Supply lines had apparently re-opened.

Since her interview with the inspector, Hortensia was being very well-behaved.

"It doesn't seem right. She's just not herself. Too calm. Too controlled. I think she was traumatized by

Isabella's death," Suzanne said. "Oh, my goodness, what if she feels guilty for her part in it?"

"Eh... I'm not so sure it's bothering her." Throughout the night, Brad's dreams had been haunted by the scene in the convent. His distinct memory at the end was a look of triumph on his little daughter's face. Not to mention her immediately demanding to get her sneaker back. She hadn't for one moment looked frightened or horrified. Or guilty.

When their dishes were cleared, the concierge entered the room. "*Monsieur* Brad, I am very delighted to say that my cousin has solved the case!"

"Really? What did he say?"

"He will announce it to all, *tout de suite*!"

"Just tell us now. We're tired and want to finish our work and get the fuck out of Dodge."

"Where is this 'Dodge?' I thought that was a truck for the cowboy, no? Well, never mind, the inspector wishes a gathering in the dining hall so he can address to the entire group!"

"But we don't want the entire group addressed!" Brad squealed. "Can't he come talk with us first? We're in charge of everyone working on our show!"

The only reply was, "*Monsieur* Irwin, he approves, so come, come! The inspector, he is waiting!"

Brad collected his daughter and Suzanne from their bedrooms, where they had gone to dress. Hortensia yawned and moved like chilled molasses. The previous day's events and the forced confinement had tired her even if they hadn't perturbed her. She was like a thousand-watt bulb gone dim. Suzanne looked exhausted, also.

"Are you okay?" Brad asked.

"Just tired," Suzanne said, stretching. She was a cute stretcher, her shirt riding up over her soft little mound of a belly, so different from the hyper-crunched torsos of the contestants. The little warm pot of feminine flesh made her belly button wink at him as she arched backward and then bent over. It reminded him of a peach, his favorite fruit. If he nibbled would that dimple be as sweet?

CHAPTER TWENTY-TWO

The dining room was full. Everyone associated with *Grab the Groom* was there. The remaining manor house staff stood at attention near the perimeter of the room. They were wearing what looked like their best uniforms, white shirts tucked into black pants and overlaid with crisp starched half aprons for the men, the same for the women but with bibbed aprons over skirts, sleeves rolled as if ready to dig in and help the police punish at least one American.

The inspector from the *Gendarmerie Nationale* stood in the center of the room, his gray suit even more wrinkled. He cleared his throat, a very French throat-clearing. The sound could be catalogued under "authentic."

A hush fell over the gathering. "All of you know by now, a number of unfortunate incidents—murders, in fact—have occurred here at the manor. The victims were innocent, delightful young ladies, just as so many assembled before me now." He cleared his throat again. "The murderer of these young ladies was, of course, not local. Normandy did not ever have such horrors."

As always, when faced with a situation where

someone else was the star, Brad interrupted, raising his hand like a high schooler. "Didn't Joseph Vacher, the French Ripper, operate around here?" he asked. "I mean, you're not unfamiliar with suspicious death."

The countenances of the locals—manor staff and police—lowered as if they were a troupe of marionettes controlled by the same string.

"Shut the fuck up, Brad," Irwin whispered, desperately.

"Vacher was French, not 'local!' Not Norman. An outsider." The inspector's voice was shrill. Agitation brought out both his family resemblance to the concierge and also his slight French accent. His tone indicated this was a finality and not to be discussed further. "To continue, if *Monsieur* Hudson would be so kind as to remain silent, there were no eye-witnesses to the crimes. But we in the *Gendarmerie* are used to ferreting out the truth. And all of you were most helpful, ladies and gentlemen. You have been forthcoming with information, divulging events leading up to the deaths. All of which we have taken into the record. There was one common link besides the victims all being female contestants. That link being: each victim argued with the killer shortly before her death." He gazed about the room. One eyebrow was raised for emphasis.

"So who is the killer?" Brad called out, only to be shushed by the collective assembly.

"All in good time," was the answer. It was impressively theatrical. Shame no cameras were rolling. Or were they? Irwin smiled. Their Australian cameraman kept his hands below the table, periodically looking down to check the viewfinder. Good boy! Shame Inspector Durand had said no filming—but there would be enough great footage if they weren't discovered.

"There was, however, no hard evidence until we searched the body of the guilty party." With one languid,

Gallic gesture, he indicated Pearl.

A gasp rose from the audience. All eyes turned to Pearl. She was white-faced and appeared stunned by the attention.

"Quiet!" The inspector protested, wagging his fingers, a little close to jazz hands in Irwin's opinion—that gesture wouldn't play well. "Please allow me to continue. Several of the other girls remembered a necklace, with one single but excellent pearl, previously in Pearl's possession, always worn about her neck. A necklace which she says went missing. We looked for the item in her room, but instead of finding the jewelry, found a full glass of poisonous acetone on her nightstand. In short, ready for the next victim."

There was an outbreak of agitated murmuring throughout the room. Several of the contestants cried out, "Arrest her!"

"No, No," the inspector said, in an emphatic tone, "It was obvious that Mademoiselle Pearl was the intended victim, not the perpetrator of the heinous crimes."

Pearl gave an audible sigh, her head thrown back in relief.

"The mademoiselle is not the person who had the will to murder, who wanted to eliminate competition. She has not a heart of pure distilled evil. No, that was the person who had altercations with each of the victims before their deaths. The person who concealed the most telltale bit of evidence…" He held up the shining golden strand. "…the purloined necklace, stolen when she was setting up the lovely Miss Pearl to be poisoned—was none other than the deceased, who called herself Isabella Imbriglio. But that was an assumed name, demonstrating that she entered France on false papers, with dishonest intent. Her real name was…" He looked down at some notes in his hand. "…Britney Woodcock!"

The contestants looked around nervously. Most of them had altered their birth names to something that would play better.

"We have reason to believe that one of the deceased, Mademoiselle Hailey, was planning on exposing this Britney Woodcock. But then, instead…" Here he cleared his throat. "…instead, she fell—or was pushed—from her balcony to the rocks below. A tragic demise."

* * *

Irwin and Brad were delighted the inspector didn't mention the deceased's secret. It might be that he wished to emphasize Britney-Isabella's guilt, which they had to admit made a lot of sense. But left this way, Hailey was still a franchise secret to be revealed in a tell-all of great commercial potential.

And both were impressed with the inspector's performance. A great reveal. Just the right amount of dynamic tension. Shame he wasn't handsome.

"Mademoiselle Pearl's necklace was found on Woodcock's body after we lifted the stone crushing her. That is proof she entered the room and had the opportunity to fill the night glass with poison." He took out a cigarette but didn't light it. "Which brings us to someone, a very special someone, who prevented yet another victim falling to this so-called 'Isabella's' blood lust." He walked to the table occupied by the executive crew and held his hand out, saying, "Please come with me, *ma chère mademoiselle*."

To everyone's surprise, Hortensia rose without hesitation, a demure, pleased smile on her face. Escorted to the room's center, with the inspector's palm atop her head, she turned to face her father and Suzanne.

"Everyone here witnessed this brave little girl running from the vile murderess. You watched her put her life in danger climbing the treacherous stones in the old convent. It was by sheer luck that she did not fall to her death—or perhaps it is divine justice." He paused for a brief moment. "Or, perhaps the ancient nuns interred here interceded on her behalf!" The inspector paced a circle about Hortensia. His showmanship really was stunning—he may have had a reserved British mother, but he'd learned Gallic hyperbole somewhere. He might be more of a draw than they thought. A reality character actor!

"But none of you know the precipitating circumstance of that chase. I had to find out from the heroine herself, this little girl. It seems that a love triangle had developed, but one that existed only in the deluded mind of the insane killer. *Ma cheri* Hortensia, is that correct?"

Hortensia's face was an eyelash batting mask of charm as she nodded.

"Isabella's goal was not winning the show, but owning it, by winning Brad Hudson. The child told me Isabella planned to murder her presumptive rival, her father's intended." He pointed to Suzanne. "But brave Hortensia went up to her…"

* * *

Brad and Irwin glanced at each other. The image of a small, pudgy hand putting something long and shiny in a pocket appeared in the mind of one and the image of a little hand taking something long and shiny out of a pocket appeared in the mind of the other. They were pretty sure what that something was. Together, as one, they murmured softly, "Pearl's necklace!"

And then they both whispered, "Brad's intended?"

"…and landed a blow, triggering her homicidal rage early. The little mademoiselle was lucky to escape with her life!"

The concierge stepped up. "I have here the certificate of gratitude from all of us!" He bent and hugged Hortensia, whose face was squeezed so tightly that her plump, moist cherry mouth might just force out a pit. As soon as he released his clasp, she fled back to Suzanne's arms. And then she reached out from that secure place to take her father's finger in her fist.

The concierge chuckled as the manor staff and production crew let out a loud "Awwwww." He brought the certificate to their table. "And I assume you will all be leaving now," he said.

Irwin spoke up. "We'd like to finish shooting…"

"*Mais non*! That is not possible."

"...at double the daily rate. Extra tips to staff."

The concierge shrugged. "Perhaps such a thing could be arranged. I shall speak with my cousin, the Inspector."

* * *

Brad collected his daughter and Suzanne from their bedrooms, where they'd gone to dress for dinner. With Hortensia, he went into Suzanne's room.

"Are you okay?" Brad asked.

"No. Just tired." Suzanne's hair was a mess, falling into her eyes.

"Well, time to eat," he said. "I'm really hungry."

* * *

Irwin arranged for cinematographers to follow the police investigators and capture everything they said and did. The contestants were happy, since they wanted more screen time to increase their exposure and build their personal brands. The inspector seemed especially delighted when he was in the frame.

The problem was Durand couldn't be obviously directed, though several times, he had to be told not to look at the camera for approval. Irwin wanted him to go about his business, to seem natural.

It was a shame about the dead girls, hateful though they had been. But he shouldn't even be thinking like that—the situation was downright gothic! Grisly, gory! In other words, pure gold. He would be the one to keep it artistic instead of tawdry.

Mabel DeVine tapped him on the shoulder, or at least tried to do so. Irwin saw her finger poking out the front of his armpit. "How's it going with the gumshoe?" she asked.

"Remarkably well. How about the sisters?"

"Waiting for the go-ahead from the boss, the Reverend Mother." She lit up. "Tell you the honest truth, you wouldn't catch Mabel DeVine selling herself down the river, being put away from the world. No siree bob! Wouldn't have been fair to my adoring audience."

Irwin waited. He'd had smoke blown up his ass before by wannabee stars. Maybe Mabel was no different, just dead.

Mabel produced a small marabou fan and waved it coyly in front of her face. "I want credit as co-casting director."

"Maybe it is best if you are the one to handle the nuns and just bring the stories to me for a development meeting. We'll thrash out which ones to use then." He'd gotten pretty used to the ghostly Mabel but still wasn't too keen on a mass of the dead crowding around him. They might even have an issue relating to his altar boy shenanigans. It was always hard to know whether to believe in a forgiving God, who let you off the hook for little indiscretions if you fessed up, or the Old Testament vengeful one his parents had pushed.

"Oh, don't worry about them," Mabel said. "I'm sure they'll talk to me now, after a century of pretending I didn't exist. Why, those wet blankets used to stand in two lines, chanting away even when I shoved myself between them and their little prayer books. I got them straightened out now. Once they saw old Mabel cut a rug and heard me sing the latest tunes, they wanted more. Don't think they want to go back to their boring old afterlife."

"So," Irwin experienced a frisson of irritation, "how are you doing on the stories? We need a solid fifteen to twenty to have enough for a season. If the show takes off, as I think it will, we'll need more." He pondered for a second. "This dump must have been built seven hundred years ago. It would take a fortune to make it safe for production. We'll have to use CGI."

"CGI?"

"Drawing on the computer. Stick the character in front of a green screen, bring in more CGI to create any background you want, a city, wilderness, an alien planet, or this place, and no one will know the character's not there. Voila! You've created reality."

Mabel was impressed and a little, just the merest smidge, intimidated. There was a lot to learn. Maybe it was good she'd given up the tiara. She'd have to get a beret somewhere if she was to be a real director.

CHAPTER TWENTY-THREE

"Pearl for certain. Now Isabella's gone, she's the top contender. We'll get this season over with. Next one will be a surprise." Brad described the deal he'd made with Lucien.

"Wow, that's pretty close to brilliant," Irwin said, reaching for another bit of creamy *escalope a la normande*.

"A kind of Cinderfella story with true love thrown in. Rags to riches. It might even come across better if they actually are in love, which he claims to be." The French kid might have come up with the idea, but it was okay if he let everyone assumed it was Brad's genius idea.

"And I agree about Pearl."

"For God's sake," Suzanne said. "Pearl's been tooling you guys. I've found out she's engaged to a guy from Hong Kong. And besides, The Groom won't go along with it. He's fallen for one of the other girls."

"Who?"

"Rosita."

"Perfect! A biracial romance. We were behind the other show in the stats…" Things were shaping up better than Brad anticipated.

"I really was voting for Pearl." Irwin took another

helping. "One of the prettiest to start with, she's also one who hasn't let herself go."

"Pork up, you mean? Over-indulging on the food here? All the butter-heavy pastries and stuff? You better watch out, Ir, or all the work you did keeping fit in L.A. will be wasted. You'll look plus-sized like your father."

With a wail like the epic storm's wind, Hortensia burst into tears, drops running down her jam-covered face. She slid from her seat to hide under the dining room table.

"Hey, hey!" Brad lifted the white cloth to look beneath. "What's the matter?"

She didn't answer. Her crying intensified and he dropped the tablecloth. A sudden jab made his shin smart. Suzanne had poked him with the toe of her shoe. Hard.

"Why'd you do that?" He protested.

She tightened her lips and, with sharp, commanding movements of her head, indicated Brad should join his kid under the table. Another jab in his shin and he complied.

Down on all fours, he crawled to where Hortensia was sitting with her arms wrapped around her knees. Her face was wet with tears.

Just a short while ago, she'd been so happy to be in his arms, so happy he'd saved her when she jumped from the tower's wall. Now, when he went to hold her, she tried to wriggle free. He held her firm with one hand and pulled his linen napkin from the table with the other. To his surprise, wiping her face wasn't disgusting at all. Even with raspberry jam colored snot.

"Shh, shh," he murmured, looking at the assorted knees. He'd never seen people from this vantage point before. Everyone wore jeans, except for Suzanne, who was in her usual skirt. From where he sat, he could see that, beneath its pleats, she was wearing pink panties.

Not a thong, just regular old panties, kind of stretched out, bagging down her thighs. Faded. That wasn't surprising, but what was surprising was how endearing he found it, how private. She didn't expect anyone to look at them, they weren't for show, he was probably the only man to have seen them, and that gave him a boner.

It was an even bigger turn-on and even more endearing when she slid from her chair and joined them. She sat cross-legged, pulling her skirt to bunch between her thighs.

Too late to hide those granny panties. He stifled a smile. Keeping an eye on Suzanne, he hugged Hortensia against his chest and said, "Now tell us why you're crying."

Not a peep from anyone sitting above and no creak from the chairs or clink of silverware. Just the muffled sounds of chatter at the other tables. The stillness above them was so profound that Brad figured they were listening. Annoying. This was exclusive family business.

Hortensia sniffled some more, giving her father a chance to reach out and draw Suzanne's leg against his side. Just for support. "So, babycakes," he went on, "why the sobbing?"

Hortensia leaned her head against him and pointed through the obscuring tablecloth at the surrounding contestants. "Pearl is pretty. More than all them other ladies. Is that why you want The Groom to pick her?"

"It's the business, the way things are supposed to go..." he began

Suzanne cut in, "No, no! Of course not. He really likes her because she's sweet. She's nice to everyone."

"But still pretty on the outside, like all the others, right?" Hortensia paused, inhaled a string of mucus back into her nose. "They don't look like normal ladies. They all look like Barbies."

"Yeah, so, I don't understand what the problem is." But Brad had the beginning glimmer of an idea.

"You didn't want somebody like me. You never did."

Suzanne leaned over and stroked Hortensia's hair. "I'm sure your daddy wanted you. He brought you here to be with him."

Hortensia shot Suzanne a scornful look. "Mommy made him. He only cares about pretty ladies. I'm not one."

"He never came to see me at my mommy's."

"I did when you were born."

She shot him a look that made his heart hide in his chest, looking for protection from his conscience.

"Anyway, you're not a lady, you're a little girl," Brad said.

"What if I never am? One girl died. Somebody said, 'It's a shame because she was so beautiful.' What if I died? Not a 'shame' because I'm fat and ugly?"

"You're pretty on the inside," he said, though that was a novel concept when it came to Hortensia. He tapped his fingers against her chest. "Where it counts."

Hortensia looked at him as if he was an idiot. "So what? Nobody gets to win for being pretty on the inside." She rubbed under her nose with her hand and wiped the snot on Brad's leg.

A small ripping sensation began in his upper belly and continued upward until it rent his chest. "Daddy would be so, so sad if something, anything, happened to you." She was his baby, his daughter. How could she wonder if he'd feel that way?

Sniffling, Hortensia blew a bubble from her nostril.

Brad sat for a moment, rocking his daughter in his lap. Then he whispered, just for Suzanne and Hortensia's ears, "When I look at the two of you, I see people I love. I see family."

"I want to eat now." She ducked out from under the cloth. Her stubby little legs flipped up as she clambered onto her chair.

"But I didn't think she needed me. She seemed so tough from the moment I met her."

Suzanne was quick to answer. "Oh, for God's sake, Brad, what else could she have been?" She was on her way out from under the table before he could answer.

His joints, stiff from sitting on the floor, thwarted Brad's attempt to follow quickly. That gave him time to think. He was glad she hadn't reminded him of his neglect in the years since his daughter was born.

Suzanne's voice floated down. "Hortensia, the man who wrote your *Beauty and the Beas*t got it all wrong. I think your daddy needs to read to you again, this time with the real ending. We all see things the way we want to see them."

* * *

After everyone had gone to bed. Irwin put his feet up on a neighboring chair, slid his buds into his ears, and began to play Caro Emerald's *That Man* for the one thousandth time. Once back in Hollywood, he'd play it aloud, yank the headphones from his husband's ears, and make him dance. Irwin was done playing second fiddle to medicine, done taking "no" for an answer.

"We all see things the way we want to see them" was a very good line, one he could use. He'd seen himself as a failure, but his husband saw him as someone worthy of love. Still, it didn't hurt that Irwin was going to be a auteur of the streaming kind, an indie success.

* * *

Mabel was happy. She'd been unable to defeat New Hollywood, it was true—absolute schlock corrupts absolutely—but if you can't lick them, join them.

She levitated to the tower, lit a cigarette, and gazed out over the tranquil English Channel, her fan, trimmed with marabou feathers, stirring gently in the light breeze.

A voice beside her interrupted her reverie. "What the fuck? I'm still in this lousy dump?"

Mabel's head snapped about. "Oh, it's you, the murderess."

Isabella stood beside her. "What are you talking about? I never killed anyone!"

Mabel laughed. "I know that, of course."

"I don't understand. Who died?"

"Some of the other vamps invading my home. The estate my husband Max bought for me. We first saw it in 1925…"

"Yeah, yeah, whatever! How did they die?"

"They were each playing the role of an innocent looking for love. And each died of greed combined with stupidity. You were the most successful and might have won, but for a particularly ballsy little tot." Mabel grinned. "The advice always was, *never agree to share the set with a child*. They'll crush you. Box office wisdom."

"That horrible little shit Hortensia!"

"As I was saying, none of you could have held a candle to me in my prime, back in 1925 when…"

Isabella looked as if the light was finally dawning. "You're saying I'm dead?"

"You and the rest were always just ephemera. Only I, Mabel DeVine, Goddess of the Silver Screen, will live forever in the hearts of those who love theater!"

"Mabel DeVine?" Isabella squinted and looked at her closely. Just as she opened her mouth to say more, a vortex of flames opened beneath her and, before she disappeared downward, Mabel just caught her voice asking, "Aren't you Gloria Swanson?"

* * *

Brad awoke, sensing eyes staring at him. Hortensia sat next to him, clutching her doll to her chest. "You up?" The hoarse little voice rumbled.

"Am now," Brad said. The clothes he'd slept in were wrinkled and damp. His face felt the same and his boxers were decidedly damp. His dreams were patchy, tearing and dissolving like wet tissues, but one thing was memorable: they'd involved exploring every protuberance on Suzanne's body and a few of the hollows as well.

The good news was, he definitely didn't need Viagra.

Fifteen minutes later, waiting for breakfast to be served, Brad was still in bed, learning cat's cradle from Hortensia.

Concentrating on winning, she pursed her lips. Her top chin looked like a prune, and with her under-chin, like a prune with a bib.

"Wow! Tough," Brad exclaimed at the woven pattern. "Think I'm beat."

She pondered the string for a moment and then showed where he should insert his fingers. He followed her direction, pulling the string into a new shape. Keeping his tone casual, he asked, "Did you deliberately set up Isabella?"

"What's 'set up?'" Hortensia's tongue clacked with satisfaction as she made her next move.

"I saw you pick up Pearl's necklace…"

"In the dead lady's bathroom? The lady in the tub, drownded?"

Brad nodded. "Yes."

"Found it on the floor. It was pretty." Hortensia looked up from the game. "If the lady was dead, that wasn't stealing."

He wasn't sure what to say, especially as the necklace was already stolen. "Why did you give it to Isabella?"

Hortensia untangled the string from her fingers. "Gave it to her to stay away from you. Ladies like fancy things, especially ladies who look like Barbie. She said it must've cost a lot of money."

"But why did you kick her?"

"Mostly because I was mad. She promised that if I gave her the necklace, she'd leave you alone. She was a cheater and a liar, and cheaters and liars are very, very bad."

Hortensia, testing the string's knot, making sure it was strong enough to last, was the picture of pediatric innocence. Surely, she couldn't have planned the outcome of her actions. Or could she? "So you kicked her to make her run away from me…"

"And Suzanne. People keep being mean to her and she doesn't do nothing about it." She looked up again. Was there a glint of cunning in her eye? A rapid chill ran up his spine, just as she smiled and said, "But now that Pearl lady has her necklace back. Everything is alright again." She held out the string formation, which looked like a spider's web. "Suzanne makes a very good mommy. I think you like her. I think you like her a lot."

He decided to change the subject. "First choice in pastry should be determined by competition, you against me. Winner of the next game of cat's cradle gets first choice."

Suzanne brought in a tray of croissants and coffee, with a glass of milk for Hortensia. Since Brad was still a beginner, and not a very good one at that, he got all the plain croissants while Hortensia and Suzanne feasted on the chocolate- and raspberry-jam-filled ones.

When the pastries were gone and the bed littered with crumbs, Suzanne said to Hortensia, "Time to get dressed so we can see what the others are up to."

Hortensia nodded. "Daddy, you coming?" she asked. "I'll put on my clothes real fast."

"Think I'll stay here and get dressed first." He didn't want to go out in the hall wearing his rumpled clothes.

She looked from him to Suzanne and the sly look flashed across her face again. "I'll go look for Uncle Irwin. Suzanne can bring you down when you're ready."

"You know," Brad sat thinking for a moment, thinking thoughts that still bothered him. "Isabella's death. Do you think Hortensia planned..."

"No!" Suzanne's tone was emphatic. "She's not the devil spawn people seem to think she is. Isabella's death was an accident."

"I didn't…"

"Yeah, you did mean to imply. But she's just a lonely little child. Maybe smarter than most." She leaned back against the pillow and Brad followed her down. "No one was taking care of her, so she did what she had to. If that meant being obnoxious to get her father's attention, then she sure did that well, didn't she?"

His index finger, with a mind of its own, began tracing little circles on her left breast. Round and round…

She didn't stop him. "You really believe Isabella was the killer?"

"The inspector sure made a good case. Lots of circumstantial evidence stacking up. I'd vote yes," he said. “There were no witnesses to any of the murders. And we’ll be sure if they stop.” He considered pursuing the matter, telling her that, though Isabella was the logical choice for murderer and was certainly a raving bitch, she could have been set up. But he stopped himself. Suzanne was sure, surer than he was, that Hortensia, a five-year-old, couldn’t be that devious.

His thoughts were buzzing like flies caught by a spider. But his hand had switched from one finger to the whole palm, rubbing across her nipple and then going lower and lower in lazy circles. Pretty soon the buzzing was drowned out by the sound of her breathing. And he stopped thinking about anything at all.

CHAPTER TWENTY-FOUR

Mabel DeVine sighed with nostalgia as she sat on the dresser, smoking, and watched Hortensia's father make love to Suzanne. It was obvious that Hortensia was well on the way to getting what she needed, whether she knew it or not. And Mabel was pretty sure she knew it.

"Max, how I miss you!" she exclaimed as one circular movement of Brad's hips brought a sharp little animal cry from Suzanne's lips. "You wouldn't have taken as long to climb in the saddle. But as my old mama would have said about Brad Hudson, 'He's so dumb, he could throw himself on the ground and miss.'" She looked down again from her vantage point seated on the dresser. "Oh, my! Ah, well, at least I can see why women go after him."

A few minutes later she was on her way to the convent to speak with the Reverend Mother, escorted by the usual assistant spirit.

The head nun seemed to still be slumbering, but Mabel found her tiara on the chamber's floor, lying in a puddle of dirty water.

"Hey!" she said. "That's no way to treat a gift from my Max."

The Holy Relic's eyes opened slowly. "Take it back. I will not keep it a moment longer. And from this moment on, this sacred place will be closed to you."

"Why?" How would she get the stories she needed?

"You wish to corrupt us, turn us from our work praying to allay punishment for the world's sins. Just as our Savior suffered on the cross."

"But I thought we had a rapport, a collaboration. A friendship."

"We had a moment out of time, a brief respite. A bit of fun. We really liked your *chansons*, the dancing, too. Very alive, the sort to lift the spirit." Her voice grew more conspiratorial. "Sometimes we do suffer from the doldrums. Eternal service, even of the Lord, sometimes feels eternal." Her color grew more florid. "Not that praising Him and His works grows tedious to us."

"Of course not." Mabel was stunned. She could see where this was going.

"But it is time for us to return to our calling." The Reverend Mother's eyes closed again, and the chamber filled with mist. Competing Gregorian chants filled the air as the room grew dark.

Mabel found herself in the cloister, her heart somewhere down around the silk stockings that were always a tiny bit baggy, her tiara firmly back on her head. She looked around and saw the two lines of nuns, facing each other, chanting away. Trying to attract their attention didn't work—things were as before, when she was ignored.

She longed to escape, but how? She was trapped here, in her purgatory.

* * *

Irwin was in an uncharacteristically chipper mood when Mabel winked into view.

"What's got into you?" she asked.

"Oh, let's just say all our problems have been solved and, as far as our show goes, it's green light all the way. I hurried here to tell you the good news."

"Uh, there's a little hang-up. The head nun says no, uh-uh, no way, ixnay."

"The Holy Relic? The Reverend Mother? The Prioress?"

"One and the same."

"Let me talk with her. I'll dangle enough in front of her to make her sign."

Mabel sighed. "I have such a good title for it, too. *Grab the God.* Even a Busby Berkeley dance sequence in the cloister, filmed from atop the tower. Imagine, black habits opening like flowers to reveal the white surplices beneath." She sighed again. "Men are never allowed in the Reverend Mother's presence. You can't go to the chamber beneath the tower to talk to her. Think I'm banned, too."

Grab the God? Busby Berkeley? Sounded trashy, lowbrow to him, not to mention derivative. Also, not the elevated concept he thought they were going for. But did he want people to watch or not? What good was great art if it failed to find an audience? Reality shows already mocked everything else sacred in life: true love, marriage, even survival itself, so why not God?

It was all over. Irwin's face seemed to fall into his hands. His shoulders shook as he began to sob. He must be an idiot to have joined into the fantasy of a flapper's ghost.

Mabel waxed philosophic. "I think we should be realistic. A serious show wouldn't get a whole lot of viewers. One thing I realized, as the pinnacle of cinematic success, was the value of the *experience.* Movie goers want to be awed, entertained, made happy. They didn't want sadness, they want sex, music, dancing.

They crave leaving their mundane lives behind and being part of the glory that was Hollywood. Doesn't mean we can't chuck in some redeeming or meaningful uplifting stuff somewhere—just gotta be delivered with pizazz!"

He was crying, tears dripping between his fingers.

"But get this, I had an idea that's the cat's meow." She paused, maybe to make sure his sobs didn't interfere with hearing her. "It'll make little Hortensia happy."

"What's that?"

"Let's do a reality show that's not about the beautiful. Like in my day when plastic surgery was out of reach for most. We could have people, ordinary people, just live together for a while to see if they can make it as a couple. Really talk to each other and stuff."

He lifted his head. Who said there were no new ideas in show biz? A non-superficial reality show. There was nothing like that.

"We could call it *Ninety-Day Spouses*!" Mabel said triumphantly.

EPILOGUE

Deep in the wall, near the still-warm stones of the fireplace that was once part of the ancient convent, Cleopatra was awakened by thumping—a metal headboard hitting the wall behind. In her primitive reptile brain, even more ancient than the building, the vibrations signaled *move and resume the hunt*.

Her owner, Jocelyn, was forgotten as was the snug leather carrier in which she'd once slumbered. Spring would come, warming the stones of the cloister. Where once half-starved nuns had rubbed chilblained hands together, plump summer rodents would scamper, exploring the garden in the summer sun. That sun's rays would warm Cleopatra's cold-blooded body and let her slither sleek through tall, concealing grass. Meanwhile, there was game aplenty in the manor. A veritable feast, rat after rat after rat.

www.ingramcontent.com/pod-product-compliance
Lightning Source LLC
LaVergne TN
LVHW090600110826
845146LV00001B/206

* 9 7 9 8 9 9 0 9 8 6 5 0 3 *